Prisoner of the Stone Palace

by

Alexandria May Ausman

This book is a work of fiction. Any references to historical events, real people, or real places, are used fictitiously. Other names, characters, places, and events are products of the author's imagination, and any resemblance to actual events or persons, living or dead, is entirely coincidental.

Book cover illustration by Alexandria May Ausman
Editor: Jon M. Ausman

Library of Congress Control Number: 2024912149

ISBN: 978-1-963335-17-0 (ebook)
ISBN: 978-1-963335-16-3 (paperback)

Published By:
Ausman & Cousins LLC
1700 North Monroe Street
Suite 11, Box 284
Tallahassee, Florida 32303-0501

For author interviews: ausman@embarqmail.com

Charlotte, Designer Palace Diorama

Das Kaiser Haus Series

The Rise of the Priceless (Chapters 1 to 10)
Metal Illness (Chapters 11 to 19)
Jonas the Vampire (Chapters 20 to 29)
Prince of the Elders (Chapters 30 to 40)
Leo's Lamb (Chapters 41 to 50)
Mastermind Malfred (Chapters 51 to 58)
Priceless Lost (Chapters 59 to 67)
Broken Silver (Chapters 68 to 74)

The Collar King Series

Return to Das Kaiser Haus (Chapters 1 to 7)
Felicity's Child (Chapters 8 to 14)
Tears of the Violin (Chapters 15 to 22)
The Golden Collar (Chapters 23 to 30)
Rise of the Mortar King (Chapters 31 to 38)
Prisoner of the Stone Palace (Chapters 39 to 46)
Mortar Transformation (coming soon)

The Psycho Series

Cemetery Kid (Chapters 1 to 20)
Stop Calling Me Psycho (Chapters 21 to 33)
Motor-Psycho (Chapters 34 to 44)
Delusion of the Collar and the Key (Chapters 45 to 53)

Brutality's Prisoner (Chapters 54 to 64)
Aesthetic Akathisia (Chapters 65 to 74)
Metallic Burden (Chapters 75 to 83)

27 Masters Series

Anita the Benevolent (Chapters 1 to 7)
The Beast and the Witch (coming soon Chapters 8 to 16)
High Priestess of Schizophrenia (coming soon)

Book 6 Characters: Prisoner of the Stone Palace

Almut: a black collar Torture Master
Altergott, Dr. Reese: a clinical psychiatrist
Annette: a Haus black collar
Birgit: a Haus Dungeon Mistress
Byron: a Haus Dominant, a Voting Council member
Cary: a black collar door guard
Christian: the anger and lust shard
Christian Axel: a Haus Dominant, the Priceless
Claus: an Elder of the Haus
Cora: a FemDom of the Haus, the Fur Queen
Der Goldene Hund: the Voice or the Boss shard; the Conscious shard
Der Makellos: Leo and Christian's German Shepherd
Felicity: a lamb
Fiona: a deceased Haus FemDom, spouse of Oswin
Florian: the first Priceless in the Haus
Friedrick: a Haus Dominant, friend of Byron
Geraldine: a hard working lamb that cooks for Maxximillian
Gerard: a deceased sadistic stepfather to Christian Axel
Gretta: a Haus FemDom, the Silk Queen
Hanno: a deceased brutish black collar yard worker
Henner: Gretta's German Shepherd
Hubertus: a black collar Torture Master
Ivan: captain of the Russian Guard (outdoors)
Jakob: a Haus Dominant

Jonas: an Elder of the Haus
Kilian: an Elder, psychiatric rehabilitation counselor
Kloe: Marc's deceased big sister, a black collar, also the name of Marc's lamb
Lambs: Abelard, Annette, Geraldine, Milo, Ryker
Leo: an Elder of the Haus
Lucus: a Haus Dominant, a royal
Mad Max: the sadistic shard of Maximillian, aka the Heart and Judgment
Mad Maxx: husband of Meine Liebe; a Haus Dominant
Mad Maxx: the masochistic shard, aka the Brain and Guilt
Malfred: a Haus Elder
Marc: a deceased Haus black collar
Matz: a Haus Dominant, a pimp and loan shark
Max: the Soul shard
Maximillian: the submissive name given to Christian by Peter
Maximillian: the seductive shard, aka the Libido
Maxximillian: the submissive adopted by the Elders
Meine Liebe: submissive and spouse of Mad Maxx
Noethan, Dr. Anselm: the Haus doctor
Peter: a Dominant of Der Kaiser Haus; best trainer of submissives
Petrov: a Russian Guard
Rachel: the niece of Malfred
Rolf: a Haus Dominant
Roland: a first floor Haus Dominant, a violinist
Roselina: a Haus black collar, spouse of Cary
Ryker: a deceased Haus trainee

Sebastian: a Haus Dungeon Master
Tadeas: a Haus Dungeon Master
Viviana: a Haus Dungeon Mistress
Xavier: a deceased Fur King

Preface

Most people reach a crossroad at least once in this journey we call life. Mad Maxx has already come to several points in his story where a wrong move could have resulted in losing it all. The little loving boy that was hauled away to the Mortar Palace has disappeared and been replaced by a cold hearted, brutal man. The reasons for his rapidly changed approach to life and those around him, are as simple as they are deep. An obscene birthday surprise had brought the unbreakable Priceless to his knees. Unable to deal with the horror he was forced to endure, he found he couldn't just get over it as he had always done before. He is led to believe he is a life-time prisoner as the Mortar King of Das Kaiser Haus. With a broken heart, he seems to have finally accepted defeat in the face of seemingly unbeatable odds.

But has he really given up his fight against the horrible darkness that has come to claim his unwilling soul? It will soon become clear to everyone that nothing is more dangerous than the cornered Mad Maxximillian.

Language in italics is a conversation between the adult male Master Mad Maxx and his female submissive Meine Liebe.

Chapter 39: All the Kings Men

My eyes went wide in terror at the sight of those two criminals standing there outside the gate. I felt my heart speeding up more than from the fear of what they had come to do to me. It was not clear why they were leading the lamb Geraldine like their pet behind them. I knew with these brutal men whatever they had planned to do with her was going to be horrific. I can take almost any terrible thing from torture to twisted sex but seeing that hatchet they carried sent me right to psychotic hell.

I was wailing in pure misery before the Dungeon Masters Sebastian and Tadeas came up behind the Altergotts to let them into the cell. I backed into the wall not bothering to hide my rivers of tears as the four came into the "Palace" together. I realized the brothers called in muscle to assure I would give them no trouble during their cruel games with me.

I shot a look of desperation to the Vampire that had taken a seat on my Mortar Throne. He was smiling at me with sadistic humor. There was no doubt he was enjoying my predicament. I didn't care anymore that he was unjustly angered at me. I thought only of saving my poor helpless Geraldine from the slaughter that I was certain the evil Altergotts had planned for her.

I crawled across that floor with rapidness and grabbed Jonas's ankles. I gave up all attempts to maintain any dignity. I wept on his boots caressing his calves in an honest pleading for mercy. Jonas chuckled appearing most thrilled to witness my pathetic behavior to lobby for his aid in this serious matter.

He snorted. "I see you are demonstrating quite a bit of regret over your recent choices. Well, too bad for you son. Get off me and take your medicine like a man. You should have thought about the enemies you were making on your lofty climb to the top. That Lucus got Reece fired from his job, and his license revoked simply because you paid what was owed to them. Messing with a man's source of income is low, Christian. Your retaliation for their having a little fun with you was going too far. Now they come to seek revenge they have earned. Admit it to yourself. You have this coming, and you know it." He kicked me in the head with force but not hard enough to knock me out for the second time since his arrival.

I covered my face fearing a second kick but didn't bother to retreat or get off the ground. I laid there at his feet weeping uncontrollably into my hands unable to get a hold of myself. Sabastian and Tadeas lifted me to my knees by pulling me up by my upper arms. I kept the boys head down and eyes to the ground. I was sobbing so hard I couldn't even make out their boots through the watery veil flowing fast and furious.

Kilian laughed loudly as he took a place in front of me. "Greetings Maxx. You know I was out in the stable today and ran into an old friend of yours. Geraldine here seemed real concerned about you since she had not heard a word of you in many days. I thought it would be a kindness to bring her along for a visit. I am sure you missed her as much as she misses you, ja?" All the men around me laughed as Geraldine called out sounding frightened.

I flashed a terrified look at the lamb and saw her breathing was shallow. She was scared. I suppose she was reading my mind. I tried to clear out the fearful thoughts that ran through it but no matter what I did all I could think was please don't slaughter my lamb.

Reece saw me glancing at Geraldine. "I was sure you were wrong about the boy's attachment to such a filthy beast brother, but I see there is something to your observations. Look at him. I bet he would do anything to protect that nasty thing. Like maybe accept torture in her place. Am I correct in that assumption Maxx? Are you willing to do what you are told to keep this lamb safe from injury?" He smiled menacingly at me.

I shuddered in the Dungeon Master's hold. I was not surprised that it was going to come down to this unbearable choice. I took a deep breath and closed my eyes while nodding that I was agreeable to whatever as long as they left Geraldine alone. Seeing my resignation with that agreement to torture made all the men laugh hard, including Jonas.

Kilian knelt down and grabbed my bonded crown forcing my head to look at him. "You are going to do everything that Reece or I command without a fight, or I kill that precious sheep of yours. In a moment Sabastian will remove that gag. You will only use your tongue the way you are told to and one cry for aid, rude statement or sound other than screams of pain will result in Geraldine's quick departure from life. You will not be told twice or warned again. I mean it. You understand me, boy?" I nodded but was nearly convulsing from the strength of my crying jag over this horrid humiliation.

Kilian smiled with wickedness and nodded, "Good, Sebastian, unlock the gag and you boys stay handy. Reece and I may be in need of aid to restrain him to hold still for our sport. I know this idiot well. Even when he realizes the odds are not in his favor he eventually fights the loser battle. It is in his nature. Fucking schizophrenics are never to be trusted." Sebastian reached into his pocket and took out the ball gag key.

I didn't move a muscle when the man released my arm and began working on the lock. Within a few moments my mouth was free of that rubberized monstrosity. I silently watched as he went to put the padlock and key into his pocket. He didn't notice the key missed the mark. It fell to the straw at his feet.

I darted my eyes to check on the other men. No one dare noticed this mistake but me. I had to think fast. I pulled forward falling to my hands with a loud vail at Kilian's feet. In a single rapid movement, I dug into the straw taking huge handfuls of it. I rubbed it into the boy's face then threw it to each side of me. I was pretending to be in full begging mode but actually was trying to bury that key before anyone saw it laying there in the open.

That act worked. My powerful mourning caused them all to break into fits of cruel laughter. None of them discovered Sebastian's clumsiness. I continued to behave bereft hoping that this open display of defeat would curb at least some of the violence they had planned for me.

Well so much for hoping, ja? Nothing I did convinced them to go easy on me. I received no mercy in their vicious thrills at my expense. They began with a sadistically ferocious double team rape. I kept my vow to give them no quarrel, but that did not stop either of them from making the sexual assaults hurt as much as humanly possible despite my compliance with their every order.

When the brothers had been sated to gluttony I was weeping, groaning in agony and bleeding from both ends. To my dismay they immediately made it clear they were far from done with dare torturing. The Dungeon Masters aided them by holding me down as Reece and Kilian took turns employing various painful implements to my flesh and worse, the boy's manhood.

I screamed in torment until at last there was really no further need for the gag. I had wrecked my vocal cords. All that came out was a raspy rush of air as they broke out into another round of the gang raping with the Dungeon Masters deciding to get into the act this go round.

The entire time Jonas sat there watching the horror the men inflicted upon me. I was forbidden to call to him or anyone for aid or risk the Altergotts turning their aggression against the helpless lamb Geraldine. I instead looked to him many time using my eyes to pled with all I had, begging him to make them stop.

At first, I found the expression he cast back at me as one of humored satisfaction. As the four of them continued their brutality, however, I found his smile had melted to one of disbelief with what I read to be a tinge of fear. Even the usually unflappable Vampire was beginning to find their sport with me to be over the top.

I sensed Jonas's was softening his original stance to see this punishment of his Mann through to completion. I kept my begging eyes focused on his own as the men took their turns ravaging my flesh without care or kindness. I was not hallucinating. This horrific abuse he was witnessing was definitely starting to get through his thick skin and piece him right into his black heart. Reece and Kilian had just switched their positions off with Sebastian and Tadeas in their horrible four man tag team when Jonas finally broke.

The Vampire let out a loud roar. He then rushed Sebastian grabbing the rapist by his shirt. The Dungeon Master appeared startled to dumb as Jonas wrapped his arm around his neck. He offered no reasonable resistance to the Vampire tossing him off me from his mount. Tadeas that was forcing the blow job backed off me in fear after watching his brother's treatment. The Altergotts, however, maintained their tight holds on my upper arms to restrain me from escaping the men's assaults.

Jonas was observably pissed the brothers didn't take the hint. "Kilian, that is enough. You motherfuckers already got what you wanted. The boy is busted up. You let him go and take that animal back where you got it."

Kilian squeezed my right arm more tightly as I panted and moaned from the aching that seemed to emit from every inch of my flesh. "Jonas, you mind your business. You cannot tell us what to do. We are finished with the boy when I say we are."

Jonas's eyes lit up with fires from hell. "How dare you refuse to listen to me, Kilian. I think you forget it is my Mann you hold and fuck over. I have the right to demand you end this bullshit and you know it."

Reece chuckled as he flashed a humored look at Kilian. "Let it go Kilian. You need not rile up Jonas to gain the Dungeon Masters. We got our cocks and anger satisfied. These other fellows can fuck on their own time. I say we get to the main show and call it a day. This idiot isn't going anywhere. Tomorrow we can come back without your Ex watching and finish the show, ja?" Kilian nodded with barely controlled irritation in his expression as the two of them harshly pushed me face first into the floor letting go of their hold for the moment.

I rolled to my side slowly. Doing my best to watch the brothers while I pulled up my breeches. With the ankle bracelets and wrist cuff none of my clothing could be removed. The attackers could only push them up or pull them down, but they could not remove them, a minor mercy I guess. Jonas stood there glaring at them refusing to leave his spot in case the Dungeon Masters, who had retreated to the wall farthest from the angered Vampire, decided to try to finish what they had been interrupted from completing.

I trembled and wept in silence as the brothers went to collect their earphones, blindfold and stereo. When Kilian turned and began to head back in my direction holding the objects I let out a loud wail of fear. I realized they were not leaving but merely changing the nature of their terrorizing. Jonas managed to end their punishing of my flesh but not their desire to distress my mind.

Jonas shot me a look of pity, then set his fury back on Kilian. “I think you have gone deaf brother. I said enough. You pack up and leave right now. Christian needs rest.”

Kilian, that had been grinning at me with evil thrill, glared at the Vampire with irritation. “I will go when I am ready. If you have issue with it then you may go take it up with Gretta, Jonas. I agree with Reece that these two nothings won’t be permitted to use our time with the Priceless to stir up your anger, but that is where I put an end to your control of this situation. I suggest you either go fetch the Head Voter or sit down and watch quietly.”

Jonas took a step toward Kilian appearing ready to blow a gasket. “You come any closer to Christian and Gretta will have to come down to identify your remains, cocksucker.”

That made the snake stop dead in his tracks. "You dare to threaten a fellow Elder? This is getting out of hand. You need to back off Jonas. I tell you the boy is agreeable to meet our demands. Let him speak for himself. Tell him Maxx. You will be most happy to give me and Reece whatever we want, ja?" He shot a grin at the shivering lamb tethered at my cell gate.

I caste a frightened glace at Geraldine. "Please don't hurt the lamb. I won't argue or give you quarrel if you let her return to her family uninjured."

That response made both Altergotts smile in triumphant glee. "You hear that Jonas? The boy says he is up for more sport. I think you need to remember you have no power over Maxx now that he is the Mortar King and Master of this Haus. You know the rules. You must mind his orders." I flashed a look of shock at that snake wondering if this was truth or merely another underhanded trick.

The Vampire took another step toward Kilian with murder in his expression. "Christian may be the King, but I am the King's Mann. He is not above me, but I am certainly above you asshole. You touch him anymore this day and I will see you whipped for it."

Kilian shot me a look of wantonness then sighed. "Alright, I hear you Jonas. I suppose Reece and I can hold off the rest of our sport till tomorrow. However, I think I am in the mood for veal. We will take this lamb to the back and make her into our dinner." He turned and motioned

Reece and the Dungeon Masters to follow him out of my cell.

I saw Kilian take up the anxious lamb's leash and let out a loud wail of terror at the sight. "Nein, nein, nein. They will kill my Geraldine. Jonas, I do whatever they want for the life of my lamb. Come back, Kilian. I will comply if you swear to stay your hand on your blade and satisfy your stomach with another meal instead of the taste of veal. Do you hear me speaking, snake? I am begging for the mercy of serving all your desires for that price."

Jonas pushed me backward with a sudden movement. "Shut up, Christian. They are leaving you alone and you beg them to come back to torture you some more? You are out of your Gott damned mind."

I nodded at that statement. "This I am told all the time. I am insane, Jonas. I demand you leave me to my despair. Isn't that what you wanted? To see me loath my birth. Well, you see this way we all get what we want. I save my lamb, the snake brothers get their twisted thrills, and you can be assured I wish for death more than I could have imagined possible. Besides, I am to understand that as the Master of the Haus you have to mind my commands. Then fucking do as I say. Stand down and stay out of this. Watch if you like. You better realize just because I am the schizophrenic doesn't mean I am the retarded. I am fully aware that this nightmare with these snakes is you Gott damned fault to begin with. You let them into my shitty life and now the only way they will go away is if they find for me the grave. I am forced to reap what you sowed cocksucker."

Jonas's eyes went so wide day nearly fell out of their sockets. "Christian, you dare to raise your voice and accuse me of such dishonor. I will not stand here and put up with the insult of it."

I chuckled bitterly through my tears. "Then go elsewhere and be pissed about it. I am tired of your constant refusal to admit to your mistakes while you are chronic about pointing them out as my own. I am the fuck up of that there is no doubt. However, I refuse to accept the cross that is not mine to bear. This motherfucker is able to visit his wrath on me because he is an Elder. How did that happen, Jonas? Did he suck Claus or Malfred's cock to climb that ladder to the top? Nein, it was your bed he warmed to earn him the title he honestly doesn't deserve."

Jonas growled at me in with fury rising. "He was a Voter already. He still would have access to you even if I had not raised him."

I scoffed. "You forget that I am familiar with Peter. The man told me he received the title of Voter thanks to you not him. He hates this man and for all his faults Peter knew he was a backstabbing snake when you ignored the signs of it. You don't want to admit that you raised this bastard twice. That is because he has bitten you double, hasn't he? Deny the facts all you like Jonas. You tell lies only the walls will believe. This idiot knows the truth of it.

You are more the fool than me and that took some work, Jonas."

Jonas backhanded me with strength sending me right to the floor. "Shut up, Christian. You go too far with that insolent mouth of yours."

I shook off the blow but didn't raise my face for a second helping. "You only have issue when it doesn't agree with your pleasures. Leave me to my fate, Jonas. I tire of your pretending to love me when in reality you care only for your own best interests. Let them do their worst. I fucking hope they send me to permanent psychotic hell or better yet, kill me. It would be a mercy I have wished for so many times I've lost count." I began to weep loudly in a fresh crying jag at the truthfulness of my statement.

Jonas stood there appearing confused as to what to respond to that. Kilian chuckled then began to clap. His brother came to join him in the applause. I covered my face with the boy's hands and wailed like the lost kid. I no longer cared what they did or that Jonas was one of my only hopes of escaping this nightmare. I just wanted it all to go away for good.

The Altergotts wasted no time pushing the confounded Vampire out of their way. They pulled my hands out of the way and slid the blindfold over the boys streaming eyes. I heard them yell to the Dungeon Masters to come aid them in restraining me once more. I offered none of them struggle as they put the headset over my ears. They had some trouble with it thanks to the crown but managed after several attempts.

Within only a few moments the now familiar sound of many voices speaking all at once filled my consciousness. The Dungeon Masters held me tightly to my spot as the volume increased to eardrum busting levels. I shook in their grips feeling the voices shattering the boy into tiny particles that were sure to blow away in the high winds of the tapestry vortex.

I was afraid of becoming the dust of the universe, but for Geraldine I was willing to suffer this hellish fate. She means everything to me and is the innocent. I realized I was a nothing and eventually, the darkness of the void would consume me anyway. I no longer wished to fight it off. I had lost the will to live, of that there was no longer any doubt. Better to be the lost than the tortured, ja?

Just when I was sure I was about to blow into billions of pieces the voices went silent. I trembled with a gasp at the sudden quiet. I couldn't see anything nor move. All I could do is wait for the noises to start again, or the earphones and blindfold to be removed.

Then with an unearthly shriek Geraldine bayed in agony. I screamed as I heard the sounds of the hatchet cutting the air multiple times. Each time it made contact with something Geraldine cried out in terror. I realized with full on horror that Kilian and Reece were slaughtering my lamb.

I began to struggle with all my strength in the Dungeon Masters' grips. They held me tight while I begged and screamed for them to stop hurting my lamb. I heard several more blows from that axe then Geraldine gurgled and went silent. I heard her flesh hit the stone floor with a loud thud. I wailed incoherently, uselessly flailing against my subduers.

The voices then began with vigor as I went into the deep psychotic fit. That only caused my struggle and attempt at screaming to become more frantic. My throat was already devastated by the long hours of howling and oral rapes. I could barely speak much less make the insane noises. By this time all the men heard the boy do is rasp with hoarseness with many pauses in my calls for mercy caused by air rushing out without the capacity to carry the sounds of anguish.

I could hear Kilian and Reece's laughter rising above all the others voices. This further distressed me. The sorrow was overtaking my senses, and I could feel the darkness of unconsciousness looming like an eager lover greedy for our embrace.

It was then that a wet, wooly thing was forced into my screeching mouth. I attempted to recoil from the invading substance. Someone grabbed the metal crown and held my head tightly. I closed my lips with force, but the man pried open my jaws. They pushed the unknown thing into me then covered my mouth so I couldn't spit it out.

My tongue informed me this was a piece of raw meat based on the taste of blood and texture. It took a second but finally it occurred to me this was a chunk of my Geraldine. I went into a spasm of desperation. I had to spit my lamb out of the boy. This nightmarish force feeding was all I could take. I lost all consciousness of my humanity and became the mindless beast.

The hand came off my mouth and I spit the meat out. I then began to gnash my nubs with vigor trying to bite anything, even the empty air around the boy. I writhed and spasmed uncontrollably in the grips of those that held me without care of injuring the flesh or joints. Guttural noises emitted from my chest and the drool flowed like a fast moving desert flood.

Throughout this entire scene the voices spoke none-stop and the Altergotts laughed with great humor. I was broken at last. There cruel trick had gained them the victory day had been seeking since my return to the Haus. I was the incoherent hebephrenic sure to never recover or so they thought.

It was almost too late to save me from this hellish fate when suddenly the blindfold was ripped off my eyes. I tried to bite the hand that pulled the bondage device free. The Vampire stood there holding that bit of black cloth staring at me appearing terrified. I couldn't understand what was happening or who this man was though I knew I should have knowledge of both things.

Jonas's mouth moved but I couldn't hear him over the sounds pumped into the boy's ears by the earphones. He apparently realized this and in a stunning move snatched the side of my crown and forced my face and attention to the other side of the palace cell.

It took a few moments for me to understand I was looking at a healthy though very scared baby Geraldine. The slaughter of her had been staged. A trick of the headset and props of forcing me to eat raw steak pieces.

Despite my dangerously deteriorated mental state, this mercy registered deep within. The Altergotts hadn't murdered my lamb. None of this was real, it was merely a contrived hallucination. This re-invigorated the inner strength and need to survive at all costs. I took up the wheel once more and dug my feet far as they would go into the boy's brain. The chaos all around the wheelroom began to abate and the psychotic fit slowed.

The furious Vampire rushed at me. I cowered thinking he intended to strike. To my surprise he punched Sebastian and then Tadeas until both released me. I snatched off the headphones as I watched the two Dungeon Masters flee to the Palace gate to escaping Jonas's continued blows and loud promises to do worse to them if they didn't release me at once.

The sounds of the voices and laughter ended immediately. The sudden rush of mild noises further calmed the turmoil within me. I collapsed to the floor panting, sweating and drooling full of fatigue from the heavy battling of my symptoms of schizophrenia.

As I laid there too worn to rise, I could hear Jonas dressing down the lot of them. He told them all he would kill the man that dared to lay a finger on my lamb. Then to my utter shock he said to be assured that they shall never abuse me by the use of Geraldine as he was confiscating her and putting her under his personal protection.

I wondered if I was still hallucinating as he continued to assure all the men my lamb would thrive and grow into the adult. He said if not the Haus hallways would run red with the river of blood he would spill in revenge. I rolled to my side to get a better view of the Vampire taking up the shivering lamb's leash. I gasped in disbelief as I saw him pet Geraldine and softly whisper reassuring words to ease her terror. This was a side of the Vampire I never had seen before. He was actually demonstrating honest kindness to a helpless creature beneath him.

I closed my eyes and rubbed them with vigor. This had to be another trick of my diseased mind. Jonas was a lot of things but a caring mothering type never. I was sure I was cracked beyond repair at this point.

Yet when I opened them back up I witnessed the Vampire waiting with feigned patience for the Altergott brothers, that had been packing up their tools of torture, to leave. He loudly stated he was following them out to be assured they were not left alone to employ any further insult to his misused Mann, Christian Axel.

I shot a look of confusion at Florian. He stared back at me with a wicked grin. The Vampire coming to my aid was more than a little unexpected, but I was grateful for the mercy of it. A bit of hope that he would find a way to see me free of that cell soon rose within. I was sure that whatever resentment he still held regarding that Lucus business, or any of the men in my life, had been trumped by the realization I wouldn't survive the level of brutality inflicted without restraint thanks to my position of helplessness.

This, along with knowing that Geraldine was safe for good from the Altergotts, brought me back from teetering on the brink of eternal madness. Though I was worn out to weakness, I was able to hold my demons to a controlled calmness. I allowed the peaceful silence and break from anxiety wash over my ravaged flesh even as I saw Sebastian coming back towards me.

Jonas saw him approaching too. "Hey, I told you to leave my Mann along, asshole. Are you deaf or do you have a death wish?"

Sebastian winced and halted. "Uhm, I apologize to you honorable Elder Jonas, but I am merely following the orders of the Silk Queen. The King is to be gagged at all times when not in use for, uhm, when it is not necessary for him to use his mouth. She wants it assured that a madman's ideas never become the laws of the Haus."

Jonas nodded slowly. "Ah, so that is what this is all about. Gretta fears that Christian will see her toppled from the throne by his word becoming the rules that outrank her own. That clever bitch thought of everything." He stared at the ball gag still tethered to the scold bridled crown.

Sebastian nodded. "I cannot speak of such things only to say if I deny her commands it will be my ass. I beg of you to allow me to do my duty without further quarrel or question. I will reattach the gag and nothing more, I swear it to you."

Jonas scoffed. "You will keep your hands off till the second my back is turned there is no doubt of that. I saw the familiarity you demonstrated while coupling my Mann Sebastian. I am not a fool. You have been sporting before this afternoon at his expense. I won't interfere with your assigned duties but let me give you this warning. That boy better not suffer serious injury from you and your brothers foul interest in him. The Priceless blood is my salvation. You spill a drop of it, I will boil yours for the insult."

Sebastian looked at the floor but rushed toward me as he said, "As you say Elder Jonas. I swear neither Tadeas nor I will impair your Mann nor allow any significant injury to his flesh." He took up the ball gag and forced it into my mouth while retrieving his tiny padlock.

I didn't attempt a struggle. I laid there glaring at him in open hatred as he locked the horrid thing back into place. I recalled the key was hidden inside the straw. All I had to do is dig around till I found it. Then I could remove that fuckin gag at will, at least till he noticed the key was missing. I would need to work out a plan to keep that from happening.

Sebastian smiled at me appearing every bit the brute. “See you tomorrow screwball. It has been a real pleasure.” He turned and let the entire group, including Geraldine, out locking the cell door behind them.

I didn’t move other than trembling from the pain and fucking cold air for many moments. There was no blanket, you know. I strained the boy’s ears making damned sure the sounds of any life bigger than the dungeon rat was stilled. When I was sure I was alone, other than Florian, I forced my flesh to sit up. I groaned as the truth of their fun and games washed over the boy.

Florian chuckled at my obvious discomfort. “You better watch letting that hodensack of yours grow too big King Maxx. Those boys seem hell bent to see you castrated. Not that it would matter much, ja? They already treat you like the frau.”

I shot him a look of irritation but decided to let that insult go. Besides, he was right. I couldn’t deny the humiliation he witnessed as they used me as their female in the intercourse. My tortured manhood reminded me most rudely they had nearly made me the eunuch on top of everything else.

I slowly crawled to the spot I recalled seeing that key drop from Sebastian’s pocket. There had been much activity and struggle over the spot since it was misplaced there. It took a bit of digging but I managed to find it pretty close to where it had landed in the first place. I didn’t hesitate to unlock that padlock and remove their cruel gag.

I took many deep breaths of relief as Florian sucked in his breath. "Ah, that was clever. Yet you are surely aware those brutes will discover it is missing soon. Then what will you do? Hard to ask for aid with that thing blocking your attempts."

I glared at him with animosity. "If you have nothing more to say then the obvious I demand you shut the fuck up. I am aware this solution is temporary. You know what else Florian? I refuse to take any crap from one that is such a failure he managed to lose his head."

Florian snorted. "Hey, you need not take your anger out on me brother. Save that fire fuel for the ones that earned it, motherfucker."

I laughed sounding as insane as I truly am. "I am no motherfucker, Florian. You need to stop calling me that. I am the fatherfucker or did you miss the gender of my lovers? I think it funny you see everything but the important shit."

Florian gasped. "Holy hell, you are mad. I thought it only an act, but you clearly are cracked. That horror show I saw in this cell today appeared anything but romantic. Yet you call those rapist your lovers? Fuck, you are crazier than me."

I nodded with vigor as I winced and tried to stand up. "I am the King of insanity, brother. Never forget it either. I was thinking a lot about what you said, you know that this, uhm, palace was built for you. I agree, this throne, crown and cell is meant for the foundation bones not the modern

Priceless. I tend to prefer a softer life. You know things like running water, a stove and mattress have spoiled me from this rough living. So, tell you what brother. You help me get out of here and I will return the service. Do we have a deal?" I managed to hold the boy up by the wall and began the painful process of relieving my water through that ravaged chunk of meat that had been my cock.

Florian sat there in silence watching me for a moment then said with hesitancy in his tone, "Alright, I will aid you but only if you sweeten the deal a bit. I need only wait a moment and I will have the flat mate no longer. The men are coming back tomorrow. You won't live much longer at the level of torturing they are unleashing on you. I want more."

I turned my head to stare at him in shock. "You greedy bastard. I offer you the place as my most trusted court Jester, full occupancy of this Palace, my place on the throne, the Metal Crown and this is not enough for you? What fucking more do you desire? Name your price Florian before I change my mind and bash you into dust as I should have the second I fucking saw you in here with me."

Florian scoffed. "There is no need to threaten me, Mad Maxx. I tell you what I want. What you have. I desire to have the Dungeon Master guards, a couple doctors on call, and maybe few other courtiers of my very own."

I buttoned up my breeches slowly while shooting him a glance of sudden understanding. "Well, now that sounds completely fair brother. I beg your forgiveness for thinking you should be satisfied with less than I am enjoying as the Mortar King. Okay, deal then. I give you all you ask and if you are patient, extra I think. I am sure I can see you are well served by a royal inner circle for the next two hundred years. That said, I am all ears. What is your plan to see me out that gate and back above?"

Florian smiled with thrill as he sang out, "One was the sorrow. Two wanted the blood. Three wore the gowns. Four was true love. Five for the future. Six still holds the Gold. Seven will never happen if you remember the secret that metal holds."

I narrowed my eyes. "The perverted Lucus? You are saying he is your plan to see me free of this foundation hell? Well, I can certainly swear you are playing the role of the court fool to perfection. You idiot. Even if Lucus could get access to see me, which as the fourth floor nothing he cannot, why the fuck would the man want to aid me after I broke his jaw? That is if I would be willing to endure his nasty advances any further, which for the record I am not."

Florian scoffed loudly. "Oh? You think Lucus is a worse suiter than the men I saw abusing you today? What exactly is the nature of the foul shit he is asking of you that makes you recoil like that? I ask out of morbid curiosity. If he is desiring something from you that has not already been inflicted on you or at the very least promised to be coming in the near future. I definitely want to hear it described in detail immediately."

I groaned at the honesty in his wisdom. “Fuck you, Florian. Don’t you think I have stroked enough cocks to thrill for today without adding your own to my ever lengthening list? Wait, you don’t have one do you?” I trembled as I looked about the cell worried that he maybe was the lustful ghost and capable of carrying out a supernatural assault on me.

My obvious terror made him break out in cackling laughter that echoed off the rock walls. “Damn, you are one paranoid bastard. I must say it is hilarious that you would think I am desperate enough to stoop that low. I prefer my lovers to be of impeccable pedigree and fine moral behaviors. Give me a little credit would you? I most certainly don’t want to be with a whore like you. Shit, you are beyond soiled goods. Hell, there are circuited silvers that have a less impressive list of those that tasted their skills. I cannot believe you fear I want to fuck you. Well, forget that. Nein and yuck. I would be greatly insulted by your even thinking it, however, I realize you are the psychotic. A creature such as you cannot help their disordered thoughts. It is merely the curse of schizophrenia, ja?” Florian had read my mind obviously.

I turned around to face the skull leaning into the wall for support. “Gosh, I don’t know what to say. Thanks ever so much for the gracious compliments, Florian. You sure know how to make a man feel self-confident and desired. That said, I must ask you kindly to keep any future attempts to raise my spirits to yourself. Another series of flattery of your type will no doubt cause me to consider suicide. I am not in need of reminding of just how disgusting and unworthy of life I am brother." I glared at him not attempting to hide my sarcastic tone.

Florian laughed wildly at me. "At least you are entertaining I have to give you that. Not a lot going on around here for many a century. I think I may even miss you a little once I retake my throne. Promise me that from time to time you will come back for a visit. Maybe just to fill me in on the gossip?"

I shook my head in disbelief. "What the fuck. You think we are girlfriends now, Florian? I think not. I may be a little weak minded but coming down to the dungeon to discuss rumors with a skull is even too nuts for Mad Maxx. In fact, it just occurred to me that for the last several minutes I have been arguing with a fucking cranium while my own blood from torture runs down the back of my legs. I am trapped like the beast in a cell and forced to suck my dinner through a straw. I wear a King's crown of recycled metal that I cannot take off, but I rule nothing but the rats and rape. Ah, help, someone please, Gott dammit. I am fucking insane. Kill me, I am begging for anyone to end this pain. I don't want to live anymore. Make the voices stop. Leo? Rolf? Jakob? Cary? Where are you? I am lost." I fell to my knees and began weeping into the boy's hands as the tapestry began to ebb and flow all around the cell.

The floor trembled with the quakes of madness. I wailed in terror and hopelessness unable to get ahold of myself. Above the boy's head the roof began to rotate, and lightening flashed from the eye of the vortex. The stress of my poor treatment had finally gotten to me. A psychotic storm was building with incredible speed threatening to engulf me for all time.

My ears were assaulted by the whispers of the Haus residents living above that dungeon hell. I could hear them laughing at me and saying the most dishonorable things about my character. I screamed, as best I could given my hoarseness, begging them to shut up.

At first, I tried to block their cruel words by holding the sides of my head tightly. When that failed to silence the noise, I grabbed handfuls of the straw and buried my head under the piles. I could still hear them all, taunting and mocking me no matter what I did to end their torment.

I felt the boy's flesh unraveling. My arms and legs became alien to me. The confusion of all that sound, the flashing lights of the storm, and sensations of shattering into thousands of pieces blinded me to any coherent thoughts of my own safety. I had to make this nightmare stop any way possible.

I came up from my straw grave with a roar of the madman issuing from my ravaged mouth. I ignored the agony and stood up using all the remaining strength left within me. Then without hesitation I ran at the wall head bowed. The resulting collision with the stone was cushioned by the metal crown pinned to my head. I bounced backward with only the boy's neck seriously jarred. As I took another run at that wall, my railing mind was degrading to levels not witnessed since the onset of my disease.

Despite my disordered psyche it was not lost on me of how completely evil Gretta's designs to keep me alive but unable to challenge her had been. She had made sure to bond that crown on my head to keep me from injuring myself seriously if I tried the head banging. That bitch made damned sure I couldn't find the mercy of death through suicide nor even the comfort of unconsciousness.

I bashed into the wall with all my might, but that metal crown held. I finally accepted this was not going to work. I changed gears and attempted to find the grave by slamming my forehead instead of rushing the wall like the bull. This too was impeded by my bonded metal headgear. The base of that fucking thing extended out just far enough to prevent me from making direct contact with the wall. That crown was designed to act like the helmet. Yikes!

Several minutes passed before I wore myself out trying to do the impossible. I wailed in misery and slid down the wall face first to my knees as I admitted my latest defeat. I wept uncontrollably in my kneel thinking wildly of ways to end my life.

Briefly I toyed with the idea that I could wrap the collar chain around the boy's neck, pull to the end of it and choke the pathetic life from my bones. That thought was quickly extinguished when I realized I would pass out before finding death.

You see, even intensely psychotic I was not completely stupid. It occurred to me that likely after I went unconscious the chain would go slack. That would allow me to gain access to oxygen and the reflexive lungs would resume their function against my will. This would allow for my continued existence with a far worse disability of probable brain damage as the result of my botched hanging.

I held that key to the ball gag padlock tightly in my hand as I sobbed there next to the wooden privy at my hellish situation. I stared at it wondering if somehow I could use it as a tool to find my release from the mortal coil. Through this entire psychotic episode Florian had remained uncommonly quiet while observing my fit.

He overheard me trying to decide if the key could open an important vein. "I wouldn't do that if I were you Mad Maxx. Here, give me the Key to hold. You are going to get out of this cell, trust me. Doing something stupid lets your enemies win. Is that what you want? To be the loser for truth? You are the King, Maxx. You must be the honest leader you were born to be."

I rolled the key through the boy's fingers feeling fatigue that went right to my soul washing over me. "You don't understand. I don't want to do this anymore. The baby lambs and green fields avail me. I can be with my Annette, Marc and Kloe if I take the river trip. They wait for me to come home. This brutal world is the foreign land to Christian Axel. Leave me alone and let me find the peace I surely have earned. If I have not, then please tell me what more I must do to earn it. I am so tired, Florian. I want to go where they cannot hurt me anymore," I wailed.

A hand gently laid on my shoulder from behind me. I let out a shriek thinking one of the voices had come to lay claim to the boy. I hit the floor and rolled up defensively while screaming in my raspy voice bloody murder from the startle.

Birgit jumped backwards reflexively from my outburst of fear. “Oh, my Gott. I apologize your Majesty. I realized it is poor protocol to lay hands on the King, but I thought a bit of true affection would bring you some comfort. I ask you again with profound respect to allow me to have that key to your gag, Sire. I can protect it for you as I have said but even more I can have a copy made of it. Surely that brute Sebastian will discover it is missing. He will come looking for it. If you can trust your loyal servant Birgit, then I will see at least a small amount of the Masters cruelty eliminated for good.”

I gasped as I slowly realized it was Birgit and not Florian that had been speaking with me for Gott knows how long. “Birgit? Is this real? Are you really here or am I hallucinating this?” I hazarded a look by pulling the boy’s hands away from my eyes.

Birgit was kneeling there next to me with a sweet smile on her wrinkled face. “I am really here, Sire. I saw the others leave a while ago. I waited till I was sure the Masters were not likely to return for the night before daring to come check on your welfare. I see that my worst fears are realized. I can no longer find comfort in the lies I tell myself. I can clearly see these dishonorable men are taking advantage of my King in the most deplorable of ways. I am ashamed to confess there is nothing I can do to stop them, Sire. I was raised to my position by the men of the late Xavier. The men in power that gave me immunity from the severest of punishments are no more. Gretta would like to see me, and my sister Viviana laid low, and replaced with her own FemDoms. The Dungeon Masters Sebastian and Tadeas are her men. They have the position of favor and given a chance would aid the Silk Queen in seeing us all used to fertilize the grounds. I don't tell you all this my King because I desire to make excuses for my lack of aid to my Lord and Master, but merely to explain the truth of your dangerous situation and my own." She extended her hand in offer to aid me.

I groaned in pure agony while she helped me sit up and lean into the wall. "I understand Mistress. I thank you for the mercy you do offer this worthless man, no matter how little you think it may be. Sometimes even the smallest kindness can make the biggest difference. I know you cannot bust me out of this cell, that I have already figured out. However, I will allow you to carry out the plan to copy this key. If you could find it within your power, could I ask one more small favor of you honorable Birgit?" I handed her the small padlock key.

She grinned and bowed her head in reverence. "Of course you may ask of your servant anything you want Sire. If it is within my ability I will see it done immediately." She slipped the key into her apron pocket.

I nodded. “My Felicity? Have you been able to find her for me? If I had my lamb I think I could find the strength to endure what I must. She will know what to do.”

Birgit frowned and shot a confused glance at me. “Uhm, Sire, I think you require the aid of your powerful connections in the Haus, not the toy lamb. However, I will dare not question your good judgement. That is why I am here Master Maxx. I have contacted your Shadow King. I have managed to slip him past the watchful eyes of the dungeon guards, and he awaits my signal in the Palace ritual room just down the hall. If you can assure me that your visit will be brief, quiet and never spoken of to a soul beyond the three of us, I will go get the man this moment. Be warned. The Guards go on break in fifteen minutes. The timing of our escaping the cell must be precise. There will be no other chances. We need get out of here the moment I give the signal, or he and I will find our deaths by pyre.”

My heart nearly floated from my chest with hope. “Then waste not another second seeking to aid me in comfort. Fetch Cary. Go and hurry, Mistress. I will attend my own hurts and thank you forever for the mercy you grant me this night. I will never forget the kindness.”

She smiled as she rose with a wince. Without hesitation she rushed from the cell down the hallway to guide Cary back to visit with me. I did my best to wipe my face of the tears of humiliation. There was no mirror to seeking out the horrific reflection I was sure I would caste.

I smoothed out my dirty, torn clothing. I was grateful for the black color of the vampire outfit for a change. It managed to hide the many stains of blood, urine and semen that coated almost every inch of the material. However, it couldn't mask the smell of my shame. I winced as I listened to Cary and Birgit's footsteps coming down the stone hall. There was no way to camouflage the signs of my being the victim of torture most brutal from my Dark Bonded Shadow King.

I saw his smiling face at the gate as Birgit opened it to let him enter the cell. She said nothing as he rushed across the room eager to embrace his lover. I whimpered in pain as the strong guard dropped to a kneel and wrapped his arms around my waist. He ignored my sounds of discomfort while pulling me to his tight embrace. To my surprise he was seemingly oblivious to my disheveled state.

Cary held me for a few moments taking deep relieved breaths. "My love Christian. I thought I was never going to see you again. I have been worried out of my mind day had killed you, or worse you had died by your own hand. You have no idea how good it feels to hold you in my arms this moment. I swear I never want to let you go," he whispered into my ear.

I groaned from the sharp pains ripping through my flesh from his handling me. "Please brother, let me go. I am not in the condition for your affection. As you see I am not dead. Not yet anyway. We don't have long to speak. I need you to focus. There are a few things I require be done or this maybe the last moment we will ever have together for truth."

Cary gasped and released his hold rapidly. "Ja, I hear you Christian. It is my true honor to carry out your orders, my heart. Tell me how I can help and be assured it will be done. Wait, holy hell, Christian. What have those devils done? Baby, you look like shit. Who has done this? Tell me and I will send the cocksucker to his grave for daring to lay a hand on you." He caressed my cheek softly wincing as his eyes ran across the horrific indications that I had not been treated well.

I held my tears in check over the look of horror in his expression as he examined me with his eyes. "It is not important what has happened, but it is paramount it stops. I will not survive much longer if I cannot find aid in releasing me. I need you to go to Matz on the third floor. Tell him Mad Maxx has sent you to request his aid in speaking to my Master Lucus. Inform Matz that he must lobby the man to take me back under his protection. Make it clear to Matz that I am willing to pay any price for his intervention and there is no limit to what I will grant Lucus to receive his favor. Matz will know how best to approach and speak to the Dominant. I only need you to make sure Matz agrees to do it. If he tells you nein, hound him or even threaten if necessary. This man Lucus is my only real way out of this nightmare. Gaining his forgiveness will not be easy. Matz likely will have to work at it, far harder than you will on him to get this ball rolling."

Cary frowned but nodded. “As you wish, Christian. I will make sure Matz goes to Lucus or see him swimming with Fiona and Hanno in the well.

I chuckled bitterly. “Had I realized how foul life could be I would have spared Fiona her swimming lesson. Instead, I would have gifted her the Metal Crown and a seat on the Mortar Throne brother. This fate is very fitting for a child killer, ja?”

Cary nodded with sadness in his expression. “Ja, I think you are right, my heart. Almut and Hubertus wanted me to give you their apologies brother. They are near suicidal from the guilt their bad advice they gave to you. They said if they had known the truth of the Mortar Throne and the terrible fate they sent you to by instructing you to demand it, well…”

I interrupted Cary. “You tell my men they are forgiven. None of us knew this was a trap set by the Silk and Fur Queens. I hold no ill will towards those that caused this injury by ignorance. I reserve all my hatred for those that use this misstep to fill their twisted greed, ja? Almut and Hubertus can rest their troubled souls knowing that their King Mad Maxx loves them as his own brothers till the earth claims his bones.”

Cary flashed a weak smile at me. “That is why I love you so much Christian. You are fair and just as well as wise. Surely there is something more your lover can do besides seeking out Matz and speaking to your men that will bring you comfort. Please, my love, I cannot bear to see you suffer like this. I feel so fucking helpless."

I nodded. "There is one more thing I need from you Cary. When you visit with Matz, ask him to go to my apartment and use his old key to get in when Lucus isn't home. In the closet in my bedroom, he will find my lamb Felicity. Tell him to get her then find the Dungeon Mistress Birgit. She will smuggle Felicity to me. That, my lover, is the only comfort I can hope for at this moment."

Cary looked deep into my eyes then before I could stop him pulled me by crown forcing a deep kiss. I had been severely traumatized by the cruel abuses from earlier. That caused me to flashback to the terror suffered at the hands of the other men. To Cary's shock, and my embarrassment, I recoiled as if he were biting rather than kissing me.

He sat there holding on to me tightly, afraid I would harm myself if he let me go he would say later, with an expression of disbelief while I wailed in terror and struggled against his grip. Cary had no idea what he had done or what to do now that I was behaving like the loon I truly am.

I wasted several moments of our visit freaking out like that. When at last I was able to get myself back under control, Birgit had already come to the gate to warn Cary time was nearly up.

Cary shot the Mistress a look of fear then glanced back at me appearing shamed. "Christian, I should have realized that with you here in chains that maybe others saw it as opportunity to, uhm, never mind I wasn't thinking. There is no excuse for it. I lost my good judgement. can you please forgive me for taking such liberty?"

I wiped my wet eyes and panted still feeling anxious, and truly shamed at that unmanly display in front of my Dark Bonded. "It is already forgotten. The mistake was mine and I pay enough for it for the both of us. I thank you for the mercy you show me by risking your life to see me. I owe you more than I can ever hope to repay." I looked at the floor feeling overwhelmed by despair.

Cary smiled with adoration in his eyes. "All I ask in return from you Christian is that you survive and escape this cell. You swear to do that then I will consider us even, ja? I don't want to hear you say this isn't something you can promise me either. I have brought you the thing you told me will assure this is possible." Cary reached into his guard jacket and pulled out my lamb Felicity.

I nearly fainted in amazement as my Shadow King handed her to me. "How did you get her Cary, or for that matter know about her in the first place." I took Felicity into my shaking hands and pulled her tightly to my chest marveling at how her softness made me feel better immediately.

Cary snorted with a mild chuckle. "Marc told me about the lambs. He said that Felicity lived in your jacket pocket like his Kloe did his own. Birgit told me yesterday when I tried to get permission to visit that you were asking for a lamb called Felicity. I realized this was the one I had heard about. I went to your apartment and told Lucus that the Dungeon guards sent me to fetch a fresh jacket for you to wear in your cell. I took the chance the Dominant would grab the correct one. He gave me the coat and slammed the door in my face. As luck would have it, your lamb was indeed in the pocket along with two others I recognized at belonging to Kloe and Marc. You need not worry love. Their lambs are safely in Roselina care until you return to claim them. I bring this one, Felicity to give you some comfort in what seems like the never ending misery."

I looked up at him as the overwhelming grief – of loss of my black collar children, my freedom, everything – overtook the boy. "I thank you for the comfort you brought to Marc, and now to me." I fell into the crying jag.

Cary pulled me into his embrace allowing me to weep in his arms. He softly assured me that all was going to be alright I needed only to be strong a bit longer. He kissed my ear softly as he whispered a promised. Cary said only death would prevent him from finding a way to get Lucus to pull his powerful strings to see me free again.

I had faith in my Shadow King. I had no trouble believing everything he said to me in those dark moments in that rotten cell. His words of hope, and solace I found in his embrace, re-lit my blaze to fight for my life. I will openly admit it was Cary's gentle touching and thoughtful heart that deserves all the credit for my survival of that horrible incarceration after being coronated as the Master of the Haus.

To be truthful, I couldn't have been more blessed than to have the loyalty and love of such fine men as Cary, Almut and Hubertus. There perfect service to your unworthy Master has never wavered since and without them, I would not be with you here tonight, but we get ahead of ourselves, ja?

Birgit broke up Cary's nursemaiding his grieving lover with a demand that they had to move quickly or be trapped for good. I let my Dark Bonded lover go from our embrace with fresh tears breaking out.

It was touching to see he was wiping his own eyes of their sorrow as he rushed to follow the Dungeon Mistress out of the cell before it was too late to escape. I watched him shoot several glances full of regret at me as the two of them ran like hell down the hallway to sneak out before the guards returned to dare posts.

I pulled my trusty companion Felicity out to examine that she was unharmed. My lamb was fit and well fed as ever. I snuggled her back to my chest sighing breaths of great relief. I was no longer alone in that cold, damp tomb. Florian and Felicity made for fine roommates. Having friends to share your pain with and to break the hell of loneliness makes even the worst nightmares tolerable. I fell asleep in that rodent riddled floor cuddling my lamb while Florian sang ancient lullabies of faraway lands.

A panicked Birgit abruptly awakened me. She shook me with hurried harshness begging me to entrust my Felicity to her care before she was confiscated. I was confused and half asleep as the Dungeon Mistress attempted to pry the lamb from my hands.

I wailed out in fear as Birgit managed to snatch Felicity and pushed her roughly into her apron pocket. "Nein Mistress, I beg of you. Don't do this. Felicity is mine. Why do you steal from me." I lunged at the Mistress, but she had managed to retreat beyond where the heavy weights would allow me to go.

Birgit frowned at me then whispered loudly, "Sire, please allow me to replace your gag. I don't dare steal from my King, I swear it. I merely aid his Majesty in offering his toy sanctuary until those who would take her away from him are no longer a threat. I beg of you, listen to your servant Birgit. The Voter Peter and that dishonorable doctor Noethan are coming with their guards Sabastian and Tadeas. Hurry, they are heading for the Palace, Sire. There is no time for explanation."

The names of those two men stopped my wailing immediately. "What? Peter and Noethan are with those brutes? Oh, bloody hell. They come to attack me together. I am doomed. Ja, I thank you for keeping my Felicity safe Mistress. Forgive my ignorance of the mercy you offer by your quick actions." I shuddered as I dropped to a kneel of resignation in front of Birgit.

She frowned but came forward taking up the ball gag on the scold cage. "With your permission Sire, may I?" I nodded and the Mistress locked me back into silence before my stealing of the key was caught by the Dungeon Masters.

I watched the frightened Mistress move with speed to the cell door carrying my precious cargo in her pocket. I closed my eyes and tried to stop trembling in terror. I knew the four men coming were not on their way to enjoy a well-mannered tea party with me. I hadn't recovered from the last round of assaults the day before and already the cycle of rape, torture and psychological abuse was beginning again.

As I braced and waited for the first shift of nightmares of the day, I wondered how long I could last. It was only a matter of time before the flesh became infected to sepsis, or I stroked out from the stress and pain. Could I keep my promise to Cary to survive for days? A week? A month? A year?

I watched the four men approach the gate. Peter and Noethan were smiling with wickedness. The Dungeon Masters opened the cell door and then stepped inside. I didn't move from my spot, nor did I take my eyes off the group as they approached. Peter carried a handful of college books. Noethan held a doctor's bag with a premeasured syringe ready to deliver the sedatives to my flesh to keep me slow, confused and groggy. No need to have to fight to extract their thrill when modern medicine could make their sport with me a no contest. I didn't even offer struggle as Sebastian and Tadeas rushed and restrained me by the upper arms. Peter stood there watching as Noethan approached with his needle. I couldn't take my eyes off the cruel smile on the face of a man that could have been my own reflection in a mirror. My own father had come to see me dishonored in such a brutal way. I felt the prick of the sedative. Then weakness flowed through the boy's veins as the doctor chuckled. He watched my flesh tremble as it was forced to relax by his drugs. He then signaled to the Masters to hold me just in case I still had any fight left in me. I winced as that pervert proudly announced their raping of the Priceless could commence if only Sebastian could figure out where the fuck he put that key to my ball gag.

Chapter 40: Beyond the Limits of Madness

Sebastian cursed under his breath. I didn't move a muscle nor take my sight from the floor as the Dungeon Master let go of my arm. I felt the fear rolling down my spine when he began to tear through his pocket seeking that padlock key. I just knew he would somehow figure out that I had managed to snag it from his possession.

Doctor Noethan sighed loudly. "What is the holdup, Sebastian? Why are you stalling? The medication I gave to this idiot is most potent in the first half hour or so. You are wasting valuable time. I desire to have my cock sucked before he become alert enough to shave some off the top, if you catch my drift."

Sebastian nodded wildly appearing to have become a bit anxious. "I know Anselm, I know. I am trying to hurry dammit. I cannot find the fucking key. I swear to Gott that damned frau of my has the stickiest fingers. She apparently has been rummaging through my pockets again. I think the bitch has either taken it from me or allowed it to fall onto floor at our apartment perhaps?"

Peter scoffed. "Christ, this is ridiculous. Why the fuck is the boy in a gag in the first place, Anselm? Not like anyone is going to fucking hear his insane pleas for mercy down here. Cut the fucking lock off with the bolt cutters and be done with it. You fear his chewing on your manhood, then put on the spider rather than the ball gag fool. Shit, for that matter, threaten to beat the fuck out of him if he dares to demonstrate hesitation. The Priceless is well trained. You all behave as if he were the unseasoned novice. If I didn't know any better I would even go so far as to think you three big brutes fear this little nothing at your feet. Look at him. By the condition of his flesh, I hazard to say someone or more have already soften him up quite a bit as it is. Yet still you feel the need to sedate him and use unnecessary tongue teething? What the hell is wrong with you boys?"

Doctor Noethan shook his head. "Peter I won't insult you by saying you are in error. These precautions are necessary for our safety when extracting our interests from the unwilling Priceless. Don't let his quiet demeanor lull you into believing he will maintain compliance with your lustful demands. I have fallen for that false trick twice already and have the injuries for such stupidity. I don't desire to go for the third helping of his attempts to prevent me from what I want from him."

Peter's eyes went wide in disbelief. "You admit openly to fear this boy? Seriously Anselm? I can see clear as the bell Maximillian doesn't have even a toenail left in reality. He is drooling heavier than the newborn babe and his eyes are empty of intelligent thoughts. It is pretty obvious this boy is psychotic as shit. The insane are too confused to lodge a willful assault on anything other than themselves. Kick him around a bit and he will comply just fine. You forget I have dealt with him for years. Maximillian is beyond useless at causing a fuss when the acute cycles come on him. He is already chained down and tethered to the wall and weights. What the fuck could he even do if he could even collect a single coherent thought to behave like an insolent asshole." He shot a look of disgust at me sitting there on my knees at his feet.

Tadeas chuckled but held fast to my other arm while his brother continued to search his pockets. "I agree with Peter, brothers. The loon is a big fellow and definitely strong. However, there are four of us and only one of him. Go get those bolt cutters from the ritual room and cut off the padlock. I say fuck it. We can always replace it later. I am eager to finish that business that got interrupted yesterday by his grumpy Mann."

Peter shot a look of worry at Tadeas. "What? Jonas was here yesterday. Am I to understand he ended your sexual assault on Maximillian? Why would he do that?" He seemed confused by that information for some reason. Apparently he doesn't know Jonas as well as he thought he did. The Vampire is a jealous bastard. He is not the generous one with his things despite what everyone seemed to think at the time.

Tadeas snorted with distain in his tone. "Oh, that snotty motherfucker thought me, Sebastian and the Altergotts were getting too rough with the nutball is all. They brought in this lamb to torment him with you know. That made the Elder all nervous. I have to be honest. I am unsure who is the crazier, this fruit loop or that freakish Mann of his."

Peter's expression twisted to one of fury. "You dare to speak of your better in such a derogatory fashion. I should see you whipped for such flagrant disrespect, you worm. For that matter, bringing Geraldine here to torture the Priceless was not only stupid it was beyond dangerous. Is it your plan to kill the boy? If so, then you and the Altergotts better watch your backs. I will see all three of your worthless hides made into feed for the pigs before I allow this boy's life ended."

Tadeas began to stammer in fear as his brother stopped searching and backed away from me. "Uhm, I beg your mercy Peter. I, uhm, didn't think the Altergotts games with the sheep was that serious. Though I confess the Priceless did appear quite disturbed at the threats they lodged at the animal. I don't understand the nature of his affinity for the beast, but I assumed the Elder and his brother knew what they were doing. The Head of the Voters has strictly forbidden any attempts to fatally injure the Mortar King. I swear Sebastian and me were only having a little harmless sport with the boy. Neither of us desire to see him to the yard, that I can promise."

Peter glared at the men then glanced hatefully at Doctor Noethan. "You know what? I change my mind. All you leave. This bullshit of your raping the Priceless isn't going to happen while this Voter has any say so. I think the boy has likely had enough of you fellows as it is."

It was Doctor Noethan's turn to appear stunned. "What the fuck. Nein. Tadeas, Sebastian, don't you listen to this arrogant asshole. You don't tell us what we can and cannot do Peter. This is not the Haus floor brother. Down here you are not above any of us, nor do we have to obey your orders. Gretta granted us permission to use this boy anyway we want. If you have a problem with that, then I suggest you take it up with the one that is over you."

Peter nearly lost his shit when that pervert said that. "You little nothing cocksucker. I intend to take this up with Gretta. Pack it up boys. We are all going to see the Queen of the Silk. Until she straightens this bullshit up no one is to lay a hand on the Priceless."

Doctor Noethan put up his hand demanding the Dungeon Masters hold their positions as Peter began to storm to the gate. "I already said we don't have to mind your words, Peter. You go see her and be prepared to find I tell the truth of it. We have permission to do as we please as long as it is short of killing the King. See you later Peter or maybe not. By the time you return I am certain I will have had my fun for the day." He and the Masters snickered as Peter tore through the gate slamming it with vigor behind him.

I winced as the Doctor then turned his sights back to me kneeling before him. "Well, more for us boy, ja? Find that fucking pair of bolt cutters Sebastian and stop fooling around. You can get another padlock on your own time. I have the clients shortly. I don't want to keep them waiting while you hold your dick in one hand and scratch your head with the other."

Sebastian nodded. "Okay, fine. I think there is a pair in the receiving room. Tadeas, hold that fucker tightly. I don't want to come back to find the loon choking the shit out of the two of you like yesterday, ja?" Tadeas nodded with a chuckle as the brute headed for the gate as Peter had moments before.

I closed my eyes bracing myself for the coming horror. I knew the second they cut off that padlock all my trouble liftin that key would be useless. The replacement would require a fresh key. I was about to lose the tiny bit of freedom I had managed. There was nothing I could do about it but feel like the loser I truly was at the time.

My eyes were snapped open when I heard the sound of sweet Birgit hailing Sebastian as he started down the hallway. "Brother, I thought I may I find you here. Last night Viviana came to make sure the King was drinking his water, and she came across this key on the floor of his cell. At first she didn't think it of any importance and nearly tossed it away. Then I recalled that ball gag padlock and wondered are you missing the key? If not then I suppose it has been discarded by past workers in the palace and somehow overlooked for years." She held out the tiny key appearing to be distracted by something down the hallway that I couldn't see.

Sebastian smiled with thrill as he took the key from her outstretched palm. "Ah, Birgit you are the angel. Ja, this is the key I have been seeking. Thank Gott your sister came across it when she did. Tell her I owe her a beer."

Birgit frowned at that. "I will tell her, but I also will warn you brother. You are lucky that the King didn't find it before Viviana did. Do you realize the damage he could have done to himself with that object had he noticed it laying for anyone to discover? Be more careful with the tools of his restraints. He is very disturbed at the moment, and I dare say a little more than stressed. If he were to be injured, I need not say it do I? I am in no mood for being cooked to well done, and I bet you are not the willing bar-b-que participate either. Don't forget what Gretta threatened if he were to be severely injured or killed."

Sebastian nodded and spit in the floor. "Ja, Birgit I need not be reminded. Damn you are a bigger nag than my fucking frau. If there is nothing else, I suggest you be getting to your other duties. Tadeas and I have the King covered for now. You can come make sure he eats in about an hour in a half I think. The doctor should be through with his treatments by that time." He chuckled a bit at what he thought was a clever statement.

Birgit shot me a look of worry. "Treatments you say. Is that what the doctor calls his rough treatment of our Lord and Master? Humm, this modern medicine seems to be akin to the ancient methods of healing the mentally ill if you asked me."

Doctor Noethan narrowed his eyes when he heard the Mistress say that. "No one did ask you, did they Birgit? I suggest you do as Sebastian told you. I will be finished attending the Mortar King then you can finish your own duties to him. Be on your way now thank you." He waved her off with his nose in the air.

Birgit snorted as if angered but offered no quarrel. I watched the lady stride off while Sebastian re-entered the cell grinning with triumph holding that blasted key in his outstretched hand. The doctor nodded and smiled back demanding that the brute unlock the gag with speed.

He shot me a look of glee "Yesterday you were forgiven the foreplay. Today you will give me a demonstration of the legendary oral skills that were denied me that day in my office. You better not skimp on the blow job either. I expect you will not neglect any of my sensitive parts. I want you to attend everything with vigor and talent or be sorry for it."

I held still as he undid the mouth restraint but the second I was free of it I glared at the perverted physician and said, "Suck your own cock and have one of these brutes lick you hodensack and asshole motherfucker. I won't do it and I don't care what you threaten. Do your worst. I am not afraid of you." I knew that refusal would result in a beating but that was the point. I would rather be kicked to death then put any part of that nasty pervert in my mouth, ja?).

Well, that insolence at his command resulted in a rapid and brutal kick right to my own mangled manhood from the brute Sebastian. after that recent session of the sexual torturing by the snake brothers, I must say the usual discomfort of a kick to the balls was more than excruciating. I let out a wail that surely reached the heavens and fell to my side unable to catch my breath from the agony of it.

Doctor Noethan chuckled as he stood over my writhing frame. "What is that you say, Mad Maxx? That was merely a taste of what I am willing to see done to you in an effort to get what I want. Do you desire to test my resolve further? Still not afraid of me?"

I could barely breathe out in a whisper, that fucking hurt you know. "I tell you to go fuck yourself Anselm, and I mean that. You put anything of yours in my mouth and find it chewed for your trouble." I groaned and did my best to guard my nearly broken male parts.

Doctor Noethan frowned at my continued refusal. He ordered the brutes to rough me up a bit without doing acute damage. I endured a painful but non-lethal series of backhands and a mild beating for several minutes. That did nothing to change my mind. I had decided the Dungeon Masters could use me as their football all day if they liked.

I maybe couldn't stop them from holding me down for their unnatural intercourse, but I could block them from forcing me to prepare them to dishonor me like they had been. I was not going to put up with anymore forced oral sex with the doctor or anyone, Gott dammit. I thought as long as Felicity and Geraldine were safe they had nothing of worth to use as incentive. Nope I wasn't going to give them my honest skills of the special services. They wanted to taste my tears they would have to rape with violence to get them.

It was my disturbed thinking that if I were the lucky one, sooner or later the men would accidently kill me trying to extract their pleasures. I decided to be satisfied that the fatal blow would result in the fiery death of the one that sent me to the peace of my grave.

I finally had come to understand this was the only way I could find any honor in my compromised position. Giving in to the demands of the rapists over the fear of being beaten or tortured had not prevented them from doing that after they got what they wanted anyway. I really had nothing to lose but my dignity or a life I no longer really wanted. I was damned tired of the shame of handing that over without a fight, you know.

When I still refused to do as I was told, the doctor dug deep into his twisted soul to seek incentive to gain my compliance with his demand. I laid there on the floor panting nearly blind from the pain of the Masters' brutal thrashing as the doctor whispered something in Tadeas' ear. I watched the man chuckle, then head for the wooden privy.

I groaned in disgust as I saw him reach into the bottom of it pulling the drawer that caught the wastes. I didn't need to be told of the plan to realize this was unwelcome news. I was already painfully aware the perverts were willing to do almost anything to see me on my knees minding their orders like the little bitch. Though this disgusting new threat was lower than I had expected them to go to get their way.

Doctor Noethan shot me a thrilled smile and crossed his arms as Tadeas approached me with that full waste drawer. “Mad Maxx tells us he will chew anything of ours we put into his mouth. I had forgotten he has not had his breakfast yet. I think the problem is the boy is hungry and fearful that he will mistake our advances as food. That is easily solved. We merely need to feed him till he no longer has the empty stomach, ja?” Sebastian chuckled with evil humor while I tried to crawl away from the advancing Tadeas.

Needless to say, he easily caught me. He called on the aid of his brother. Between the two of them, with the aid of my heavy restraints, I was no match for their cruel sport. I was held down tightly, and my mouth forced open. They poured the entire contents in sending me right into a wild spasms of revolting sickness. I was literally puking the shit up faster than day could force it into the boy.

The men were nearly on the floor with gut splitting laughter when they finally let me off my back. I went right to my hands and knees puking till I was sure I was going to upchuck my organs. In my desperation to get that nasty taste off my tongue I grabbed handfuls of the straw that was unaffected by either the waste or my vomit and shoved it into my mouth. That deplorable action only made the three brutes laugh even harder to see me grazing with insanity like the sheep. I think it is unnecessary to say it was not one of my finer moments, ja? Doctor Noethan allowed this to continue a few moments until he got ahold of his humor.

He walked over to the mess that used to be the proud Mad Maxx smiling with cruel triumph. “Well King Maxx?

Are you full yet or do you need a second helping? I am sure the boys and me can find you more to eat, perhaps fresher this time? If you think your hunger is sated, I will ask you once more to get to seeing my commands followed to the letter. You have only a few moments to decide. Then I will get to work making that last meal seem like the supreme delicacy."

Well, I hate to admit it, but I found that I was willing to put up with agonizing torture, and even the cutters. Yet, that business of being force fed solid wastes I couldn't handle. Doctor Noethan didn't have to threaten twice. He got what he wanted, and so did the Dungeon Masters. I gave none of them any further quarrel as I endured their demands for the foulest of special services be granted to each of them.

When I had finished playing the sex doll for the last man, two things happened. First, I found I had wept so much there was no more fluid left in the boy to making the tears. I could only sit there in the kneeling position shuddering from the deep despair that had overtaken me from this latest failure to maintain any sense of human dignity.

Second, I found that the men were still not done with the lording of their conquest of my soul.

Doctor Noethan smiled with wickedness as he stood over me. "I thought the rumors of your artistry surely overrated, but I am pleased to say there is much truth to the stories in this case. You know Mad Maxx, you have done such a wonderful job, I think it only fair to grant a little mercy to you. That business with the privy drawer surely left you with a foul aftertaste. I bet even the straw couldn't clear that from your senses, ja? Tell you what. Before we leave, I think we will aid you by offering the mouthwash to sweeten that amazing tongue of yours." He nodded at Sebastian with a chuckle.

I whimpered and tried to retreat but as usual Sebastian moved faster than me. I struggled with all my might as he pushed me to my back. Then with great brutality he forced my jaw open. Tadeas came up next to the two of us and undid his pants. I could do nothing but choke and gargle as the man relieved his water into my mouth like the living latrine.

The foul encounters with the threesome of Doctor Noethan, Tadeas and Sebastian would become the daily nightmare for the next three weeks of my sorry life. Most days I fought the good fight but inevitably they got their way in the most gruesome of fashions.

The sickness, perversions and revolting things they did to me still bring me to a place of distress to this very day. Of all the bastards that took advantage of me in the Palace, not even the Altergotts can lay claim to the level of obscenity enforced upon the boy by that despotic doctor and the Dungeon Masters.

Their interests were so deplorable I think I will refrain from further discussion of the things that happened. Not because I am ashamed of it, Meine Liebe. I was the helpless victim in their sport with me like you are now. You have encountered some of debauchery I endured at their hands already and need no stress added by knowing of what other horrors can be enacted by one human on another.

I know Mad Max said you wouldn't be granted any kindness with regard to the hard road you must travel with your Master Maxx, but I take that back in this instance. It is a true mercy I grant you tonight by keeping this nightmare for myself for now. When you are older, I will discuss it with you if such things come up, and sadly, knowing that horrible mother of yours they inevitably will.

The last thing I will say about them is if you can imagine it, they did it to me in one way or another over the next twenty-one days. Between their perversions and the Altergotts cruelly tampering with my acute symptoms, I nearly broke from reality forever. It is a miracle I managed to hold onto even a shred of sanity given the strain that was put on the boy.

Well, that is not completely the truth. It was not divine intervention that saved me, but special nature of my disease that I can give the credit to, but we get ahead of ourselves again, ja? We are almost to that discussion.

I will end this deplorable part of the story of the three rat bastards by saying that from this point on in the story of the Palace, when I discuss their visits, I will simply say the monstrosity continued and leave it at that, ja? I nodded in agreement with Der Hund's statement.

NOTE: For the record Mad Maxx did keep his promise and in time told me the entire story of Doctor Noethan and the Dungeon Masters. I will tell you what he told me about it when I reach it in my own childhood trauma. So, for now, enjoy the mercy Der Hund granted meanwhile you can. He wasn't kidding when he said there was nothing held back by those monsters. Yikes!

On with the story (shudder).

Sebastian relieved himself into the boy's head then quickly locked the ball gag keeping me from spitting out their foul urine. It was the final cruelty the doctor had up his sleeve, for that day anyway. The three of them left full of loud laughter at my predicament. I immediately took to the floor, shaken my head and retching on my hands and knees helpless to do a thing about their nasty trick.

I shivered in my torment, praying to the Gott that doesn't exit, when my dear Birgit would be coming to visit shortly with breakfast. I knew she had given Sebastian the key to my gag, but I rightly assumed she had made a copy of the original. If only I could hang in there a bit, the Mistress would come to save me from my misery. I had to believe that, or I surely would have had the heart attack that very second from the stress of it all.

I had covered the boy's head with straw in the floor trying to calm down the inner turmoil when I head the familiar voice of Peter call out to me. I popped up from my hiding spot sure that I was hallucinating him. At least hoped I was. I was in no mood for a fourth assault so close to the horrid last three. To my dismay my father stood there staring at me while holding his nose.

His expression took on one of abhorrence as his eyes ran across the cause of the foul smell emitting from the soiled straw. "Holy hell Maximillian. What has happened? Did you miss the privy? Gott dammit. Where the fuck are the Dungeon Mistresses? They need to get their asses in here and clean up this shit hole they call a Palace. You will get sick if open sewage is allowed to be left unchecked." He started to head for the gate appearing to truly believe that in my psychotic state I had lost all sense of decency.

He didn't even get halfway to the door when Birgit and Viviana were spotted rushing down the hallway headed for my cell. The women noticed the smell before they even entered. I saw that Viviana carried the tray of my water and gruel while Birgit dragged the basket of fresh straw behind her. I closed my eyes and silently thanked whatever supernatural being had put the fire under the women's asses to get them there in haste that morning.

Peter bellowed out to the ladies. "Christ Mistresses, the Priceless has made the mess most foul. Hurry up and clean it up before it draws the flies or worse. That boy's conditions down here are not fit for the rats. He has no blanket, bed, running water nor even the decency of freedom to reach that shithole privy with speed thanks to the heavy weights. This is unhealthy. I demand he at least gain a little damned comfort. I will bring some blankets, fresh clothing, and if you will not do it then I will give the boy the sponge bath. I don't give a fuck what Gretta says. This bullshit is not going to be tolerated."

Birgit rushed to my side wearing an expression of extreme concern. "Sire, what has happened here? There is sickness in the straw. Are you in need of a purging? Shit, sister, go watch the main door of the Palace. I am going to remove this gag so the King can vomit with safety. You stall Sebastian or Tadeas if you see them coming and give the whistle, ja?"

Viviana dropped the tray on the Mortar Throne while nodding and shooting Peter a worried look. "As you say sister but what of the honorable Voter? I don't desire to be whipped for releasing the King's tongue without the Dungeon Masters' permission."

Peter scoffed. "Go do what Birgit told you to do Viviana. I am no stool pigeon. I know nothing of rules about the King's ordered restraints. I am not even here to lay witness to anything his Mistresses do for his best interest. This you understand?"

Viviana nodded and rushed for the gate. "I thank you for the mercy of it, honorable Peter. I will do my best to keep the brutes at bay. You hurry up and attend his Majesty to as comfortable a level as possible."

Birgit didn't waste a moment. She produced the copied key and released that fucking gag. I doubled up vomiting the urine onto the floor uncontrollably the moment the boy's mouth was free. The poor Mistress's shoes were assaulted by the fast flow of my stomach contents before she could escape to a safe distance.

I blew the chunks for many minutes until at last there was nothing coming up but air. Birgit approached me and gently pulled me by the upper arm out of the foul straw that was absorbing my shame. I gave her no struggle and allowed her to maneuver me to a dry, clean area. I moaned holding my aching stomach while she rushed to grab the water from Viviana's abandoned tray.

Peter took a few steps my direction. I saw his attempt to approach. I whimpered and weakly scooted backward till the wall prevented a further retreat. I feared he had decided to take his sadistic urges out on me before I could at least recover for a few moments from the killer stomach pains that were plaguing me.

He stopped in his tracks and took on the expression of pity. "I didn't spend years training you only to see you fall prey to the whims of nothings like those brutes Sebastian, Tadeas and Anselm."

I glared at him with hatred. "You didn't? Well interestingly the skill you forced me to learn sure is the thing they all come here seeking. You will have to forgive me for not thanking you for the mercy of it Peter."

My father scoffed. "I spoke with Gretta about this dishonorable situation she has created. The woman wouldn't relent her orders to see you neutralized through brutality. She cannot kill you outright without setting off the Haus collars. However, she can send her dredges to torment you to a psychotic mess. I do believe she intends to see you made the hebephrenic, then parade you in front of your admirers, drooling and shitting your pants while ranting incoherently. Once your support in the Haus has turned from their Madman ruler, Gretta can quietly send you to feed the trees. I am sure this sad fact has occurred to you at least once even in your deep state of the acute cycle."

I nodded never taking my angry gaze from that bastard. "I have had a lot of time to think of many things Peter and to plot my revenge on those that did this to me, all of it. I do believe before you go spouting anymore information that you think will change your place as number one on my list of those I will murder, you realize nothing you say will curb my fury. You stole my life and innocence from me. You set me on this path of destruction through rape, torturing and lies. There is no one on Earth I hate more than you Peter. I will not rest till I see your rotting corpse growing the next generation of flies. Now that you hear the truth of it, you still desire to speak to me, or shall you just get right to your latest sexual assault?"

Peter dropped his gaze to the floor appearing unusually regretful. "Nein, I don't intend to force or ask for the special services from you Maximillian."

I guffawed loudly. "Oh? Is that so? What is the matter? Not feeling the urge to fuck me over as the one man band? That is not a problem. I am sure if you hang around for a bit, the second shift will be down here shortly. Maybe you can join their violent gang bang."

That word made him wince. "Maximillian, I am a man of honor. The special services rights you grant me are in return for the services I give you. It is an honest and contracted equality between us. I do not force you against your will, I take what is owed only. This bullshit of you being held down while helplessly psychotic and assaulted in chains is not something I condone."

I heartily laughed at that insanity he spewed. "Really? Is that how you view what you been doing to me for the last near six years? Equality of service return? You don't agree with taken your lust out on me when I am restrained you say? That is interesting since I seem to recall that is exactly how this fucking nightmare of mine began, in your ropes bonded to your bed I believe. Go ahead Zeus tell your cup barer Ganymede all about your lofty morality and repugnance at the deplorable treatment of the Master of the Haus by his betters. I could use a comical story to lift my broken spirits. I say it is funny, but it is anything but. I do, however find it perplexing how you think both raising and lowering this worthless man through your vile training program was the equal trade for what I have received in return from your slick person. To think all this horror merely to satiate your greed for power that as you can see was not worth even the sweat off Xavier's hairy hodensack. Peter, do you not realize you are the loser just like me? You are still on your knees at Gretta's feet while Mad Maxx is on his to everyone else." I stared at him in fury feeling I may swoon from the unreality of my predicament in life thanks to this idiot.

Peter sighed loudly and crossed his arms. “Look Maximillian, I confess you and me have not always seen eye to eye. I have been guilty of taking advantage of you from time to time. That I will also freely admit. I have allowed my anger at your constant refusal to adhere to my plans for the Haus take over and that betrayal of running off with Jonas color my good judgement. That pettiness of taking revenge on you where I can get it has come back to bite you in a way I never thought would happen. I should have warned you of your dangerous situation as the King of the Collars. I was so busy punishing you for fighting me over the enactment of our contract and that business with Matz then Lucus. Well, I left you ignorant of the things you needed to know with speed. I cannot undo any of the harm I have caused both of us by my losing control of my temper. I have failed you as your trainer and as your trusted friend.”

I almost choked when he said that. “Friend? You dare call yourself such a creature in my presence? Holy shit. I am not the fucking psychotic around here if you truly believe that shit you just said. I think you are going deaf, old man. I say again that I hate you. I have always hated you and if I lived to be a million I would still loath you like no other. Everything I have done, or will do, is in an effort to escape ever having to see your ugly fact again, motherfucker. Is that clear enough for you Peter? Or do I need to be more specific and detailed in what I would do to you if given half the chance. Tell me what I must do to prove how much I desire your slow, painful, horrible death." I sat there in disbelief at the hodensack on this asshole. Wow, and they call me delusional.

To my shock he smiled then chuckled bitterly at that. "Ja, I had that coming Maximillian. Go ahead and get it out of your system. Tell me how you would torture, whip, beat or even rape me as I have done to you, my heart. I am sure whatever you want to do to me, it is not foul enough for the horror I have brought upon your pretty head. Once you are satisfied you have said all the foul things you have desired to voice all these years to me, then I believe we can start this relationship fresh. You know, do it right this time. What is done cannot be undone. I was wrong to use you like I did. At every turn I was unjust and cruel. If I could go back and do it all again, I would have trusted the man that masterminded your existence. As it is, fate interfered with what should have been and here we are. You can choose to continue down this path of destruction by seeking revenge against me, or you can ally yourself with the man that holds the key to a future that has been thus far denied you."

I watched him as he walked over to the gate and picked up the college books I had seen him carrying earlier. Peter slowly approached and dropped them next to me keeping his eyes to the dungeon room floor in reverence. I was confused a great deal by this man's unusually tempered behaviors and honest appearing apologetic mood.

I finally found my voice after a few more moments of awkward silence between us while Birgit looked on from her perch on the Mortar Throne. "Uhm, what the fuck are you doing, Peter? Do you not see that I am as low as I can get? This game you play is beyond cruel even for the likes of you. You came here to rape me. I heard that Anselm plain as day say that. Well, get on with it and then leave me to my pathetic lot will you? Bad enough you force intercourse with my flesh, but fucking my mind is a damned shitty thing to do."

Peter shook his head. "I am not trying to mess with your head Maximillian. My offer of friendship is an honest one. I do understand your hesitancy to believe in anything I tell you given the water under our bridge. Therefore, I will simply demonstrate my sincerity to make things better between us. I bring your studies as you asked me to. I have included the assignment sheet and will come down here to give the testing in a week's time. I have been told by Leo that you have a dentist appointment to fix those wretched teeth that keeps being delayed. Since your guardian Jonas is showing a lack of care for your good oral hygiene I will gain permission to see this work be completed immediately."

That name caught my attention. "Leo? You spoke to the Elder? When? I have not heard a thing from my uncle in weeks. I thought perhaps he had abandoned me to my fate as Jonas has."

Peter scowled. "Leo is a busy man Maximillian. He has no tolerance for the man that has it all. You are the King and Master of the Haus boy. What the hell could the lowly Elder Leo or your humble servant Peter do for you that you don't already have at your disposal?" He put his arms out to motion all around the cell.

Florian began to laugh with insane humor at that sarcastic statement. The giggling was infectious. I found myself breaking out in the maniacal sounds of mirth unable to stop the bubbling crazy that oozed from the boy's every pore. Peter and Birgit joined in with dare own anxious sounding chuckle as they witness me losing my capacity to stop the budding madness from blooming into the schizophrenic shit show that had become my reality.

I held the boy's stomach in pain as the laughter dug deep into me refusing to relent its hold. Tears began to fall as the flesh squeezed the last ouches of fluid from its cells. I fell over to my side writhing in torment from the force of the unstoppable flood of hilarity. There was no doubt I had lost my mind and this time I was sure not even Felicity could stop the coming shattering.

I laid there on the floor weakening against the rising call to madness. I could barely make out Peter and Birgit's alarmed faces that hovered in the chaos of my sensory overload. All around the room the webs of the tapestry broke through the false world eating away the walls like the glowing tsunami. I was helpless to stop its coming to engulf me for its dinner. I couldn't tear my eyes away from that catastrophic scene. I was frozen in a paralyzed panic trapped at the wheel.

Just as the first fingers of the insanity reached the boy, I was flung with force from the spot to the wheelroom floor. I shrieked in blind terror and struck out with my fists trying to fight off what I perceived to be my attacker. I halted my battling, almost too frightened to believe my ears when the familiar voice called out at me from the wheel.

"Master, it is me Mad Max and I have brought Max with me. We are here to help you navigate this atrocious situation. Your pleas for aid have awaken us from our slumber. I beg of you to rest yourself, Master. I have the strength to handle this abysmal existence for a bit. I think you certainly could use a break, ja?" Mad Max shot me a smile as he dug his feet into the boy's brain and took possession of the flesh.

Max shot me a look of pity. "Master, allow Mad Max to shoulder this. He has the experience with the acute stage of the disease. He can be trusted to see the boy through till you have regained your strength."

I began to weep uncontrollably both from gratitude to my shards and the sheer fatigue of the horrors I had already endured. "I cannot find the words to thank you for the mercy of this appreciated aid, Mad Max. You are wise to assume I need the pause from the torture. However, I must caution you the environment is beyond anything the boy has yet encountered. If you feel at any time you cannot handle it, don't hesitate to hand the control back to me."

Mad Max snorted with irritation in his tone. "I already feel the flesh's discontent, Master. The boy's eyes see that motherfucker Peter, and I dare say the memory is speaking to me of things so foul I dare not utter them aloud. Despite my fear of this nightmare I find the flesh deeply engaged in, I am here to serve you or die trying. Allow me to handle the current distress, and you prepare to spell me when my own reserves are tapped out. Between the two of us the boy has the fighting chance to escaping the vortex of the nothing, ja?"

I continued to weep but nodded at his wise words. "You are right, Mad Max. Deal with Peter, and brace for the snake brothers. They will return today for more psychological warfare. Our father states that Gretta intends to drive the boy to the point of no return. She desires to discredit us to the collars, then quietly end our life. This must be prevented no matter what must be done. That bitch must not win. I sent our Shadow King to speaking with Matz and Lucus. I have faith Cary will find a way to see the boy freed of this dungeon hell."

Mad Max shot me a look of trepidation. "Holy hell, Master. Shadow Kings, Mortar Thrones, Palaces made of stone? I see the well and our beloved Marc and Kloe have found there death as have their killers in the most gruesome of fashions. I don't know why you need your sadist Mad Max. Seems you have the blood of the brutal flowing fine through your veins without my miniscule aid."

I nodded my head and wiped my eyes with a bitter chuckle erupted from my throat. "I have been a busy man, Mad Max. Things have been strange since you and the Maxx brothers began your well-earned slumbering. I think my absence from running the wheel caused me to make many unforgivable errors in good judgement. I fear there will be no undoing the terrible damage I have done."

Mad Max smiled with wickedness. “Master, I beg you to not allow these foul fuckers around us to wrangle you into the cycle of carrying the burdens that belong to them exclusively. You don’t want to be a part of their brutal world, but they keep the boy as their captive. Whatever you did to survive another day is acceptable and without fault. In fact, Mad Max intends to endure the obscene, lie, steal, even kill if necessary, to see the sun give the flesh a tan and feel the rain on his face. You would not hold me guilty of the crime of doing what it takes to be free now, would you?”

I shook my head as I realized the shard spoke the truth of things. “Nein, I would not Mad Max. You are a true blessing to this worthless man. What would I do without you?”

Mad Max’s eyes glowed with evil thrill. “Well, without the talents of your Mad Max, you would still be unaware of the joys that await us in the arms of a Frau. That alone should keep all us shards fighting for freedom, ja? Enjoy your nap Master. I need to focus on this wily fucker that is working to rake our ass over the coals yet another time. Gott damn Peter, thank goodness for Annette and our lucky sadistic brother shard or that man would have been completely successful at keeping us the ignorant catamite.” He winked at his reminding me he was the only one of us shards that was not a virgin to the penetration sex and by that act alone had managed to outfox that bastard father of ours in the past.

I laid down on the wheelroom floor closing my eyes, “Okay then I leave the boy’s continued survival in your capable and skilled hands.” With that I slipped off into a much appreciated dreamless state of unconsciousness.

I glared at Peter defiantly and effectively ended that loony laughter the boy was engaging in immediately. “You got me there brother, Peter. What the hell could the Master of the Haus require given the luxury palace and fine cushioned throne he sits on? For starters, a blanket, perhaps some material that doesn’t reek of the toilet and rape would be appreciated. However, I am not willing to pay your price for those merciful services. I suppose that concludes our business, unless of course, I hallucinated that you don’t intend to force yourself upon me. If I did, then be ready for a fight asshole. Your attentions are not desired this day. You can say I truly have reached the lofty height of ruler because I have a royal headache.”

Peter scoffed as he kept his gaze locked into my own. “I will bring you the blanket and fresh clothing, along with soap and water for a fucking bath. You can consider it a gift. I ask nothing in return other than you smelling better the next time I see you.”

I snorted at that. “Well, aren’t you the generous one these days, Peter. I suppose this is goodbye then. I must ask you to be on your way if you find our business complete. I am hungry and the Mistresses need to clean up this pig pen before my next abusers, uhm, visitors arrive. I fear I would be more than a little embarrassed for them to find my Palace in such disarray.”

He shot a look of concern at Birgit. "I leave this precious cargo in your capable hands Frau Birgit. I thank you for the kindness you and your sister show the boy. I am in your debt for the mercy of it."

I growled out in irritation. "Nein, the payment is owed by the Mad Maxx, Peter. Be gone with you. I swear your company stinks more than the soiled straw. I bet the second you are gone the air will sweeten almost immediately despite the contents of the privy strewn about the cell." I chuckled with dark humor over that open insult.

Ta my shock Peter merely nodded and took off for the gate. "As you wish, Sire. I see you tomorrow for that dentist appointment. I will send the items you asked for through Viviana within the hour. Try to rest all you can today and don't forget your studies. You are behind, and need to catch up if you intend to graduate before the end of the decade." I sat there in pure stun watching the man storm off, unable to believe he didn't backhand me, bitch, nor even correct my nasty comments to him. Peter was like Jonas, showing a side of him I had never seen before.

I didn't have the time to ponder this strange tolerant side of my father. The gate had barely swung closed when Birgit approached me with the bowl of water. I tried to refuse the stuff, but the Mistress insisted despite the gross smells and my still rolling stomach that I needed to drink to ward off dehydration. I groaned in misery as I realized the frau was correct. That vomiting, sweating and stress had used up all my fluid reserves. I knew that going without adequate water would result in delirium, which the boy didn't need any more of, and eventual expiration.

I gave her no quarrel as she aided me in finishing the entire bowl of liquid then the second one full of the gruel. The good news was that porridge crap may not have been the finest in cuisine, but it sure broke that disgusting residual taste out of the boy's mouth. I can never say it enough, but you got to take the small mercies where you can, ja?

I sat there with my back to the wall where Der Hund had fallen watching the Mistress quickly rake out the mucked up straw and replace it with fresh tick. I thought despite her lack of handsome physical attributes she maybe was the most beautiful woman in the whole Haus, at least at that moment. She seemed to genuinely be looking out for my best interest wherever she could. Her sister Viviana's gentle care was nothing to overlook either.

I wanted to thank them for all day were doing for me, but I decided words were not good enough. I decided if I ever got out of the Palace I would keep my promise to raise the Dungeon Mistresses of the Mortar King to a place of ease in the Haus. I was deep in thoughts of ways to reward her for the loyalty when the middle aged Mistress turned her attention toward the gate appearing a bit anxious.

That caused me to turn my head to see what or who the hell had stirred her to panic like that. I saw Viviana approaching carrying a black Vampire outfit from my closet with Peter following quick on her heels. I gasped sure that the man had reconsidered his thoughts about raping me. I tried to use the wall to stand but found Doctor Noethan's sedative was serving it function to the optimum capacity. I slid back to the dungeon floor with a thud as my knees gave way under the weight of trying to hold me up.

Peter came into the cell rolling up his sleeves with a large key in his hand. "Okay Maximillian, here is the deal. You are going to bath and change out of those repulsive clothes. You can do it the easy way or the hard way. Up to you."

I snorted at him hatefully. "Well there big stud, I would be most happy to wash but you see I am unable to take the damned things off and unless you are hiding the shower in your back pocket I believe bathing is also a pipe dream."

He smiled and nodded at Birgit. "Ladies, I do believe the King is in need of bath service. Tie your aprons on tight and Viviana fetch us a fresh pitcher of water will you honey? Your sister and I will get his Majesty stripped down and ready for the cleansing while we wait."

Viviana rushed over and retrieved the water pitcher from the basin. I watched the frau rushing off to find the facet in the main dungeon area to fill it up as Peter ordered. I turned my confused attention at the two fast approaching adults that seemed determined to see me accept their offered bathing service, like it or not.

Peter had to restrain the boy at first as I didn't understand what the two of them intended for truth. He held me tightly by the arms as Birgit used that key Peter held to undo the ankle and wrist shackles. The moment all but my collar chain was free of the heavy chains I stopped acting the raging fool. I held still hoping they intended to let me out of the leash to the wall as well.

I resumed my battle with both of them when Peter reached around my waist and began undoing my breeches. I yelled like a loon demanding he let me be and stop trying to rape me. The Dominant ignored me as he continued tearing at my trousers and the frau began tearing open the buttoned up blouse I was wearing.

I would knock one off and the other would attack. I kicked, gnashed, wailed and fought with vigor trying to keep them from stripping off my befouled clothing. My wild thrashing only managed to slow their progress. It didn't take them long to have me down to the boy's birthday suit. Birgit threw my clothes, including my boots, which were nothing more than smelly rags by this point, just beyond where the collar chain allowed me to go.

I struggled out of their hold and stormed off after the discarded flesh covering. I hit the end of the chain with strength. The force of the sudden break in allowable movement sent me sprawling naked into the straw strewn floor with a yelp of surprise and pain.

Peter snickered and yelled out to me, "Settle down, Maximillian. The second you are fresh we will put the clean ones back on you. Damn, you are behaving like the shy violet. Birgit has seen plenty of naked men in her day, and I never knew you to be the prude anyway. What the fuck are you fuming about?"

I lifted back to the sitting position and covered up my exposed flesh the best I could. "Give me the new outfit, Peter. I don't want that radiated water rubbed on me. I have had enough contamination for today dammit. I am clean enough."

That made Peter gasp. "Oh shit. You are not back on that delusion are you, boy? Ficken Mich. Okay, Birgit, this is going to take all three of us. We cannot allow Maximillian to go unwashed. Look at the extensive open wounds all over him. Shit what have the brutes been doing to him down here? You know what? Watch him for a moment but stay clear till your sister Mistress and I return to aid you in subduing the boy. I am going to grab that alcohol in the ritual room." Peter took off for the gate once again nearly knocking down the returning Viviana carrying the filled water pitcher.

He warned her to give me room to wail until he was present. I sat there glaring at all three of them, pissed beyond imagination at the indignity of their forcing a fucking whore bath on me with that radiation water. The Mistresses stood near the door out of my reach staring back in silence.

Peter returned in record time. I got up and attempted to run the three of them in circles as they came at me to force the bath. Of course, I was captured, knocked to the floor, restrained and scrubbed with vigor.

Through the entire process I cursed, spit, bit and struggled in their hold. None of the big adults paid me any mind. To my complete shock not even Peter struck me for that childish fit I threw as day washed down my ravaged flesh and treated the numerous open wounds.

When Peter felt they could do no more given the tools available to them, I was released from their hold. I rushed to the end of the chain and stood there glaring at them in anger and fear. I took the stance of aggression daring any of them to try to regain possession of me and see what they would get for it.

Peter snickered and picked up the pile of fresh clothing including clean boots. "Put these on Maximillian before you go killing the three of us. It would be indecent for you to be found over our corpses naked and screaming like the loon, ja?" He tossed them at me.

I stood there staring at the clothing for a moment. When none of the three took another run to recapture me, I quickly reached out and took up the breeches from the pile. There is no doubt I dressed in record time, but between each article I stood there eyeing them with suspiciousness before I would attempt to add more cloth to cover the boy's flesh.

The second I had buttoned up the clean black blouse Peter cleared his throat loudly. "All right Maximillian, you are adequately cleaned up. Come back over here and allow Birgit to re-cuff your bonds. Don't give us any difficulty or

I will be forced to call in those bastards Sebastian and Tadeas to aid us in the task."

I wrung my hands and shot nervous glances at the cell gate. "Nein, don't do that. I am restrained enough with only the throat leash, ja? Please Peter, I beg mercy. Those weights keep me from escaping the lusts of the men to have sport with me. I thought you said you desire we be friends. Brothers don't chain up their buddies."

Peter chuckled bitterly and shook his head. "Ja, I know that Maximillian, but I have no choice. It is the orders of Gretta. For now, I am unable to stop her from this dishonor. Listen to me boy. You can allow your gentle Dungeon Mistresses to do this necessary bonding, or the brute Masters will. I dare say they are likely to take advantage of your spiteful and useless fighting them. Use your brain for a moment. You are the clever one. If you think on it you will agree your friend Peter isn't telling the lie."

I whimpered and stole another look at the cell gate. "Peter, please help me get out of here. I beg of you. I will do anything you ask of me without complaint. The Altergotts are coming soon. I cannot take much more of them or that nasty Noethan and his Dungeon bastards."

My father frowned "Maximillian, I swear to you if I could see you out of here, you would already be dining in the Great Hall sucking my cock under the table instead of that idiot Lucus's cock. You surely realized that before this moment. I have poured over the rule books. There is nothing I can do other than try to protect you from the infections and add minor comforts."

I nodded my head and rushed at him dropping to a kneel at his feet. Which caused him to back up in a startle and the Mistresses to flee beyond my reach. "But there is a way Peter. I can give you the recency for my Throne, ja? Here take it. I swear it to you right here in front of the Mistresses. Then you go get Gretta and tell her to let me out. Please let me out." I fell to my face on his boots weeping like the kid.

Peter let out a groan of misery and reached down dragging me back to my knees. "Fuck. I have waited my whole life to hear you say those words, Maxx. However, it is too late. I am the Voter, a Prince of the Silk Throne. If you intended to name me the regent I would have had to resign my post a full seven days before the announcement of your coronation as Master of the Haus. This is why I should have told you of the dangers. I made the stupid assumption that since you didn't know the Mortar Throne existed the threat that you would demand the Metal Crown was nonexistent or so I thought anyway."

I shook my head as I heard him decline my honest offer. At least I knew Peter and what the man was capable of, ja? "Nein. Nein. Go tell Gretta you resigned. I name you my regent and you waive that week wait as the voice of the Master of the Haus Peter. Please do this before they kill me or worse." I embraced him around his knees holding on for dear life out of total desperation.

Peter motioned for the Dungeon Mistresses to pry me off him. “Maximillian, you must not behave in this manner. It is far below your station. You are the Mortar King and Master of the Haus. You do not kneel to anyone. They kneel to you. I also have to tell you I cannot aid you the way you ask of me. I admit hearing I could have been the Master of the Haus like I always wanted if only I had used more care. Well, if you desired to punish me for all I have done by torture you just managed it. Now I must watch my beautiful Maximillian fade away taking all my dreams down to hell with him as he is slowly assaulted to death. A crueler punishment for this idiot Peter couldn’t have been contrived by the cleverest of minds. This matter is closed. Don’t ever utter it to me again.” He grabbed the sides of his forehead and rushed for the gate never casting a single glance behind him as he fled the throne room.

I wailed in misery as I saw what I was sure was my only chance of escaping out the door. The Mistresses took the opportunity while I was weakened with grief to lock me back into the weighted restraints. I was so heartbroken I didn’t bother to give them a run for their money. I merely sat there on my knees sobbing like the punished child.

Viviana removed the soapy basin and pitcher for cleaning while Birgit collected the discarded soiled clothing. In moments, the hard of hearing Viviana rushed back to the cell her eyes wide in fright.

Birgit saw her sister’s distress. “What is it? Spit it out, dammit.”

Viviana shot a terrified look down the hallway to the receiving room. “One of the Princes of the Silk Throne is coming sister. Gag the King and hurry. The man is moving with speed I can see him already halfway here.” Birgit rushed me and in a single swoop locked the scold bridle gag back in place.

She shot me a look of pity. “Forgive me, Sire. There is no time for formality. Remember what Peter told you. You are the Master of the Haus and King of the Mortar Throne. No matter what these brutes pull they cannot change that. Be prideful and show honor in all you do. They only humiliate themselves by acting as the barbarians they truly are.” I sniffed loudly and nodded, though I didn’t hear a word of what she said.

I didn’t have to hear the name of the Voter speeding to my cell to enjoy his private visit with the King. I already knew his identity. Rolf and Friedrick had refused to acknowledge my place on the Mortar Throne, so both of them were forbidden access to gain audience with me. Peter had already left, and Viviana knew him by first name.

That left only one capable of coming to take his sport out on me with the blessings of the Queen of the Silk Throne. I trembled and took shallow breaths as Birgit rushed to join her sister in their retreat. They were not permitted to linger in the Throne Room when the King was occupied with important Princes of the Haus, such as the love struck rapist Byron. I let out a mournful wail as the huge brute entered the gate wearing an eager smile and sporting a single tail whip. I looked at the silent Florian with fear rising. He smiled back as he said, “Come one, come All. Bring the Big. Bring the Tall. Mad Max volunteers for the cruelest torture. He is the Master of pain since birth. The King is the greatest show on earth.” I winced and trembled as Byron took a stance before me. “Did you miss me, Mad Maxx? Well, I can assure you I won’t miss you.” He cracked that whip, announcing it was time to let the games begin.

Chapter 41: The Rise of the Schizophrenic Master of the House

Byron had cut the air with his cruel weapon of torturing, that single tail whip, once. Likely he did the crack of the whip to let me know he meant business. I held my breath as the brute Voter approached me kneeling next to the privy. His wicked smile told me that he was feeling rather fond of finding me at this horrible disadvantage.

It was a great loss to know I had spent all those months running from his lustful grips only to lose the battle in the end. Byron had made it clear during the coronation whipping that he was most angered by my continued thwarting of his unwanted advances. Thanks to my misstep of foolishly demanding the Mortar Throne, I was helpless to prevent him from taking out his wrath from my flesh at long last. There was no doubt in my mind that is exactly what he had come to do too.

Byron put his foot on one of my leg weights and pushed it with effort till it rolled a bit. "Well, looks like you have finally fucked up big time, ja? This rat hole is not what you expected when you demanded to be the Master of the Haus I am willing to bet. Tell me Mad Maxx, how are you enjoying Gretta's hospitality to her Lord and Master? Is there anything your servant Byron can do to make your stay more comfortable?" He said in a mocking sarcastic tone.

I stared at the floor and offered no change in my position. He could see I was gagged and unable to respond to his mean statement. My lack of visible response only caused him to laugh with evil humor.

He cracked the whip aiming at me but purposely missing. I still didn't move a muscle but did close my eyes. "You know I think. I kind of like it when you cannot speak. I don't have to listen to you tell me nein anymore this way. I wonder something though. You said during that brutal beating that you would reconsider my offer to take care of you as my lover. You have had some time to think on your error of denying me what I want. So, you ready to admit your mistake and take your place in my bed?"

I lifted my eyes and glared at him with hate. I knew he was being the asshole. Byron for all his bragging had no power to see that gate door unlocked for good. He was aware I understood he was there to take his intercourse with me, whether I gave permission or nein. This bullshit sadistic mind game he was trying to play with me only deepened my disgust at sharing the same air with him.

My angered expression caused him to chuckled once again. "Oh, you are sexy when you are pissed. I confess it turns me on a great deal when you run from me. However, for any hunter there is nothing more thrilling then making the kill. We both can see there is nowhere left for you to flee Maxx. You are cornered. I hold the whip, and you wear the chains."

I rolled my eyes at that which made him snicker even more. He came closer to look me over but didn't appear to be readying himself to soften me up with a beating. At least that is what I hoped. I resolved myself that this re-visiting a situation with this man that still caused me nightmares was going to happen like it or not.

As he walked around examining me with his wanton eyes, I braced best as I could for his rough couple. All I could do is consol myself that if I didn't comply with the brute's interests, he would use his whip on me. There was no way to win a battle with him and I still bore the pain of the last encounter with that torture tool wielded by his well skilled hands.

Byron reached out and snatched the side of my crown by the bridle shaking it with vigor. "I want this gag removed. How am I supposed to be adored properly with half my lover's ability to pleasure me denied? Where is the key to the lock" He pushed me backward hard enough to slam me into the wall.

I trembled at his quick anger as I shrugged at his question. Not like I could answer him anyway. This temper tantrum was a side of the Voter I had not encountered before. It seemed that lately I was witness to many alternate sides of the men that haunted my worst memories.

I didn't attempt to return to my original position. I held still as death against the Palace wall doing my best not to make the eye contact as Byron yelled and railed about the locked ball gag. I won't lie. This scared the hell out of me.

Byron pace back and forth as he grumbled with fury. It was no small matter that he was working himself into a frenzy. I began to realize this was going to result in me losing an inch or two of flesh from his whip if Sebastian or Tadeas didn't show up soon with the fucking key.

I listened in helpless silence as he accused me of personally requesting that my mouth be kept covered so he couldn't enforce his kissing nor receive the oral special services. I was sure this motherfucker had lost his mind thinking I would want to be painfully gagged in the locks. I mean I do hate this Byron but his weird belief I would go that far to continue to deny his pleasure was pure insanity speaking, even for me. Not to mention a bit more than narcissistic.

I began to steal glances at the gate wondering if the Dungeon Masters would hear the angered Voters shouting. This was the only time I would have been grateful to see either of those bastards coming. It was bad enough to have to endure the raping but the fear of worse by this time was more than a little upsetting. The way Byron was carrying on I began to think he may end my pathetic life over the inability for him to force me to blow him. To end one's life over such a trivial thing was more than I could handle.

When several more minutes passed without any sign of my so called care givers arriving to save me, I decided I had to do something to calm this bastard down. I lifted off my hindside back to my knees and fell into the prostrate position on the floor in the path of the Voter's pacing.

Byron bellowed out in anger. "What the hell do you think you are doing, Maxx? I can see you are no doubt the sorry one now for the insults you ruthlessly hurled at me. Well, I got news for you. This act is not going to work. I refuse to forget that after all I did for you my payback was laughter behind my back. You made sport of my honest feelings for you with that shady Matz and the with snotty Lucus. I know you only fooled around with them to make me jealous. Of all the Dominants you could have chosen to rub into my face, you pick a low-down thug and a smug fourth floor nothing. You could have at least given me the dignity of selecting someone handsome, rich, or talented, but nein. You make me look like the love struck fool in front of all my friends and the entire Haus. But the high and mighty Mad Maxx is finally knocked down a peg, isn't he? It takes crawling with the cockroaches and eating with the rats to finally get you to appreciate the affection I had for you. That is right, had. I look at you know, dirty, bruised, and begging, and wonder what the fuck I ever saw in you." He grabbed the back of my collar and lifted me flipping me to my back with violence.

I whimpered in terror and put up my hands to try to block any blows to the face. Byron stood over me glaring with pure rage. I thought for sure he was going to attack with his whip or fists but after several moments of terrifying silence he stepped away from me. I shook in fear as he looked about the room as if searching for something.

Then I saw his gaze settle on my Mortar Throne and his infuriated expression broke into a wicked smile. "All my life I wondered what the Stone Throne of the Master of the Haus would look like. Well, there it is. It is not exactly what I had envisioned, but I think I was not the only one surprised by the literalness of it, ja? Tell me something Maxx, is it more comfortable than it looks? Was it worth all you paid for it?" He glanced at me with his eyebrows up as if curious for truth.

I shrugged and trembled unsure what the hell he wanted me to answer. The strangeness of the question he asked at that tension filled moment really threw me for the loop. I had worried the man was a nut, but now I was absolutely sure of it.

He scoffed. "What is this? Indifference? You know, maybe that is your problem Maxx. You never seem to be capable of making a decision and sticking with it. Never a ja or nein. With you it is always maybe. I am thinking that I have made an error in assuming you were purposeful in antagonizing me like you have. Perhaps, you merely have been fickle because you always had everything handed to you. That can stunt emotional growth, you know. You are immature and spoiled, that is the problem. This little trip to the reality of cruelty should wake you up to the honest kindness I have offered you all along. Tell you what Maxx, I am willing to be generous one more time with you. You choose to be my lover and we can forget all the sowing of the wild oats you as the boy did. Mad Maxx the man will stop acting the idiot. Are you finally ready to be the monogamous and eager lover to Byron?" He knelt down staring into my eyes with a tinge of madness in his expression.

I shivered in full on terror at this insane bastard. How the hell could he demand such a thing with me in chains. I was helpless to stop anyone that wanted from using me as the human sex doll. I had no idea how to respond to his inquiry.

If I nodded ja, then if he caught any of the criminals in their raping of me, would he kill me for what I couldn't prevent? Then if I shook my head nein, did he intend to murder me on the spot? With no way to know which answer was the one that would keep me alive I became frozen by my fear. I could do nothing but stare back at him shaking like the newborn colt in the early Spring winds.

Byron took my confusion as a sign of continued apathy that he had determined was part of my historical approach to all offers. Rather than the truth which was lack of choice in most matters. Ugh, what a moron. That caused him to burst out in a fresh series of incensed behaviors There was no way to avoid provoking this crazy man's fury. He is the unreasonable idiot. For all his accusing me of immaturity, he is completely the baby himself, unable to accept the word nein.

He swore, railed, and stormed at me for a few minutes. Byron worked himself back into a blind rage as I lay there unable to escape his wrath. Then he reached down and snatched up my collar chain. He dragged me along after him to my Mortar Throne. I gasped and whimpered as he pushed me face first into the seat pushing up my shirt and tearing down my breeches.

Byron growled out from behind me. “Stay on your knees boy and hold still. I intend to whip you till you grow the fuck up. Moving will only cause me to miss the mark. You will be sorry enough with the blows I lay on you, but I assure you the pain will not end your life like fighting me would. Take hold of your fucking throne Master Maxx and don’t let go till I say I am done. Do it now, damn you.” I wailed in terror as he cracked his single tail striking the arm of the Throne indicating where he expected me to gain traction against his coming agony.

I felt the tears welling up as I spread out my arms taking hold of the sides of the Throne. I dropped the boys head and took shallow breaths, closing my eyes doing my best to prepare for Byron’s rage filled whipping. I flinched, despite my best efforts to hold still, when he cracked the whip once again, this time striking just to the left of my exposed backside.

The sweat rolled down the boy’s face and I gritted my nubs, wondering if this was a warmup or psychological torment. Expecting the lash is bad but being caught off guard by it is far worse. I was sure that was exactly his game when, yet another crack cut through the air but as before, the tail struck the throne and missed my flesh.

The third strike fell harmlessly to the right of me. I took a deep breath thinking the fourth would find its aim true. It took all I had to remain still on my knees holding on to that fucking throne like that. All I could think is how bad I wanted to run, and let that bastard try to beat me with his whip. The only reason I didn’t is I knew that Byron would do far more damage trying to hit the moving target. It would result in serious injury and no doubt another visit from the pervert Doctor Noethan. It was that fear alone that strengthened my resolve to endure this torture no matter how rough that motherfucker got.

It seemed like time stood still as I awaited his next blow, the one I was sure would make the connection. It goes without saying I wailed in pure shock when instead of the sting of that leather tail I felt Byron's huge hands grab the boy's waist. It took hearing him spitting loudly before I realized the man was not going to mark me with his whip after all.

I wailed out in pain as the brute roughly penetrated the boy. In a reflexive move I attempted to pull forward to escaping his forced entry and harsh thrusting.

Byron grabbed the back of upper arms pulling them tightly behind me holding me hostage to his lustful intercourse "Where you going, Maxx? Your lover is right here. I have decided to fuck my King while he is bent over his throne like the dog he is. You are going to take it and thank me for the mercy of granting you my affection rather than my beating you like you deserve." He plowed into me with all his strength sending me right to hell. Remember he is a big fellow and no lube, yikes!

I screamed and wailed uncontrollably though the gag kept the sounds of it muted compared to what it should have been while he raped me with unrestrained brutality. Throughout his sexual assault he yelled out the obscenest things and made promises that every day he was going to visit to fuck me over in the most painful ways possible. He assured me that if I would not agree to be his willing lover, then he was content with forcing me to be his tormented bitch instead.

Needless to say, I was more than a bit upset by this woeful turn of events. I was not an idiot. I knew the man wasn't going to leave that cell without getting his cock satisfied at my expense. That said, I was grateful he had gone right to what he came there to do and spared me his lashing.

In a brutal world like the Haus, you have to look at the bright side of this most disturbing situation. A painful sexual encounter with this brute was punishment enough, no need to add insult to that injury. Mercy is a mercy no matter how small, ja?

Byron was, pardon the pun, deep in his thrill when the gate came open. He was so busy enjoying the misery he was heaping on me, that means taking his sweet time reaching the orgasm, that he hadn't heard the arrival of the Altergotts. I admit neither had I. I was, uhm, busy with the wishing for death and wailing, you know.

Kilian cleared his throat loudly from the gate. "Oh, my goodness Reece. It seems the Priceless has double booked his clients today. Looks like there is a line. I suppose we should have called ahead to see if King Maxx was running behind in his royal servicing the courtiers." That caused Reece and Kilian to break out in loud laughter.

Byron halted his mount in the startle of realizing he had been caught assaulting me "Kilian? Reece? What the fuck are you doing here. Don't you see I am busy? Take a power. This is a private matter between Maxx and me." He held his thrust but didn't uncouple, dammit.

Kilian crossed his arms and nodded. "You need not be concerned with me or Reece, brother. Please do continue your personal consultation with the King. We have a bit of set up to do anyway. I believe you should be finished with him by the time we are ready to begin our own sport with the boy. You won't even know we are here, we will be quiet as the mouse."

Byron scoffed. "Oh, I intend to finish what I started Kilian. I don't require your permission for it either. I am not willing to deal with you this second but when I am done here with Maxx I will make you wish you had left when I told you to. I don't like having the audience when I am enjoying myself and you damned well know that. I am aware you like to watch another get his rocks off. Fucking perverted voyeurs, the both of you." With that he went back to his vicious thrusting, but this time the only sounds he made were of pleasure. He shut up that nasty sexual speaking to me, you know.

I ignored his foul intercourse and thrilled sounds by keeping my baleful eyes on the Altergotts. I watched them bring in the stereo and headphones along with a small box that I had never seen before. I trembled at the thought of them making the voices I hear worse, but by this time I had come to realize this behavior of theirs was never going to stop until I did something to end it.

I was harshly broken from my thoughts of killing the Altergott brothers by Byron's sudden increase in his stroke. He pulled my arms behind me to the point of agony as he plowed into me with all the vigor he could muster. The brute didn't hold back anything. The boy was smacked repeatedly into the stone throne by the sheer force of his bucking orgasm. As Byron moaned out in ecstasy, I screamed from the agony of his rough treatment. My distressed sounds caused the Altergotts to stop their tasks to watch the show.

The Voter let out a loud groan of thrill then fell over on me. I crumpled face first into the seat of the Mortar Throne. If it had not been for the extended lip of the Metal crown and rubber ball gag, Byron likely would have broken my nose and busted my mouth when I crashed into the stone base. I simply was too weak from the lingering sedatives to hold up against his weight.

To my dismay, the idiot let go of my arms and wrapped his arms around my waist from behind me as if he were the grateful lover. I didn't try to hide my shuddering as he plied the boy's ears and back of neck with slobbery kissing. Byron ignored my obvious signs of disgust as he continued to cuddle and fawn over me while I lay helplessly held to the spot.

Kilian and Reece, who had been creepily watching the whole show, began to clap and jeer at Byron's perfect performance. I swear to Gott I wished that somehow my heart could stop beating right then and there. This humiliation I was suffering in the Mortar Palace just kept getting worse and worse. I didn't think I could handle much more, you know.

Their applauding him pissed Byron off. He lifted off me and uncoupled, thank Gott, with a loud bellow. I didn't waste any time grabbing my breeches and pulling them up to avoid either of those monsters deciding to go for the sloppy seconds. Not that the flimsy clothing would stop them but hey, no reason to encourage them to get to their cruel intercourse in right away. Any break in the action, no matter how short, was a mercy trust me.

He readjusted his jeans glaring at the humored Altergotts. "Cut that shit out. I will not stand being insulted like this Gott dammit. Why are you two here anyway? I hope you don't think you are going to get the chance to fuck my boy."

Kilian and Reece shot each other a look of humor and stopped clapping as Kilian responded, "Uhm, excuse me? You think Maxx is your boy, Byron? I think you are deluded. The King belongs to all the Voters and Elders. Even if he didn't I outrank you brother. You are the one handing out insults here. Reece and I will do as we please with this boy and you have no right to try to stop us. We have come for our turn at sport with him. Stay and watch us, which is fair since we enjoyed the scene with you or leave. Do you think any of us are happy to share our interests in the Mortar King equally. Nein. We want him all for ourselves just as you do, but the Silk Queen will not name any as the sole regent to his favors. There is nothing any of us can do about it."

Byron stood there a moment stealing glances of anger at me kneeling at the foot of the throne then back to the Altergotts. I gasped in terror when the brute reached down and grabbed me by the collar hauling me to my feet.

He held me around the throat from behind panting from his barely controlled fury at Kilian's words. "Nothing I can do to stop all you from taking what is mine, huh? Well, how about I break his fucking neck? I won't be able to seek my thrill with him anymore, but neither will anyone else. I could send him to the yard with the memory of my intercourse in his mind and seed inside his flesh. This way he would die completely my own. I don't desire the torment of knowing the likes of you two buzzards continually despoiling my lover."

I shivered in pure blind terror at those words. I knew that Byron was insane enough to kill me in an effort to prevent anyone else from having me for their plaything. I didn't have any faith that the Altergotts could talk the man out of ending my life. If anything, I truly assumed their arrogant statements would assure that I would be feeding the worms in mere moments. I closed my eyes and made my apologies to the slumbering Der Hund over this dishonorable death as best I could. I had no doubt at all that Mad Max had failed the Master shard.

Max frowned as I knelt in the wheelroom floor next to our sleeping Core whispering my regrets. "Mad Max, please brother, wait a moment before you disturb Der Hund. If Byron is to snap the boy's neck maybe it is a mercy that the boy that suffered so much never be alerted that the struggle is over, ja? Why not allow him the peace of dying in his sleep?"

I thought on it a moment then nodded. There is wisdom in what you say Max. Der Hund has had enough, you are right. Come what may, I grant him this final mercy. Come stand with me. I wish to have you at my side when we face the void. We have not always gotten along but overall, you are alright, brother."

Max broke out in that goofy smile of his as he approached the wheel to do as I asked him. "You are the best buddy I have ever known Mad Max, but don't tell the others I said that okay?" He chuckled.

"Tell the others what, freak," the voice of Christian broke through the wheelroom startling me and Max from that gross touching moment.

I gasped. "What the hell? Who rattled your cage asshole. Or should I say assholes." I couldn't believe my eyes as Mad Maxx came limping along behind Christian rubbing the sleep from his eyes.

Christian chortled and crossed his arms. "Do you hear that, Mad Maxx? I don't think our brothers missed us. What kind of a good morning is that you rude bastard."

Mad Maxx nodded as he yawned. “Calm down boys. Where is Der Hund?”

I pointed towards the floor drawing the awakened shards to the sleeping form of our Core laying by the wheel. “He is where you two fatherfuckers should be. This is not going to work. Go back to your beds, idiots. I don’t need two more useless sets of eyes watching my work over my shoulder.”

Max tapped me on the back. “Mad Max, let them be. In a moment, none of this is going to matter anyway. Byron, remember?”

I sucked in my breath. “Oh shit. That is right. Well, boys you picked a fine time to find your consciousness. The brute Voter is about to send the boy to the yard. I suggest you bend over and kiss your asses goodbye. This ride is over.” I grabbed the wheel with both hands and braced for the quick jolt of a broken vertebrate as Christian, Mad Maxx and Max shot each other anxious but silence glances.

Byron began to put much pressure on the boy’s neck as Kilian and Reece backed up to give him room. “I mean it, cocksuckers. I will kill this boy if either of you dare to touch him. I don’t give a fuck what that bitch Gretta says. He is mine.”

Kilian put up his hands to demonstrate surrender. “Okay, we hear you Byron. Brother, listen to me. If you kill Mad Maxx then you should know that Gretta has ordered the murderer be burned alive in front of the entire Haus.

The collars will demand revenge for taking the life of their savior. Think about what you are doing man. No matter how much you desire the boy for yourself, is anyone worth such a horrible end?"

Byron laughed out maniacally. "I can understand why you ask me such a stupid question, Kilian. You never loved anyone your entire fucking life. You used Jakob like he was a tissue to catch your jizm and then crawled into Jonas's bed without another thought of the one you jilted. I know damned well you don't care for that Elder any more than you did for this desirable boy I hold in my arms. You are forever seeking power instead of the thrill of an honest lover's embrace. I will only say this once more. Leave Mad Maxx alone and seek your perverted thrills elsewhere and take that rat faced brother of yours with you." I winced as he pulled my head to an unnatural angle but to be honest at this point I was actually rooting for him.

I know that sounds awful for me to say, but never having to put up with Kilian and Reece's cruelty again sounded pretty fucking good to me at this point. Try not to judge me over this until you are in such a situation as the rock and hard place. Byron is the goon, but he was not the mind killer the Altergotts had proven to be. I saw some benefit in tolerating his brutal intercourse exclusively if he would be capable of ending the terror of all the other men abusing me. Ja, being his bitch was looking better and better to me.

Kilian leaned over to Reece and whispered something. The man nodded, then tore out of the cell, leaving the snake standing there glaring at us refusing to retreat as his brother had done. This only managed to piss Byron off even more.

He bellowed out, “You stubborn asshole. Leave damn you. I swear to Gott I am going to do it.” I groaned as he jerked my head harshly.

Kilian nodded. “Okay I am going to do as you say. Don’t say I didn’t warn you Byron. This bullshit will not be tolerated.” To my shock the snake turned tail and rushed out the cell hot on the heels of his brother reptile.

I whimpered when at first Byron didn’t remove his dangerous hold on my neck. He took a deep breath then released me. I tried to run away but he grabbed the back of my shirt and pulled me back into his awaiting tight embrace. I dared not struggle as he held and pawed me all over, kissing like the wanton lover.

When he believed he has slobbered on me enough, he pulled my face back to stare at me with a dreamy expression. “You see that Maxx? Byron is willing to die to keep you safe. Can you dare to still refuse my offer to be your lover and protector? Are you going to deny that you love me the way I love you?”

I had learned my lesson during his assault. I quickly shook my head nein. The fear that he would carry on with his plan to kill me kept me willing to say anything he wanted me to. I wanted out of that dungeon cell, but not the permanent way Byron had offered. Not while there was still a chance I could survive this nightmare and even find an escape to the medical school as Peter had promised me.

Byron grabbed the boy's chin and took on a serious expression. "You mean it this time? You choose to love me and only me? Beware Maxx, I am the jealous lover. I don't tolerate competition for your affections. Shake your head ja if you ready to do the right thing and be all mine."

I nodded my head wildly fighting back the tears of humiliating defeat. If Byron could really keep the other rapists off of me, I saw no better option. Though I felt like my heart was breaking in my chest as a huge smile of thrill crossed his face.

He pulled my near limp flesh into a squeezing hug while yipping in glee. "Ah, I knew it. You do love me for truth, Maxx. It was only the game of playing hard to get. I could tell during our couple you were enjoying bringing me to pleasure. Your sounds of thrill were obvious even to that rat Kilian and that shitty brother of his. That is what they're angry about. I have won the heart of the Priceless and they are the sore losers, is all. Well, you need not worry your beautiful head over them. I will go this minute to see Gretta. There will be no more of this sharing shit with these other nothings. The Master of the Hau choose Byron and she will have no choice but to accept it." He released me from his hold and asked again if I was sure of my decision.

I of course nodded ja as before. That delusional man didn't seem the least bit aware that I only agreed from fear he would break my neck if I denied his offer. Byron yipped in thrill again causing me to flinch from the painful sound. He laughed at my jerking and cower, then ruffled my hair.

His fast, aggressive appearing noises and movements sent me to my knees in absolute terror.

Byron leaned down and kissed me in the ear as he whispered. "You hold that offer lover. I will be back shortly with the key to that damned gag. Then you can demonstrate your gratitude to Byron properly." He took off with speed out of the cell and down the hallway leaving me dare shaking in fear on the Palace floor.

I stepped away from the wheel for a moment to catch my breath. That was a close one. "Holy hell boys, we are in deep shit I think. I don't know what is worse, that madman ready to bust our head if we anger him in any way or the never-ending parade of rapists coming through the door. Fuck, this is a nightmare. What are we going to do? This has to stop."

Christian scoffed. "Well, maybe that idiot will get the others called off the boy. Then we need only kill the one to get out of the door. The way I see it, playing ball with that unstable bastard may be our only chance to be free."

I glared at the anger shard in disbelief. "Kill Byron with what, brother? Our bad breath? Look around you fool. We are chained to the wall and weighted down like the corpse thrown into the river. You wait and see, Byron will tire of the boy's charms soon enough, then maybe he will find an excuse to make us a true companion to Florian. I think that Priceless is right. Lucus is our only truthful escape plan. All we can do is hope Cary is successful in his lobbying Matz to do a lot of the sweet talking to that royal pervert."

Mad Maxx narrowed his eyes. "Florian? Cary? Lucus? What the fuck are you babbling about Mad Max. Cary the door guard has what to do with anything, and you think that nasty Lucus that put a collar on the boy is a coveted solution to this horror? Who the hell is Florian."

I rolled my eyes at the intelligence shard. "Christ, plug into the boy's memory brother. I would think you of all of us would wish to be caught up with the things that have happened while you slept. I expect that kind of stupid neglect from Christian, but not you."

Christian snarled out at me. "For your information smart ass, Der Hund tells me what I need to know without me having to fish for it. You would be wise to not speak about things you don't know Mad Max."

That was a surprise. "Huh? Did Der Hund speak with you this time too?" I shot a look of shock at the sleeping core at my feet.

Christian smiled with evil. "Sure did. Who the fuck do you think woke me up asshole? I am the lazy fucker that would sleep for all time if given the chance. I am only here because he came to me and said my services were required. This dumbass is chained to me, he pointed at Mad Maxx, so he got dragged along for the ride. Otherwise, the pussy would still be counting the sheep with the sandman."

I shook my head in amazement. "Der Hund hasn't moved from this spot Christian. There is no way he spoke with you much less kicked you from your bed. I would have noticed him stomping around in the wheelroom, you creepy bastard."

Christian shook his head. "You forget that I am the other half of Der Hund, idiot. He split in half to creating me when the boy was still the tadpole chained to the wall in Gerard's barn. That connection between me and the core is stronger than with any of you nothings. He can speak with me by his thoughts only. I tell you he has given me instructions and I am here to do as I always have done, protect the boy named Christian Axel Schmidt. Stay out of my way or find yourself knocked to your ass for your efforts."

I scoffed. "All right Christian, I will take your word for it. I am aware there is a stronger link with you and the core, I need not be given the lecture covering that ancient history fool. I say that if Der Hund commands it then I must obey his wishes. However, I would appreciate your sharing the information you have been given. This leaving me in the dark is rather stressful. I have to question why the Master wouldn't at least warn me that I must share space with the angry psychopath."

Mad Maxx gasped loudly as if surprised. "Oh, my Gott. I just finished catching up with this horror tale. Is what the memory shows me truthful? Please tell me at least some of the worst of it is the boy hallucinating. Holy Hell."

I chuckled with bitterness. “That is no hallucination, brother. What you see is the evidence of it. Apparently, the Head of the Voters tricked der Hund. Welcome to the party, and the Palace of the Mortar King, Master of this Haus.” I put the boy’s arms up demonstrating for the intelligence shard the nightmarish cell that held the boy prisoner in its entirety.

Christian scoffed. “Well, now that the perverted Byron has claimed the boy for his own, this shit will be over. Don’t get too comfy brother Mad Maxx. We are leaving soon enough.”

My eyes went wide in disbelief. “Are you really as stupid as you look Christian? That Byron is the Voter fool. If our own fucking father, that is above that man in station and power, cannot free us surely you know Byron is pissing in the wind.”

Christian glared at me with the flames in his eyes rising. “Peter is a Gott damned rotten liar. When the fuck did we start to believe anything that asshole tells us? Never. I say that Byron will twist that bitch Gretta’s arm like he did the boy’s during that raping shit. She will relent to his demands.”

Max frowned at Christian as I covered my face. I was getting a headache from the moronic discussions, you know. “Brother Christian, forgive me for saying this but Mad Max is correct. Byron is deluded. Gretta intends to see the boy raving mad. She has us where she wants us. There is no way she will release us to the care of Byron. The last thing she wants is one of her Prince's pointing the Mortar King's regency powers at her back. Lucus has the connections on the outside that worry the FemDom, and he is no Prince of either the Silk or Fur throne. He is our best bet to find these chains broken."

Florian's insane laughter interrupted what was sure to be breaking out into a fight among us shards. "Listen to you magpies. Hearing you arguing about which foul pervert you choose to play the little bitch to is more than funny. It is a fucking joke."

I snapped the boy's attentions to the grinning skull of the expired Priceless and screamed at him from my mind. "Shut up. Do you hear me, Florian? I am fatigued beyond imagination. I will not sit here and take any shit from the likes of you. Besides, didn't you pay attention to what that cunt snake said? There is a line to fuck with Mad Maxx. You wait your turn motherfucker like everyone else."

Florian howled in mirth at that. "Oh? Where does the line start, or end for that matter? Seems to me that you are not the picky one on who gets the first dibs. In only twelve hours I hear you swear your favors to Jonas, then to Peter. Both of them said nein. So, you go trolling to Cary asking about Lucus. Now I am to understand without hearing his likely hell no, you promise to be the sex doll exclusive to this brute called Byron. You are back to discussing Lucus despite that last idiot falling for your disgusting charms. Whew, I can barely keep up with the list of fellas you are playing mare for. It makes my head spin the speed to which you suck that cock. I must admit I am impressed, whore."

That was it. I got up from the floor and headed for Florian dragging the weights behind me. My resolve was strong to get to him, but I was moving like the man running through quicksand. It all seemed to be happening in slow motion.

I reached the Mortar Throne. Florian let out a wild scream as I snatched him from my Queen's seat. I held him to stare with his empty sockets into the boy's eyes. He could see me standing there at the wheel glaring at him in unabashed hatred. I felt him trembling in the boy's grip.

Christian giggled behind me with cruel thrill as I growled out, "Say it to my face, Florian. Go ahead big man. Scared and helpless aren't you? I can do whatever I want, and you have to endure. Why don't you do something about it, huh? I dare you to try. When you make a play to flee I will merely chase you down and fuck your mind for the insult. What is this? You have nothing witty or hateful to say to me, Florian? Does the gag have your tongue perhaps? I see you are not so brave when there is nowhere to run. Now you know what it feels like to be the Mad Maxx, asshole. Don't you ever forget that the prisoner is not the willing lover or I will forget that I used to call you an ally, ja?"

Florian nodded in my hands. "Ja, ja, I understand Mad Maxx. Please, I beg mercy brother. Don't smash me into pieces. I apologize for my rude statements. I will refrain from judgement no matter what I see in the future. I see the chains and locks. You are not the whore, you are the victim. I get it. I had no right to be so cruel."

I nodded. "That's better numbskull. You watch your mouth, and we will continue to remain friends. I don't have so much wealth I can afford to throw away even one that is in my pocket. However, I am willing to go bankrupt to keep the rumors and lies about me to the bare minimum. Think you fool. What if anyone heard you saying the crap you spewed just a moment ago? I am the Master of the Haus, Florian. The King cannot have negative gossip floating around about him. The people will rise up and see him crucified."

A shrill voice cut through the air startling me so bad I nearly dropped Florian onto the stone floor. "Look what we have here brother. It appears that Mad Maxx is fascinated with the corpses. Perhaps he is imagining his own future? Nein, I bet he is not sated from all that affection he got from the idiot Byron. He desires more kissing and without any recourse he was hoping to find a bit of adoration anywhere he can get it." I flinched as I turned and saw Kilian, Reece, Sebastian and Tadeas grinning at me from the cell gate.

I put Florian down on my throne with speed. I did my best to back away from the four brutes that were fast approaching me, but as I pointed out to Florian moments before, there was nowhere to run. The Dungeon Masters captured and dragged me back to the wooden privy where Kilian and Reece stood waiting without even breaking a sweat.

The brutes held me hostage in their grips while Reece left the cell briefly. Kilian made the small talk with

Sebastian about the weather and menu at the Great Hall while the three awaited his return. I groaned in pure dismay as I watched Reece coming back pushing a gurney bed, with restraining straps, on wheels down the hallway. He came right into the cell and parked that horrible thing within easy reach of my subduers.

I struggled with all I had as Sebastian and Tadeas forced me onto the bed and strapped the boy down despite the already overabundance of chains, damn. Kilian locked the wheels to keep my futile attempts to free myself from rolling the thing across the stone floor.

While he did that his brother Reece and the Dungeon Masters were forcing the blindfold and earphones onto me. This had become the custom with these snakes visits, but that didn't prevent me from doing all I could to make it hard for them to finish their cruel work.

I fought so hard I finally got the violent backhand treatment from Sebastian. I ignored his warning and refused to hold my head still as he tried to get the speakers set up. That blow bought him enough time, while I recovered from being knocked to stupid, to place the torture devices with effectiveness.

Once I was blind and my hearing muted except to hear only what they wanted me to hear, I felt the ball gag being removed. I held still for that small mercy, though I guess they didn't mean for it to actually be such a thing, ja? My mouth wasn't even completely freed before the familiar sounds of all the people speaking over each other began in the headphones. I took shallow breaths and braced for the coming sensory overload the Altergotts seemed so damned found of.

This time the voices lowered to barely audible rather than the usual rising in volume. I felt a bit of relief that at least I wouldn't have to endure that loud noise when suddenly a shrill scream broke out. That made me jerk in shock and pain. Fucking thing was loud as hell. This horrible shrieking was followed by a series of piercing whistles, sirens, and horns. Each blast came on with suddenness and was so loud I would struggle with all my might to cover the boy's ears against the sound.

I didn't realize it at first, but I was also wailing as each assault to my hearing happened. The background voices were then joined by rhythmic noises that sounded like the blips on a radar or perhaps the morse code.

All the while those shocking sirens and horns blasted intermittently. I admit it didn't take long to put the boy's nerves on edge. I could feel my nubs chattering from the increasing anxiety and the sweat breaking out all over my flesh.

This went on for many minutes with no change. Then suddenly, Reece pulled up the blindfold. The light poured into my sensitive eyes causing me to gasp for air from the agony. He grabbed my crown and held my head still. Kilian approached me from the other side and held my eyelids open to keep me from finding relief from the assaulting glare.

Reece then pointed a light into the boy's face. Bright colors and excruciating light poured into the boy's visual pathways unhindered by even the mercy of blinking. Tears welled up with vigor attempting to sooth the hostile conditions created by these snakes. I writhed against my restraints and wailed as the motherfuckers continued to hit me with the overstimulation of sight and sound.

Another several minutes passed until the next change in the torturing began. Suddenly the loud noises stopped, and the whispering people became a bit louder though I could only understand a word or two of what day said. A voice rose above all the others. It was menacing male voice with a monotone and deep tone.

That man said in a repeating loop, "The ants are chewing their way through." The voice kept getting louder until I was sure I was going to go deaf from the sound.

All the while Reece's strobing lights blew my mind's gaskets. I began to lose the ability to think clearly and understand my location. It felt like I was floating away and coming apart all at the same time.

The snake brother withdrew his cruel light and nodded at Kilian saying something I couldn't hear above the sounds in the earphones. He released my eyelids, thank Gott, and I blinked back the stinging tears the fell freely down my face. I turned the boy's head trying to see where that snake was going, but my vision was confused. I knew that Reece had turned off the strobe, but I could still see the colors bouncing and morphing in the boy's visual field. It partially blinded me because I couldn't see what was hiding behind the blobs.

Kilian returned within moments holding that weird box I saw him carrying earlier. I watched Sebastian and Tadeas as best as I could since my vision was still obstructed undoing the straps that held my arm on his side. Before I could attempt to fight with my newly freed hand, the brutes restrained it holding it up where I could easily view what they were doing with it.

I yelled in fear as I saw Kilian take a lancet and cut into the tips of each finger on the handheld by the Dungeon Masters. blood welled up with viciousness as I wailed and tried to pull away from his brutal assault. I thought for sure he was going to cut them off.

However, there was nothing I could do but scream in terror. Sebastian and Tadeas held me tight. while this was happening, the evil male voice in the earphones continued to repeat the ants were chewing through. I was so fucking confused by this point I couldn't tell you if I was coming or going. Kilian finished cutting, this included the boy's thumb, and smiled as he dropped that lancet to pick up the box.

He demonstrated the side of it to me making sure I could view it easily. My eyes went wide in fear as I watched through a glass window hundreds of ants crawling around inside that box. It was full of them from what I could see. After he was sure I had understood the contents he held he grinned with wickedness as he shook it with vigor pissing off every one of those insects thoroughly.

I let out a loud scream when Kilian then turned the box to show a flap large enough to put a hand into what had been cut into the back of the box. The ants were prevented from getting out by a thin film of plastic wrap material. I had realized too late, why he cut my fingers open like that and what that man was trying to tell me.

Da Dungeon Master's held my arm with strength as Kilian forced my mangled hand into the box through that opening. I railed and wailed nearly fainting from the horrific sensation of the thousands of angered ants crawling across the boy's flesh hidden within that hellish insect farm.

The repeating voice suddenly screamed, in a repeated loop as before, "The ants are tunneling inside you. Beware, beware. Do you hear them chewing your flesh?" In the background the whispering voices were joined by the sounds of chewing.

My Liebe, I swear to Gott I could feel the ants doing exactly what that man said they were going to do. They were tunneling into the boy through the cuts at the end of my fingers. The sensation of chewing from within began there and within moments spread to my wrists. The tingling of their tiny legs marched up to my elbow, then to the shoulder. It took less than five minutes for every artery, vein and capillary within me to light up with the agony of the invasion of these tiny carnivores.

I screamed wildly non-stop as I felt the ants devouring me from the inside out. The men laughed with great thrill as I thrashed uselessly begging for death to end my horrific slow ingestion by ants. Kilian removed the box, assuming enough ants to finish the job had gained entry into the boy and ordered the Dungeon Masters to re-restrain the bloody hand. Reece produced a roll of the duct tape and used it liberally to assure no matter how much I thrashed I couldn't get those earphones off my ears.

It goes without saying that the four of them took that opportunity to begin their sexual assault on the boy. Kilian took his intercourse with me first, followed by Reece, then the two brutes played that tag teaming shit. They were so turned on by my obvious terror, and watching their brothers make the greedy pigs of themselves ahead of them in the rotation, none of them required the preparation for their mounts by oral services. I was left free to scream in torment without interference.

None of the men seemed to take notice of my wailing. By the time the brutes began treating me like their sex doll, I was completely stupid with the belief that I was being eaten alive. They took their time and appeared to find immense pleasure in that abominable scene. I base that on their expressions and complete lack of hesitation to do as they wished while seeking the orgasm. There was no doubt they were having the time of their lives.

In the wheelroom things had gotten out of control rapidly. The invading ants rushed in wreaking havoc as they chewed through the pathways of the boy. I stomped like the flamingo dancer keeping the tiny monsters from reaching our sleeping core. I knew they had come to eat him for their dinner.

Max, Mad Maxx and Christian rushed about the room like madmen swatting, slapping, swearing and squishing the army of insects as fast as they could move. It seemed like for every one we killed, a hundred more came to pay their respects for their fallen comrades. Yikes!

The panic rose to excruciating levels within me. I felt the borders of my shard become ragged and I could see by the expression on Max's face, I was not looking too good. It was becoming clear I was going to shatter if something wasn't done fast.

Mad Maxx yelled out in terror. "Christian, look at Mad Max, brother. He is cracking. We have to do something, or we lose the defender of the soul. Fuck, watch out Max. The ants are breaching the left lobe. Shit, I have to let Christian off the chain and attend that or the boy will go into the seizures."

Max wailed back as he stomped wildly keeping a protective barrier around the sleeping Der Hund. "Go cut Christian loose, brother. There is no other option. Attend the brain with quickness. I will keep Der Hund protected. Mad Max, get way from the wheel. You are coming apart. Let the anger shard take control before it is too late." I nodded and staggered away nearly hitting the floor and shattering into dust as Christian rushed past me taking up the wheel with speed.

The boy's sounds of terror ended almost the second Christian took up the controls. I leaned into the back wall panting, feeling sicker than I ever had before or since. This was the closest I had ever been to the shatter and let me tell you it is not something I recommend. The only thing worse than the feeling of the impeding void caused by my instability was the loud noises of those ants chewing throughout the flesh.

Sebastian and Tadeas had finished their sexual assault and where patting each other on the back, likely bragging about the others prowess. Christian lay there in silence. I watched from the wheelroom back wall as the anger shards predatory eyes tracked each of the four men's movements with care. All of them were speaking to his brothers with thrilled smiles on their faces.

What they said we couldn't hear thanks to the voices in the earphones. It was becoming clear, when no further assault came in many minutes, they had finished with their evil plans. I, like Christian, began to believe soon they would free the boy from that restraining bed and head back upstairs to enjoy their victory over us.

I shot a glare at Mad Max to insure he wasn't going to try to interfere with my plans to attack these assholes. For that moment, I was frantic to get those ants out of the boy and the earphones off the ears. That said, I knew if I stayed patient, the chance to strike out would present itself soon enough. If the boy was to die this horrid fate of supper for the ants, I was going to take at least a tiny chuck of the bastards to hell with us.

Kilian approached the boy with his eyes narrowed. I couldn't hear him, but I could see that my sudden calm was neither something he expected nor wanted to happen. He motioned to his snake brother to undo the tape that held the earphones on the boy's head.

I winced as that nasty adhesive ripped wads of hair from the boy's noggin, but I refused to utter a single sound. It took a bit, but Reece managed to get the earphones off with only minimal pain compared to what the boy had become accustomed to, you know. The Altergotts stood on each side of me staring into the boy's face.

Reece took out his pen light and shined it into the boys eyes. I held fast to keeping the silence though that light was fucking painful. "It doesn't seem to be the catatonic fit, Kilian. Not sure why he is sullen all at once. Listen to me Maxx. I can see the ants crawling around inside you with this light. See that Kilian. Is that an ant that just crawled out of his ear?" He pointed the light at the left side of my head next to the snake.

Kilian nodded with an expression of shock. "Oh, hell ja. There are so many of them. How long do you think it will take them to finish eating up his organs? I bet that hurts like a sonofabitch. It gives me the shudders just thinking of what a terrible agony being devoured alive must be."

Reece sighed "Well, from what I can gather, by morning the ants should have him mostly picked clean. It is a terribly slow and painful process. They are already inside his brain. The good news is in a few hours, he will be feel nothing and be drooling, idiot that cannot do a thing but piss himself and shit his breeches."

Sebastian, that had come up to watch the show scoffed. "Well how the fuck can we tell the difference then? He is already drooling like the loon he is, and I must point out he wet himself when Tadeas was having his turn at him. Thankfully he held his bowels, but I don't think that he would if there was anything left in his gut after all that puking he has been doing lately." He chuckled at his disgusting assessment of the boy's sorry state.

Kilian nodded and smiled with sudden thrill. "I know. Undo his straps. I think all he needs is a little wiggle room and we will see the results of this experiment come to maturity I bet."

Reece appeared worried but motioned the brutes to do as his brother suggested. "I don't know, Kilian. Seriously, this strange silence and lack of response is not typical for Maximillian. I think it wise to give him a wide berth until I can assess this odd symptom with sureness of our safety."

Tadeas came up with Sebastian and began undoing the straps while the Altergotts retreated to a safe distance. "Are you funning me Reece? You fear this little nothing? Even out of the straps he is chained to the hilt. Not like he can do anything but cry like the little bitch he is." Sebastian giggled as he nodded his agreement at that statement.

I held my stoic stillness as the final restraint was removed. Sebastian grabbed the boy by the upper arm and flung him to the floor like the rag doll. I allowed this to happen without attempting any resistance. I landed on my hands and knees. I trembled in the spot from the strength it took to hold back the screams of terror over the chewing ants all over the place.

Sebastian and Tadeas walked over and stood over me laughing like hyenas. I shook my head slightly and watched in horror as some of the ants spilled out of the boy's ears onto the floor. They scrambled frantically seeking a way to re-enter the boy's flesh to join their fellow for the free meal.

That was all I could stand. I stood up with suddenness ignoring the weight of the chains and silver balls. I let out a banshee like wail and plowed into the shocked Sebastian with all the strength of the lion. The Dungeon Master crumbled as I released rapid blows to his stomach, sternum, face and finally kicked him in the right knee nearly breaking his leg in half.

Tadeas let out a jell of surprise and punched the boy in the lower back. I ignored the pain while hoping that his blow killed a few of the ants munching on my kidneys and turned with the speed of a cheetah. I left the writhing Sebastian in a pool of his own blood as I focused all my pent up anger on Tadeas. I backhanded the stunned Dungeon Master sending him sprawling backward into the floor.

I began to batter that bastard with vigor. He tried to block my kicks, punches and head butts but I was younger and quicker than him. Within moments he joined his brother groaning in agony nearly unconscious on the Palace floor.

Kilian and Reece had been yelling words of encouragement to their men during the fray from the cell gate. When I had laid Tadeas low I turned my attention towards killing me a couple of snakes. I took a wild run at them screeching like a madman. I hit the end of that chain, held back by the weights as well, and was snapped back with such brutal force I was jerked to the floor gasping for air. I nearly broke the boy's neck you know.

I ignored that near miss recovering with rapidness. Sebastian and Tadeas had also regained their feet. I saw them staggering in an effort to retreat from my reach. With another wild scream I came at them full force. Sebastian escaping my chain length, but Tadeas was not so lucky. I knocked that motherfucker so hard he flew across the cell, sadly out of reach at last, with a loud scream of agony.

Florian had been watching this show in silence all that time. The second Tadeas landed on his back at his brother Master's feet the idiot decided to add his two cents. I heard his laughter begin to roll across the cell floor like the tapestry flood. I turned to stare at the grinning skull in pure shock that he had the power to do this shit.

Florian's voice boomed out rocking the entire cell. "Kill them, kill them, hahaha. You are the damned Mad Maxx. An ant brings down the giant and eats him for his dinner."

Now that was a bit uncalled for, ja? I covered my ears in terror as Florian began repeating those words in the loop. Each one echoed off the walls and fell to the dungeon floor shattering into a thousand pieces of glass. The sound was deafening."

I screamed in pure desperation. "You shut up. I am not listening to you. Oh Gott, someone make him stop speaking. Shut up, Gott damn you. I swear I will smash you into the wall, motherfucker. Mad Max, Mad Maxx, Max, anyone help me please. I beg of you brothers. Make this asshole stop this nightmare. We have to hurry. The ants are killing the boy. Do you hear them? Can't you see them? Where the fuck is everyone. I am lost." I fell to my knees rocking in place and holding the boy's ears tightly screaming those words non-stop, blinded to stupid by the fear that had overtaken me all of a sudden.

I heard Reece yip out sounding thrilled. "Look brother, he is degraded to the hebephrenic. I told you the ant trick would work. Hurry up boys, pick yourself up and let us out of the cell. We need to find Gretta to report the good news. The Master of the Haus is hopelessly psychotic and ready to be paraded down the halls. That was the easiest thing I have ever done. Hurry up you idiots. You can clean yourselves up later. You should have been expecting that schizophrenic would lash out in the fit. Bet next time he won't get the drop on you. Told you the insane are strong bastards, ha." Tadeas and Sebastian limped to the cell door to do as Reece commanded.

I didn't stop my disturbed ranting and behaviors as the four men took off with speed while taking that bed, box of ants and other torture tools along. I could hear them excitedly yelling of their victory as they rushed to find that bitch Gretta. It was registering somewhere deep within the boy that I had better get my shit together or I had a lot more to worry about then that ant invasion.

Mad Max came up and stood next to me with an expression of determination. "Brother, this situation is too much for one or the other of us. Allow me to help you steer the boy. If we combine our strength we can beat these ants and the Altergotts plans to see us dishonored in front of the collars."

I glared at him full of despise for the shard I had once called a true brother. "I will not work with you as long as that thing is on your chain Mad Max. I have told you this many times. Max will drain me, and he desires to see me shattered. You know that."

Max stomped on a bundle of ants headed for Der Hund's sleeping frame. "Christian that is not true. I may not agree with all you do, but I am not such a moron I don't realize you are necessary for the boy's survival. Allow Mad Max to aid you. I swear to keep my distance and mouth shut."

Mad Max shot me a glance full of sarcastic humor. "Well, there you go brother. You must move over so I can help you. The soul accepts you as the evil that cannot be denied without serious repercussions. He gives you his oath to keep his distance. Do remember Max is a man of his word. What are you waiting for, him to kiss you and ask you to marry him or what schwuler pig."

I chuckled with humor over that much missed cruel humor of the sadistic shard. "Call me the schwuler pig, will you? I seem to recall you have the Dominant lover called Leo and that wasn't enough cock for your wanton ass, ja? You got yourself the black collar lover too. Wow, now that is impressive. I guess it is a good thing you have no more holes to fill with another or you maybe will seek out the silver boyfriend and collect the whole set, ja?"

Mad Max playfully swatted my shoulder. "Fichen Dich, Christian. I didn't choose Cary as the lover. Your butt buddy Der Hund did. I thought you said he filled you in on all that has happened while you slept. If he didn't tell you about that weird situation he got the boy into, then I guess you two are not as close as you thought, ja?" I moved over and he took the left side of the wheel to aid me in calming the boy's psychotic fit.

I glared at him in pretend anger. "For your information Der Hund did tell me that he blood bonded Cary, not you. However, he said he chose Cary because you said you loved the man."

Mad Max snickered. "Ah, I see that Der Hund misunderstood me. I said I loved the man's gun. I guess the Core thought I meant the one, never mind. The choice was genius, you wait and see. I am sure he will get Lucus to come and see us free from this prison. Wait, speaking of perverts, where the fuck is Byron? I thought he said he was coming back?"

I shrugged as I watched another ant run across the boy's visual field. "Gott, I hope you are wrong there. I cannot take another fucking. Forget that nasty business. What the fuck are we going to do about these ants that are eating the boy alive brother? I swear I am going to freak out again if that infernal chewing doesn't stop."

Florian broke into our conversation by clearing his throat. "Hey, Mad Maxx. I don't mean to stick my nose where it doesn't belong but if that radiated water is a killer. Just saying. I mean sure it will kill the boy eventually, but he is bigger. With ant size I bet a good drink of it will send them all to legs up within mere moments. It is full of chemicals like the bug spray, ja?"

I flashed a grin of thrill at Mad Max. "I don't know who that fucker is, but I think I am starting to like him a lot. He is right. Drink the water. It will kill the ants."

That idea made me tremble. "Ja, I see the wisdom in it but brother, in time it will kill us too. We trade one horrible death for another you know. I don't think we should do it. Let's find another safer way to exterminate dem."

I sneered at him. "Vait a minute. This is easily solved. We take a vote. All those in favor of being the dinner for ants raise their hands." Of course, not even Mad Max raised his paw on that election, ja?

The boy crawled over to the water bowl left to him by the kind Birgit and turned it up swallowing the entire thing in a fell swoop. He was finishing his radiation tinged solution as the noise of many people echoed down the halls. I shot a look of fear to Mad Max. He was staring back deep in his own terror. We couldn't tell who was coming this time, but no matter the identity of the coming persons it was sure to be yet another horrific scene. They seemed to be taking on extreme dimensions that none of us had even imagined in our most fevered nightmares. Mad Max and I braced as Florian chuckled and the ants began to fall dead by the droves in the wheelroom floor. One by one they succumbed, appearing to be in much agony from that radiation poisoning.

Chapter 42: The Rise of the Schizophrenic Master of the House, Part 2

I shot a look of worry at Florian and saw that his expression was also that of concern. The many voices echoing down that stone hallway sounded like the army coming. I wondered if beating up Sebastian and Tadeas had finally been the last straw for the Queens of the Silk and Fur thrones. I became convinced those disembodied sounds belonged to the Guard come to collect my worthless ass for the planting in the yard.

Mad Max and I turned the boy's head all around the cell seeking a spot to hide. There was not even the closet, or table to take shelter under. I let out a whimper and crawled like the animal across the floor putting my back to the Mortar throne. I pulled up the boy's legs wrapping my arms around them and hid his face behind the knees. I trembled in terror, hoping the bullets of the Guard would find their mark with merciful quickness. There was nothing else I could do but wait for my expected death.

The Palace silver gate stretched the entire length of the cell. Thanks to it constituting one of the four walls that held me hostage, there was no privacy whatsoever. I was trapped like the zoo creature that anyone could come to view at their pleasure. Not a soul needed to enter to watch everything I did from a safe distance.

It would be easy enough to point the rifle through the bars and unload the clip right into the boy's flesh. I assumed then the Dungeon Masters would allow the rodent's to clean up the blood and guts such a gruesome murder would leave behind.

The group of voices suddenly went silent a few minutes after I buried my face into the boy's legs. I panted in fear with my eyes closed doing the best to brace for the pain of being shot to death. I really did think they had come to end me once and for all you know. Mad Max and me gripped the wheel tightly.

I noticed we were white knuckling that blasted thing. It is likely we nearly busted it in two from that stressed out exertion of strength wielded between us. It took all we had to keep the boy still, quiet and calm during the distressful moments of sitting there waiting for doom from the unknown visitors.

The shrill voice of Gretta cut through the air causing us to flinch. "What the fuck is this shit, Kilian. You dragged me down here to this stinking hole saying that idiot is railing and banging into walls like the madman. All I witness is a battered, dirty, skinny, frightened teenager shivering and weeping in a corner. While the sight of his misery is a joy to behold it is not going to help accomplish my goals. In fact, I dare say if his precious Gott damned collars were to see this pathetic scene the Mortar King would probably gain support rather than lose any. I ought to have you whipped for bothering me with your fantastical stories of success that are just that, fantasy."

I heard Cora scoff then growl out, "I think dear Sister Gretta, that Kilian and Reece have contracted a bit of the schizophrenia handling this foul creature. They must have been having the hallucinations." The FemDoms began to chuckled sounding most humored over their dressing down the Altergott brothers.

Sebastian broke the laughter. "Nein, Honored Queens. I swear on my honor that Reece and Kilian were speaking the truth. That boy was wild with the insanity. Look at me and my brother Tadeas. See the injuries and bruises? That motherfucker you claim to be the harmless angst teen did this shit. Only moments ago, he commanded the strength of the mad."

Gretta snorted. "He gave you that shiner and nasty limp did he? Oh, come of it, Sebatian. You really expect me to believe that little nothing psycho managed to lay you and your brute partner low? Surely, you know I can see he is chained to the floor by weights and restrained to the wall. Even if he were of a size capable of beating two huge grown men, you could easily retreat out of his reach. Those chains don't allow for him to go farther than the privy and the Mortar throne. I thought this merely the joke of bad taste but now I am starting to believe you fellas are trying to openly offend me and my sister's intelligence."

Reece's voice whined out in defense of the Dungeon Master's allegation. "Nein, Honorable Gretta, Sebastian speaks the truth of the matter. The boy was in the catatonic excitement fit. When like that the psychotic can command strength far beyond the normal. I saw Mad Maxx nearly kill these two stout men with his bare hands. I have witnessed this kind of almost supernatural power come from many other schizophrenics during my tenure at Heslach."

Cora snorted sounding disgusted. "Do you hear this? Now these idiots are expecting us to believe in magic and superman. Christ, I left my supper for this bullshit? Gott dammit, I say we have the whole lot of them hauled off to their own dungeon cells for a few days. Maybe they will think twice before crying wolf to their bedders in the future, ja?"

Kilian gasped and then said in a frightened tone, "Honored sister, I must beg you to relent your harsh threats. We are all the honest men. Every day we come down here to suffer the most abominable conditions in an effort to aid you in your quest. There is no way any of us would dare to bother you with false reports. The boy was the hebephrenic when we left him. He obviously has calmed down his catatonic fit since our departure. It is unfortunate that the techniques we used to run him into chronic madness have failed to take the permanent hold as of yet. Maybe a few more sessions will result in the desired mental deterioration. I bet if only prompted mildly at this very moment the Priceless would break into the mad dog fits we told you were witnessed."

Gretta sighed. "Is that so? Well, we are already down here Kilian. Go in there and prod the filthy thing. Let's see if you are blowing smoke up my skirt or you are telling me the truth, ja?"

That made me lift up my head to get a look at the group over the boy's knees. I was curious to know if Kilian and that snake brother of his were really coming into the cell. If they got close enough I could finally take out my revenge for all the brutality they had leveled upon my flesh once and for all.

I saw five Dominants and the two Queens standing outside the cell gate. Gretta, Cora, Kilian, Reece and Sebastian were flanked by Claus then the ailing Tadeas. Seeing the Elder Claus caused my hopes to rise. If anyone had the power to see me out of that Palace it would be the first Prince of the Fur throne. I noticed he was staring at me intently with an expression of pity on his face. Mad Maxx quickly came up with a plan to gain his attention and end our incarceration while we were at it.

Kilian and Reece were deep in their excuses for refusing to enter the cell when I slowly took to the boy's feet. I kept my gaze averted and wrung my hands as I stood there trembling from the raging anxiety within. The ants were falling dead all over the wheelroom, but my stomach was rolling from the bug spray we drank to poison them. I was sure it was only a matter of time before I ended up vomiting my chewed up guts right into that would privy drawer.

Claus noticed my standing up as did the injured Dungeon Masters. "All of you shut up a minute. Look, Mad Maxx is alert and appears to know we are present. Maxx my boy, tell your Elder Claus, is what Reece and Kilian saying true or do they make up lies?"

I scoffed and shook my head wildly, like rocking it uncontrollably is more like it. It is a movement disorder of schizophrenia. "Nein, I hit no honorable man in all my life, Elder Claus. I don't know why these men lay false claims around my good name. They strike me, not the other way around. I think maybe they fall down the stairs from the wine drinking. To hide their dishonor, they look to blame the helpless prisoner for their bad habits."

Claus chortled at my response. "Railing with madness, huh? Maxx seems lucid enough to me, brother Kilian. I dare say his explanation for the condition of the Dungeon Masters makes a hell of a lot more sense than this insane tale of that boy whipping their asses."

Sebastian yelled at me full of fury. "You little liar. How dare you deny what you did to me and your other caregiver Tadeas. You better think before you say another word, worm. Soon enough you will be without the audience to hear your story telling or screams.."

I stopped the hand wringing and looked up locking my hateful gaze on Sebastian. "I think you will return to abuse me any way you please no matter what I do or don't say you perverted motherfucker. I have nothing to lose, nor can you threaten me with any effect. Claus, Elders, am the Master of the Haus. My word is the law. I demand that Cora and Gretta be removed from the Fur and Silk Throne this moment. I assign Claus to the Fur Throne and replace the Silk Queen with a king. I raise Rolf to Head of the Haus. I further move the Elder Malfred be made First Prince of the Fur throne and the Voter Peter to be First

Prince of the Silk Throne. Cora, Gretta and Kilian will be sent to the dungeons to await my pleasure for sentencing for crimes against the Mortar King. Reece, Sebastian and Tadeas are to be immediately executed by the Guard. You will release me from these chains and this cell this moment. I have spoken. I expect you to see this done with haste, King Claus," I roared out doing my best to say this with strength and authority.

You could have knocked all them down with a feather they were so shocked at what day heard me say. Claus's face broke out with a huge grin as Cora and Gretta's melted into expressions of rage. Kilian stared at his brother dumbfounded while Sebastian and Tadeas swung their head wildly trying to figure out what to do. They had fucked up and left me without that fucking gag. I was able to voice my demands without the hindrance their Queen Gretta had ordered to prevent the very thing I had just done, you know.

Claus let out an excited yup. "Ah, you beautiful boy. I swear I love you more than my own life. You heard him boys. Arrest Cora, Greta and Killian. You will then report to Ivan, the Head of the Guard, with Reece for your execution the minute these three are in their cells. Hand over the keys to King Maxx's locks. The Master of the Haus has spoken. His word is the law."

Gretta reached out and grabbed Claus's gown clad arm with viciousness. "You shut up old man. The Mortar King is stricken with madness. We do not take orders from the incompetent. Only his regent can enforce his voice and you know it. That is the law."

Claus jerked his arm from her clawed grip with fury in his eyes. "You will unhand me, Gretta. How dare you insult me by speaking to me with commonness? I should have you skinned by whip for that alone. We all know no regent stood up to speak for Mad Maxx during the coronation. Therefore, his words have no legal middleman. The rules say the Master of the Haus's words are law, period. It matters not that you are to pay for your cruelty trying to hold on to power. I intend to see his orders followed. The way I see it you deserve everything you get and more. You should have accepted with grace that the power of the Haus was lost to you the second that metal crown was place on his pretty head. Even locking him up in the center of hell didn't stop him from finding a way to seek rightful revenge on you bitches. I already respected this boy as a warrior of rare quality more than I ever admitted, but now he has my undying loyalty. There is no longer any doubt in my mind that he is the King of the prophecy legend. All hail King Mad Maxximillian. Long live the King."

Gretta roared out in anger, "Arrest Elder Claus this minute. Send him to room with Byron. A few days cooling off in the deep freeze pit will change this old buzzard's mind about his allies in this Haus. Do it now Sebastian and Tadeas or the one thing the Priceless orders, you know, your growing the trees is going to be carried out."

I watched in dismay as the brute Dungeon Masters subdued Elder Claus, who had begun to rail and curse, then drag him off down the hallway. Thankfully they did it with uncharacteristically kind gentleness. Likely due to both his high station and his advanced age.

I whimpered with deep fear realizing that Mad Maxx's plan, while valid, had failed. It had finally become painfully clear that as long as Cora and Gretta could keep anyone of strength from hearing my words spoken, I was stuck as their hostage and the plaything of those evil men. I simply didn't have access to enough Dominant or FemDom allies to see my wishes carried out.

On the bright side, if dare was one, at least I knew that Byron was no longer the threat. Apparently, his seeking out Gretta with demands for my release had not been well received. Later I would be told Reece had rushed ahead and warned the Silk Queen of his attempts to murder me to keep others from touching what he thought his. When the delusional Voter showed up to demand he be named my regent, Gretta was waiting, with the Guard. He was immediately arrested and given one week in the Pit as punishment.

Along with his vacation to the dungeons he was officially banned from coming to the Mortar Palace to visit me for life. Claus had given Sebastian and Tadeas the key to all the doors of the stone Palace to assure I was safely locked behind several gates. This was done to prevent anyone, especially the lovesick Voter, with a desire to kill rather than share, from sneaking in to say hello or worse.

I stood there unsure what to do or say now that I had been completely beaten in my latest bid for freedom. I felt the tears welling up in the boy's eyes from the hopelessness of this nightmarish situation. It seemed I had run out of options. Jonas, Peter, Byron and now Claus, all had been powerless to aid me out of those chains.

I had found the bottom at last. I fell back to the boy's backside and hugged his legs to my chest. I returned to my original spot of hiding my face from the brutal word that held me her prisoner. I sat there weeping without any attempt to maintain any dignity. I could hear Gretta and Cora laughing and joking with the relieved sounding Altergott brothers.

It was not lost on me that my useless outburst had caused the vicious FemDom's to forget all about their false alarm. It seemed the Queens were no longer angered that I wasn't quite ready for the parade of shame through the Haus. The way the four of them were speaking, all of them seemed satisfied I would break soon enough. I listened to the Queen admit that they were in no hurry to see me ended for good. Besides, the knowledge that I was being tormented at inhumane levels brought them the thrill of their lives.

The horrible things the FemDoms said were bad enough, but hearing the snakes bragging of their joy over their getting to experiment without restraint on the worthless schizophrenic only caused me to cry even harder. I seriously was almost as low in spirits as any human could go while still existing.

I sobbed loudly into my lap. All the while I was thinking things would have been different if I had been a stronger boy. I couldn't get the idea that I would be free with Annette in the green fields with the baby sheep if only I had not shattered. I should've let all that guilt over the horrid sexual and physical abuse go instead of letting it bother me into the state of the schizophrenic, ja?

I winced as the noises from that radio of Jonas's began to drift down from the Palace ceiling. It settled around the boy's ears as a whispering at first, but then it became so loud it was almost deafening.

That DJ on the radio was announcing to the Haus I was the pussy. I trembled in misery as he explained that thanks to the weakness of my mind I was not reliable when it came to reporting the reality of anything. Without the credibility owed to any human being, it had let these animals being allowed the full reign to do with me as they pleased.

At last, it was dawning on me the no one was going to come breaking through those cell bars to save the worthless psychotic called the Mad Maxx. This was my life for good. I heard the DJ say that I was lucky they kept me around as the plaything. He said that otherwise I was more trouble than I was worth. I really began to weep when he said that I am the useless creature that should be put down like the rabid dog, but that even that sad animal is of more value than the schizophrenic. At least they are granted mercy, so they don't have to suffer the madness.

I nearly choked from the tears when that radio announced loudly for all to hear, “Well, one could argue that warming cocks is possibly an excuse for allowing that thing they call Mad Maxx to waste the space. However, it is wise to keep him in the chains, so he doesn’t bother the decent folks of this Haus. They have proven themselves of worth to society, unlike this insane bastard.”

The DJ went on to point out that the snake brothers were respected and free to roam. He said I was so fucked up I hated all these brutes for bothering to finding a purpose for my meaningless existence among the winners in life. That I should be grateful they thought of me at all much less desired to fuck me.

Hell, as much as I wished to tell that DJ to shut up and argue that he was wrong in what he was telling everyone about me, I knew he speaking the truth. Afterall what could I claim to have done that demonstrated any kind of honest value? I had never held a real job, attended a real school, been off the Haus grounds, created a single kid nor been capable of finding a woman willing to couple with me.

Ja, you could say it was a real depressing moment for your Master. I sat there helplessly crying like a beaten little bitch while the Altergotts and Queens made fun of my pain. I concluded, with the help of that DJ, I am nothing but rubbish wearing the costume of a man. I had to accept that I was so terrible even though my own mother had no regard for my safety or welfare in general.

It was obvious, by this point, I was indeed pathetic and my struggle to survive insignificant. I listened while the radio told me it would be for the best to end my life the second I had half the chance, and spare anyone else the trouble, you know.

Every schizophrenic eventually reaches this conclusion sooner or later in their cycles, Meine Liebe. I had been to this low point before, back when I still wore the bat collar. The stresses of serving, torture and the enforced unnatural lifestyle had assured I was no stranger to the suicidal ideation, ja? This time, I would not find it so easy to carry out my desire to find peace the only way one of my kind can.

Gretta had already assumed I would rather choose death than suffer the torments of the perverts she sent in the never-ending parade to dishonor me. It is kind of funny to realize that this bitch that hated me so much, and wanted me dead for truth, had gone through so much trouble to make sure I couldn't take my own life.

I find humor in it because I sit here with my little frau in my lap thanks to that evil woman's desire to see me suffer as much as possible. It was her sadistic fetish to listen to the men that abused me tell her the stories of horror. You know, like the cat does sometimes with the mouse, she thrilled in the cruelty, Gretta was merely playing with me a bit before laying down a lethal blow with her kitty claws.

After all, it would have been easy enough to give me the knife, take me up to the first floor, and let the collars watch as I ended it in front of dem. That is how despondent I had become, and trust me, the Queen of the Silk knew it.

You see, the bonded crown restraining my movements, and Haus doctor on constant call all were designed to keep me breathing. Until she had been sated of her lust at hearing the perverted tales of the soiling of the Priceless Master of the Haus. She desired to demonstrate to me the extent of her Power. It was her plan to end me, but when she said, not when I wanted or needed this nightmare to cease.

I was the prisoner of a war I never knew I was fighting against Cora and her. To think all this atrocity was thanks to that fucking paradox law written by the drunken Elders as a joke over two hundred years before. The only creature that was of real threat to the Silk and Fur throne was the Mortar King.

Since there were specific and rare qualifications to hold that title, before these FemDoms none of the Kings/Queens of the thrones had ever had to be concerned about the Master of the Haus. Cora and Gretta had been trying for years to assassinate me, trick me in my metal, and stop my rise to the throne. I had not understood why they hated me so badly, bothered to notice me at all until that day in the Mortar Palace.

I had finally learned the truth of the danger I posed to them. They had to find a way to get Claus to deny he heard my words, or they were finished. I honestly had the power of the Haus within my words. All I had to do is say the words and the law was in action. I needed no votes, agreements from Princes or Princesses, nor the approval of the councils of the other two thrones. I was, and still am, the voice of the Haus.

The regent was supposed to be there to assure that I didn't make decisions as the acute schizophrenic that were full of delusions, hallucinations or paranoia. No one had managed to capture "the heart of the Priceless" which turned out to be the code word for regent, therefore I was the King with full control of all the rights of my throne. This was why all my life, all those men had battled, attacked and even abused me trying to get their hands around my leash. Owning the Priceless meant you were the Master of the Haus by proxy.

I had never learned any of this, and no one told me obviously, before it was too late to run from my destiny. I thought with much misery that afternoon I had signed my life sentence by demanding that coronation. I understood at last that I wasn't getting out of that cell. Gretta was going to keep me locked up with a gag for the rest of my life, even if she didn't find a way to see me dead. Cora and she couldn't let me out, or they would be rendered powerless and have to bow at my, or my regent's, feet. I could not be unrecognized as the Mortar King.

I know you have figured all this I have said, Meine Liebe. The reason I tell you all of it this moment is, so you understand this is all still the truth of it. I am forever the

Master of Das Kaiser Haus, and you are my Queen. I assume at this point you wonder how if what I just said is truth, the King found his way out of that Palace hell to be here with you.

I nodded my head. "Well, yeah I do wonder Master but more than that is Gretta still alive? Why don't you just order everyone to stop abusing the silver and black collars. Don't they have to listen to you? I thought you said we can leave the Haus if we want to. Is that because you are the King?"

Master Maxx laughed. "Ah, you are the clever little frau aren't you? I am going to explain the truth of all this as we go along. I promise to keep nothing a secret from my tiny Queen. Though I am the Master and you the Mistress, well after you break my silver you will be, there is complications to all of it. It is not something I can explain in a few words either. You will have to listen to the rest of this story and all that you wonder will be revealed as we go along, ja?"

I sighed. "I once heard if someone has to use more than the word yes, then it always means no, Master. I will listen to your story, but I already know something bad about the ending."

He scoffed. "Oh, and what would that be?"

I turned to glare at him for a moment. "I think the only way you and me are getting away from those mean people you are telling me about is if we run away Master. Or like you said, burn down the Haus."

Master Maxx nodded without taking his eyes off my own. "Ja, I think you have been listening closely. That said, I still would like to finish telling you the rest, or are you ready to get back to the brutal training for the Dominant selection?"

I snorted and turned back around. "Master, I could listen to this story for the rest of my life. I am in no hurry to get back to thudding, whoring and worse. Besides, like you keep telling me, I don't know everything until you tell me. Every time I thought I knew what was going to happen next, I was wrong. I don't want to guess anymore even though I don't like hearing about those men hurting you. Like it or not, I need to know all of it. These men are coming to hurt me the way they hurt you. Better to be prepared than ignorant."

Master Maxx chuckled. "As I said, my demonseed Frau is intelligent. You learn lessons quickly. That is good. Okay, then on we go with the tale of the Mortar Palace."

Sebastian and Tadeas returned from their task putting Claus into the pit. Gretta stood there jelling at the two of them for many minutes about their stupidity in not replacing the gag when they finished their sport with me. They hung their heads low and whispered apologizes, claiming that this error would never be repeated. She then told them no one was leaving till the Mortar King's tongue was restrained.

I didn't bother to attempt fighting the two brutes as they limped up to me still sitting there weeping. I knew any aggression from me wouldn't be taken lightly by the watching Silk and Fur Queens. Sebastian snatched the side of my crown bridle and held me tightly as Tadeas forced the ball gag back into the boy's mouth. I think my going limp without any resistance surprised even the Queens. I suppose they expected me to at least argue over this indignity.

Well, not this time. I was done with the unnecessary roughness. I couldn't win, so why be the loser, ja? I had decided it was best to just lay there and take whatever brutality they heaped on my head. Then maybe Gretta, or all of them, would tire of her sadistic game and just get on with ending my pain. That is the best I could hope for by this point. Ja, kind of sad I know but there didn't seem to be any other answer to escape the Palace other than the yard for good.

I watched in silent tears as the Masters shot each other looks of cautious confusion as they backed away. I didn't move a muscle nor even glance up at them. It didn't take long for the group to clear out of there headed back to their lives while leaving me to my miserable fate.

The rest of the night was uneventful. Birgit snuck down to my cell, as she did every night for the rest of the time I was there, to give me Felicity. She seemed rather shocked when I only shrugged after she asked if I desired freedom from that gag till morning. That said, she went ahead and released me from it despite my apathetic response.

Then like every morning for the next three weeks, with one exception we are about to discuss if I can find the strength to, she rushed into the cell in the early hours. I gave her my lamb without quarrel and held still to have her relock me before the Dungeon Masters caught the little mercies she kindly gave me.

Tis ritual became the only useful reality that I could hold on to. It was a bit of unusual luck that this middle aged woman was assigned to my care. I must say that compared to everyone in my life before that time, other than maybe Leo, Birgit became my only point of light. Without her I think I would have been lost in the smothering darkness that had infected me down to my soul.

I had been through many horrors and suffered indignities so terrible they are difficult to discuss. That said, I had not yet found the limit to how truly horrible one can be to his brother. Sadly, I was to be schooled in the lowest level of the obscene the very next day or should I say night. It was a gift I was enforced to receive on my seventeenth birthday....

As I said, the morning began like the other few had with Birgit rushing into cell to hide my Felicity and relock the gag. She had barely left when Peter arrived oddly without any escort. I nearly fainted from shock when he undid the locks to my ankles and unchained me from the wall and the weights that held the boy's arms. He kept my arms chained at the wrists and the gag locked tightly much to my dismay. He informed me that I was to follow him without struggle, or the Guard would see me planted.

I was so thrilled to be leaving the Palace I offered the man no quarrel. I thought he had found some way to rescue me, you know. Peter clipped a chain leash to my gold collar and pulled me along behind him partially bonded but more than a little relieved to go.

However, that emotion was short lived. I whimpered in fear when instead of taking me down that hallway that let back to the dungeon he took us the opposite direction. That hallway was narrow, dark, full of the cobwebs and spooky. Peter glanced back at me upon hearing my noise and told me to be still. I was sure the man was taking me to a worse cell than that nightmare I already had suffered for nearly a week.

To my surprise we came to a set of stairs that let up. I kept my noises of panic quiet as I followed him to the first floor on a path almost no one even knew existed. When we reached a door at the top to my shock it opened right into the dead end hallway of the Haus clinic and Dentist office.

I suddenly realized this secret path was created in case the Mortar King needed medical attention, but those that held him desired privacy because of his ill health. It would be dangerous for the collars of the Haus to be aware their King was not well. The clever founders had thought of every possibility to keep any Master of the Haus that may rise fit, hidden, and hostage for his entire life.

I began to tremble in terror thinking Peter had brought me up to be tormented by Doctor Noethan in his home base. It was no small thing the relief I felt when my father dragged me behind him into the Dentist's office. His telling me that he was going to see that my teeth were fixed had slipped my memory. Well, I had other pressing matters on my mind, ja?

Peter warned me that speaking or disobeying the Dentist would result in punishment most foul as we sat in the waiting area. He didn't need to threaten me. I was still chained for starters. I knew even if I could run away, every door was guarded, and the Guard was watching for my attempt to escape. I had given up all hope of freedom from this hellish fate. All I could do is keep my head down and nod that I understood. It was then that Peter finally unlocked the gag so the Dentist could work.

For the next several hours I endured painful shots of the Novocain and violent nub removal. When that kind Dentist finally put down his tools for the day, I didn't have a single bit of evidence left that I ever had teeth in all my life. It was a depressing moment to realize that I was not even the man yet and already the baby had more than I did in my mouth.

The Dentist smiled at me as he packed my bleeding gums with the cotton. "Ah this went easy and in a moment you will forget the pain of it. I have the birthday present for you Maximillian. Hold still while I get it."

I laid there unable to feel a thing under my nose, not like I had much sensation without the numbing shots thanks to my facial injuries but still. I had not been aware it was my birthday, but the Dentist had my medical records. I had just turned seventeen years old as that sun rose on the world that June day in 1975. I was only twelve months from becoming the man, and here I was still being let around like the fucking barn animal. I must say learning of the specialness of that day hit me hard.

The Dentist returned to find me weeping uncontrollably. He misunderstood the reason for it and did his best to assure me that in a moment I would be restored. The man begged me to end my tears as he held up the pair of temporary dentures where I could see them.

He chuckled at my look of confusion when I saw them. "This is my birthday gift to you Maxx. You will have a beautiful smile in a moment and as soon as your mouth heals we will get you the permanent pair of dentures. After that you can eat the solid foods again without pain. Now you stop that crying. It is going to be okay that I swear to you." He told me to open my mouth as he fitted these fake teeth onto my ravaged gums.

I was immediately extremely uncomfortable with these foreign objects inside my head. It was going to take some getting used to for truth. The Dentist called Peter into the room to see the new Maximillian. I had to lay there in silence while the two of them offered many compliments and words of encouragement for this fix of that dreadful dental issue I had to suffer for years.

The Dentist then gave my father numerous instruction with a new appointment set to receive the actual dentures to replace the temporary set after the healing. Just like that it was over. The nubs gone, the fake teeth in the boy's mouth, I was re-gaged despite the surgery, and off Peter dragged me back to the Palace without any further fanfare.

I wanted to plead with him to help me but even without that ball gag I knew that was useless. Peter either didn't desire to aid me or didn't have the power. I was more than a little angry at that asshole for seemingly ignoring my desperate plight. He didn't fool around getting me settled back into the Mortar Palace. I dared not go against him for fear that Sebastian or Tadeas or worse were just around the corner waiting to get me.

I was okay with being murdered I thought, but I was certain by this time no one would do that for me. Another beating or whipping I was in no mood to take. I quietly endured his slipping the locks and weights back onto the boy without any struggle. He seemed surprised by that but still behaved as if at any moment he would have to knock me down and finish with brute force.

When he had me secured he shook his head staring at me with a surprised expression, "Well, I thought for sure you would at least attempt to fight me. Good thing you learned the severe gravity of your situation without demanding to have it demonstrated to you again. I suppose even you can tire of bleeding from the needless torturing. There may be hope for you yet, ja?"

I shot a stunned look at him wondering what the hell he meant by saying there was any hope for me.

He chuckled when he saw that I didn't understand his statement. "You should never assume it is over until it is, Maximillian. Long as there is breath in you there is a chance things will be better tomorrow. I know it seems bleak and finished for you right this moment. It may indeed be game over. However, one never knows what things can change in the future. I trained you to take pain and keep going. Use what you know, my heart. It certainly came dear, didn't it? No time like now that it will come in handy. I would like to ask you to focus on your studies and do your best to not run afoul of the brutes that come here to abuse you. Stop fighting them. Give them what they want and try to avoid their brutal punishments for giving them shit. Once Gretta realizes you are never going to break, maybe then I can speak some sense into the bitch? Can you swear to try harder, Maxx? If you do, then you have my promise to do whatever possible to see at the very least your living conditions improve, if not your full release." He looked at me appearing to show some pity, which was weird as hell to see in this of all the men I ever knew.

I sighed then shrugged. Peter scoffed then went over and picked up the books he brought to my cell the day before. They were still sitting on the floor next to the privy. He looked through them a moment and retrieved a piece of paper. I sat down leaning against the Mortar throne as he approached me holding the college materials.

Peter reached out offering them to me. "Take them Maximillian. Find a place away from this misery in the pages. The studies will keep you patient and calm. I know you boy. The one thing that makes you above anyone in this Haus is that huge intellect you possess. Learn, wait and try to trust your trainer Peter. Though I cannot tell you how, I don't believe this is the end of it for either of us. One day you will be the doctor. I can feel it in my bones."

I glared at the idiot with disbelief but took the books from him with a nod. I didn't buy a word of what he was saying, but to be honest I expected him to be as bad as anyone else that came through the gate. He was just as capable of thudding, whipping, raping, or beating me as the Dungeon Masters. It didn't seem like the bright idea to disagree with his stupid words meant to encourage me to keep my spirits up. Easy for him to say. He had the keys and would be leaving the second he was done taking whatever he wanted from the boy.

Ta my complete shock Peter smiled, ruffled the boy's hair and said, "Good boy, I will see if can smuggle something tastier then that nasty gruel that Gretta orders brought to you. Remember, no matter what the brutes want, better to give it to them. You were trained to be the pleasure submissive. Be that creature and see your cuts and bruises disappear. You focus on your studies like I said. I will see you tomorrow. Oh, and happy birthday Maximillian." He turned around and hurried from the cell leaving me unmolested and completely confused at this new Peter. I was grateful for the mercy don't get me wrong.

I opened the books and began doing what he told me to. It didn't take long for me to become lost within the pages of the college level history, science and math books he brought to me. It only took an hour for me to almost believe Peter's vision of my future as the doctor. A few more hours passed, and I did buy into his assurances that this was only a rough patch in my life but not the definition of it.

Then to my dismay the Altergotts came for their daily visit. This time they came without Sebastian and Tadeas. Which was odd that I had seen neither all day. I remembered what Peter said and did my best to offer no fight to these beasts.

The only thing that did was encourage them to be more brutal. I was treated to the same thing as the day before with the only difference being two fewer rapists. The two of them didn't stop until they had me freaking out from the fresh ant invasion. I endured their sexual assault as the earphones encouraged the ants to chew on the boy from the inside out.

Luckily, I had learned the cure for this horror from Florian. The second the Altergotts finished their cruel sport and left me screaming like a madman to collect Gretta, I drank the contaminated water. As before, all the insects fell dead, saving the boy for another day of torture. Yikes!

This time Gretta and Cora were beyond pissed to find the reported hebephrenic Mad Maxx sitting quietly reading his books. If I could have smiled, hearing the tongue lashing the two snakes got from the Queen's would have made me do it. They were told that if they ever bother the FemDoms again and I was not the raging nutball, the two would find themselves rooming with Byron and Claus for the insult.

I glared at the snakes as they hurled verbal threats to me the moment the Queens had left us. I couldn't do anything but shoot looks of hate at them in return. I was gagged and by now my mouth was killing me. Even if I had the free mouth, I doubt I could have used it to do anything other than moan in agony.

The Altergotts finally left me to my solitude for the night. I got up ready to run in joy to embrace Birgit when that lovely woman showed up with her sister Viviana. I was more than ready to be with Felicity and have that painful gag out of my aching mouth, you know.

The women approached me with a smile noticing that I was happy to see them. I was just about to take my beloved lamb, I was excited to show off my new teeth to her you know, when the voice of Sebastian cut through the air.

"Birgit, Viviana, you will take the night off. We will attend the Master of the Haus tonight. Don't argue either. The Silk Queen says you are to report to her if you take issue with her orders," said the brute from the gate.

Birgit shot me a worried frown and hide my Felicity in her apron pocket with quickness "I apologize, your Majesty. My sister and I must leave you with these foul men. Be assured we will return in the morning to check on your health. Keep your chin up and remember you are the King. Be the King, Herr Maxx." With that both Mistresses departed with speed leaving me to my fate worse than any I had ever known before or since.

I trembled in terror as Doctor Noethan, Sebastian and Tadeas came through the cell gate after they were sure the Mistresses had long since left. It wasn't the brutes that caused my panic, but the buddies they had brought along with them to join in there fun with me. Five extra to be exact. I slowly stood up backing away and shaking uncontrollably unable to wrap my mind around the nightmare unfolding before my helpless eyes.

Doctor Noethan grinned as he watched me recoil in disgust of the oncoming crowd of the unnatural. "Mad Maxx, did you think we would forget your birthday? Nein. Me and the boys put our head together to come up with the perfect gift for the man that has had it al. Bet you did not foresee this though. I can see by the expression on your face this is exactly the thing you never expected. See boys, told you he would be surprised. Well, you cannot keep them, but that is okay. For tonight, they are all yours. Oh wait, I meant to say you are all theirs." The lot of them broke out into loud laughter as I screamed and tried with all I had to escape this fucking cruelty straight from hell itself.

NOTE: I am not able to continue with this part of the story dearest reader. In all the many horrific stories I have told, none reach the pure depravity, revulsion nor horror of this one Mad Maxx told me years ago. I will only say that when my Master Maxx told me what happened the entire night of his seventeenth birthday at the hands of Noethan, the dungeon Masters and five

unnatural visitors, he had a trauma driven full on melt down. To this day we never discuss what happened that night again.

The only reason I mention anything about it at all, is because in a future chapter this incident will be partly discussed in the choice of type of revenge Mad Maxximillian will level at these three. He will tell you in not so many words what happened that night when you see how he punished them.

I think it will less a traumatic for him and you to read when discussed in the capacity of why he did what he did to these three. Yeah, he will make them pay so hang in there.

For now, I don't desire to put Christian through the horror of relieving this unspeakable situation where he is the helpless victim. You can all use your imaginations and if you still don't have any idea what could be so bad even my jaded ass won't repeat it, then no worries. When you see what he does to these guys you will figure it out.

I thank all of you for understanding. The reason this chapter avoid a deeper description is I had to do a little soul searching on how to delicately deal with this birthday surprise. There is no way to sweep it under the rug, but I also don't want to hurt Christian, or even remember it myself. So, this is how I decided to manage it to move on with the story.

I pray this is to your approval Christian Axel. I know you wouldn't complain if I did write about it, but I just can't do it. I also know you understand why.

I am showing more than just my husband mercy by not repeating this shit. I know none of you really want to hear the revolting details of what could make a huge, tough, grown German man fall apart in the arms of his nine-year-old Frau more than six years after the incident occurred. Trust me on this, you really don't want to know. On with the story beginning with the next day.

The next day after the brutes had finished their heinous sport with me, Birgit kept her promise to me. She came to the cell to check on me. What she found was a nearly catatonic, drooling and broken boy. I had to be rushed to the Dentist for a procedure to remove the temporary dentures from the boy's gums. I had clenched my jaws with such viciousness I had forced the things to embed into the mangled soft tissues. The tooth doctor was horrified by the idea something could have upset me so badly that I had done such a self-mutilation.

Peter tried speaking to me. He wanted to know what caused me to show distress and traumatized behaviors. No matter what he promised or threatened I maintained my silence. I truthfully never intended to utter a word of the obscene abominations that I had to endure that night. Though no matter what I did, I couldn't stop seeing and feeling the whole nightmare play out in repeat through the wheelroom screen.

Both me and Mad Max were showing signs of the shatter. Max and Mad Maxx guarded the slumbering Der Hund with expressions of pure terror on their faces. They watched helpless as he and I began to drool, and stagger from the weight of the horrific traumas being forced onto the boy.

The vortex of the nothing was whirling at full speed within threatening to suck us all inside. If that happened, there would be no return for the boy. A mindless zombie, a shell of a human being would all be that remained of the Mad Maxx if something wasn't done, and soon.

I was returned to my cell, without the dentures and strict orders that my mouth be attended, or I would die. I suffered continued attacks from Reece, Kilian, Sebastian, Noethan and Tadeas despite the commands that I be granted a rest. They made sure to force the oral services several times in the next few days. It goes without saying they enjoyed a great deal of the horrible pain it caused me with the open wounds and a sore mouth.

On the seventh day, my men Cary, Almut and Hubertus were allowed to come to the gate to observe their King. Only ten minutes was permitted, and I was gagged to assure I couldn't speak to them. I sat there so miserable that I couldn't lift the boy's head to look at them, staring at me like the zoo animal on display.

Cary whispered that Matz was working day and night to change Lucus's heart about helping me out. I just nodded to that. I already knew Lucus couldn't help me. No one could.

The next days came like all the ones before. Horrible things were done to me by the five brutes. I don't desire to repeat them, but as I said before if you can imagine it, it happened. Some way or another I was forced to endure things so foul the devil would blush to hear them described to him. The worst came from the Dungeon Masters and that vile doctor Noethan, but the Altergotts got many cruel licks in themselves.

They used their boxes to fed me to ants, set me on fire, and even convinced me at one point they gave me the ice pick lobotomy. It seemed there was no end to what they could cause with only the right repeated words, a few props, and strobe lights. Between that psychological torment and their chronic gang raping I am unsure how me and Mad Max managed to keep that vortex at bay.

Part of it may have been the overdosing of Doctor Noethan's sedatives. He didn't realize that his medication designed to keep me weak was actually sending the acute stage of my disease into retreat. The symptoms I was showing by this time were more the PTSD than schizophrenic type.

The end of the week saw the appearance of Claus. He came to visit with me after being let out of the pit. I listened in silence, yes while gagged, while he apologized for recanting his report of hearing my orders. He told me that Gretta told him if he didn't swear I never spoke she would see me and him burned alive for it. The Elder wept while he confessed he didn't care if they killed him but that he couldn't bear to bring such terror on one so young that he truthfully loved.

I did my best to forgive him for it. That was not easy since right after that tearful begging my forgiveness he took his opportunity to demand his contracted special services rights with me. I would end up seeing him twice more. Ja, you guessed it, each Thursday at one just as I had sworn before I broke my collar. Damn him, you'd think he could forgive me that blasted contract given the situation but nein. He is an animal.

Every morning after Doctor Noethen and the Dungeon Masters finished whatever horrific sport they wanted with me, Peter came to visit. Amazingly, and uncharacteristically, my father never once demanded his special services rights. He came to check on my health and progress in the studies. I found it a useless endeavor, but I continued to follow his study plan despite my thinking I was the prisoner for life.

The weekend of each of the next three weeks Peter administered the testing. I have no idea how I managed it, but I passed each one. There was nothing else to do in the Palace but study and await the next torture/rape session. I suppose without any other distraction the information stuck with vigor in the boy's nearly busted brains.

The second visit from Cary, Almut and Hubertus was as depressing as the first. The news hadn't changed. Matz was begging, and Lucus refusing. The men left me feeling more despondent than ever. That depression was further deepened when the Vampire Jonas showed up right on the heels of their unfruitful visit to demand his bi-weekly blood couple.

I didn't give him quarrel in his demands. I secretly hoped he would nick an artery and end my torture. He did cut deeper than usual for the second time, but no luck on the bleeding to death idea. Jonas didn't bitch about my gag this time nor take notice of my despairing mood. He took what he wanted from me and left without any kindness nor attempt at small talking. I was left alone to wallow in my sorrow, alone, dejected and beyond miserable.

I fought a lot the first week in the palace. I wept a river of tears the second one. During the third, I sat staring into the nothing daring it to do its worst. Me and Mad Max no longer cared. It couldn't have seemed grimmer, but one should never say never, ja?

The men came to torture and rape the boy day after day. Peter came every morning to make sure the lessons got done for the imaginary world outside the Haus. I was sure by this time I would never know the thrill of the sun on my face, a car that I owed money on, or a laughing frau in the passenger's seat happy to see me.

As the week before Claus came to see that he was not left with the unsatisfied cock. Cary, Hubertus and Almut also came like clockwork. This time they whispered to me that Matz had failed. Lucus told him to leave him alone for good. He wouldn't even answer the apartment door for the wolf any longer.

By week four I believe with all my heart it was officially over. This nightmare was my life, and there was no escape. The Altergotts turned up the level of their torture. I started to think it was an option to fake the hebephrenia. Being sent to the yard sounded like heaven to your worthless Master by then. I did my best to convince them that I was the hopeless psychotic, but to be honest I am no actor. They could tell I was faking it.

Truth is I didn't even have enough fight left in me to appear dangerously insane. The apathy and lack of motivation had set in deeply within the boy. Those negative symptoms assured that not only my flesh was chained. My mind had joined the boy as the prisoner.

The end of that week saw Claus come for his contract, and the most violent attacks from Doctor Noethan, Sebastian and Tadeas. The Altergotts were once again threatening Geraldine. They told me that Jonas no longer gave a damn for the twisted Mad Maxx that was nothing but the whore for the Dungeon Masters.

They tried to convince me that the Vampire had given them my lamb for their supper. It didn't work. I knew bedder. Jonas is a bastard but if he really had done such horror he would come to see me suffer while he told me in person.

Florian had stopped speaking to me after that horrible seventeenth birthday surprise. I suppose he found me so disgusting he didn't want to know me any longer. I didn't blame him either. I wished I didn't know me too. That said, suddenly on the last day of the fourth week the Priceless began to yap at me like nothing had ever been amiss between us.

I was gagged but I tried to let him read my mine. He kept rambling on as if he couldn't hear a thing I was thinking. I decided to forgive him for the weeks of silence. It was good to hear the voice of someone not speaking something the obscene or demanding the revolting from the boy. I sat back and listened in mild thrill as Florian spoke of the gossiping he was hearing from the hallways above.

It no longer mattered that none of the rumors he speak of were of importance to one so low as me. It was pretty clear that the people no longer remembered either one of us. It was just nice to close my eyes and recall that one time I had been alive and had dreams. For a moment, Florian's stories whisked me far away from the stink, filth, and pain of that hell hole underground.

I was deep into focusing on Florian's descriptive tales when the sound of the gate opening brought my mind crashing back down into the boy laying on the dungeon floor. I whimpered and retreated to the wall keeping my head low, wringing my hands in terror at what disgusting thing the Altergotts, or the dirty threesome had planned for me this time.

I nearly pissed myself when instead of Reece or Sebastian's voice, that of the Mad Lucus called out my name. I looked up from the straw strewn floor to see if my eyes would agree with my ears of the identity of the man that commanded that voice.

Mad Lucus stood there at the open gate with his arms crossed staring at me appearing stunned. "Christian Victor? Is that you boy? It cannot be, you are the scarecrow. Didn't these fucker feed you at all? Come here so I can get a better look at you."

I nearly fell face first getting to my feet to follow his orders. I rushed as far as the chain allowed and fell to a kneel keeping my head bowed low in reverence. My heart was pounding in the boy's chest threatening to break through the ribcage and fall onto the floor. I didn't know how or why Mad Lucus was there, but I was beyond thrilled to see the man. Wow never thought I say that did you. Well neither did I.

Mad Lucus approached me with caution staying just out of my reach. "Well, well. Seems someone has finally learned to appreciate his Master, ja?" I nodded ja with vigor not even caring that this was meant to be an insult.

He scoffed. "You broke my jaw, Christian Victor. You called me a pervert in front of the whole Haus. You turned your back on me and demanded the coronation of the Mortar King without naming me your regent, though you promised that position to me." I looked up in the startle confused that he was saying such a lie. I didn't even know such a thing existed before that day so how could I promise it to him

Mad Lucus saw my surprise. “That is what the heart of the Priceless means Christian Victor. You said you gave me your loyalty and adoration. That is the regency boy. Then you turn around and try to take the power for yourself after sending me to silence with your cane. That gold collar you wear did you not swear allegiance to me? I warned you to be careful how you responded, boy. I am in no mood to fight with you.” I nodded that he was correct and wondered how he expected me to argue when gagged to the hilt as I was.

He nodded back. “Exactly Christian Victor. You did it willingly, but you betrayed your Master. Well, how has that been working out for you? I bet you have just had the time of your life down here with the rats and predators. I bet you know the difference between a lover and a pervert by now, ja?” I glared at him wondering what he had heard about my uhm, incarceration difficulties.

Mad Lucus snorted. “I cannot hear you Christian Victor. I asked you do you still think me a pervert now that you have endured the real thing?” I shook my head nein and caste my guilty gaze back at his feet.

The Mad Lucus smiled. “Okay, you seem docile enough. I am going to come to you and remove that gag in a moment. I warn you boy, you dare to move an eyelash against me when I do this I will see that all you have suffered thus far has been a fucking cake walk. You hear me?” I nodded and cowered in fear.

I sat still in calm reverence while the man removed the gag. I wondered silently where he got that key. The second I was free of it he backed up eyeing me from head to toe. I didn't dare move as he examined my dirty, half-starved frame with disgust in his expression.

He clicked his tongue. "You are a wreck. I thought I was getting a pretty boy. Instead, I find a haggard old man. Yuck! It will take weeks of feeding and working out to get you even halfway desirable in my bed. I will be ashamed to be seen with you. Everyone will say that poor Lucus. He is saddled with that nasty thing when he is so much better than that."

I shuddered and dropped my gaze even lower. "I apologize for failing you so horribly, Master. I dare not beg your forgiveness. I can only throw myself upon your mercy. If it be your desire to see me finished for my low behaviors and betrayals then I think it is far too good for the likes of me."

Mad Lucus nodded. "You got that right, Christian Victor. I should let you rot to death here forever. However, I am the eternal fool. I have given you chance after chance only to find it thrown into my face. This time I want to believe you have learned your lesson completely. Have you though is the real question. That is if I am to even think you would wish to leave your Palace and come with me."

I gulped back my panic that he was going to leave me there. "I beg of you Master to take me with you. I will do anything you ask without hesitation. I will never betray your wise words again nor try to escaping you. I will never call you pervert nor deny your lusting again. I swear it." I fell forward in prostrate hoping that he wasn't playing a cruel game and could take me with him.

Mad Lucus came forward and kicked me in the shoulder sternly but not hard enough to damage, "I have heard this bullshit from you before, Christian Victor. Then found my face wired shut for it. Get the fuck off your belly and kneel where I can view those dishonest eyes of yours. I want to see if I can tell you are lying to me yet again." I did as he commanded with speed.

He stood there staring at me while I did my best to avoid eye contact. "I have decided. I am going to take you with me back to the apartment. You will mind me to the letter. On your eighteenth birthday, if you survive you will be called upon by the Silk Queen. She will give you the opportunity on the date ending your minority of naming a regent. You will name Mad Lucus your regent. In the meantime, you will keep that royal mouth of your fucking shut. If you dare to ever speak to the collars again in the commanding voice of your station I will see you brought back here to rot under the care of far worse scum than you been dealing with. Next time there will be no second chances. Fuck with me ever again and you will regret it for the rest of your long, long life. You will accept that from this moment forward you are the Master of the Haus that has lost his tongue. You understand me?"

I nodded keeping my head low and holding my breath in hope.

Mad Lucus bellowed, “Say it, Christian Victor. I want to hear your words that you understand me.”

I took a deep breath then said, “I swear I will not disobey you, I will not speak to the collars, give any orders or commands, and I will name you my regent on my eighteenth birthday. I understand the punishment for breaking my word this time is life incarceration in the Mortar Palace as the plaything of the lowest creatures on earth. I thank you for the mercy of the second chance you grant me to prove my worth to you Master. I will not let you down this time.”

Mad Lucus nodded with a wicked smile. “You get all that, honorable Gretta?”

I gasped as the Silk Queen stepped out of the shadowed hallway smiling at me. “You bet I did, brother Lucus. Don’t forget the contract is in writing and I have just now witnessed it. The punishment for his breaking it will be swift for you but beyond agony for him. I will make sure of that. I do believe we have a deal, my friend. You may take home your prize.” She threw the keys to the locks on my chains into the cell.

I shot a look of confusion at Mad Lucus. “You tricked me into a contract with you and the Silk Queen? Master I don’t understand. It is obvious Gretta wishes to see my throne neutralized. If you had her ear to see this done, surely you knew I would have been happy to agree to exile. Why didn’t you offer it for my release? I asked Matz to tell you this. Did he neglect that information? Even if he did, you know I desire to be gone from the Haus. Instead, you maneuver yourself to hold me to this horrific crown for my life. I am trapped in the walls for all my life if I am to understand this contract correctly. Why do you do this to me, Master?"

Mad Lucus reached down and picked up the keys with a chuckle. "Ah, there is the truth at last. You intended to tell me anything I wanted to hear to get out of this cell. I expected you would abandon me the second you got the chance, and you are proving me right with each word you say just now. Listen to me, Christian Victor. You knew you were swearing to grant me the regency at age eighteen, and that meant you can never leave since if you did I am no longer the regent of a King that has fled his country. This Haus is your home boy. You are never leaving, your Highness." He walked over to me and began to undo the locks that held me.

I stared through the veil of rain that flowed from the boy's eyes. My hopes to find the green fields, my baby lambs, the cottage under the mountains, coming home from the exhausting day as the physician to my beautiful Annette, are all gone. I can never undo the coronation. I wear the crown of the Mortar throne and to find freedom from a fate worse than death, I traded my dreams of living in the world outside the walls of Das Kaiser Haus. Oh well, like they say, when the door closes you got to break the windows.

Chapter 43: The Dog

I sat there in silence watching Mad Lucus unlocking the chains that had kept me the hostage for little more than a month. Gretta stood at the silver gate sharing the small talk with my Master as he went about his releasing me from her bondage. I felt the anger rising within the boy's chest at this latest manipulation by those monstrous leaders of the Haus.

Once again, I had been put into the position of agreeing to a contract that was weighted to the advantage of another. I stole a look at that vicious FemDom wondering if pushing her down the stairs was not worth any punishment I got for it. I had so many on an ever growing list of people I wished to see dead. Gretta had managed to move several spaces up to the top with her unnecessary cruelty towards me. I never wanted to steal her power, nor be the Master of the Haus and she fucking knew that.

Despite her knowledge of my truest desire to be far from that hell hole filled with the worst of all perverts on Earth, she blocked every exit I ever found. Her allowing Peter, Jonas and fucking Kilian to keep me trapped within the walls had led to this inevitable outcome. That I could no longer deny. It took the power of the Head of the Voters to assure all this nightmare unfolded as it had.

I slowly came to understand none of the other brutes in my life had the ability to do anything they had done to me without the full cooperation of the Queens. Ja, you could say that day I finally realized before I took out another Elder or Voter, I needed to see that Gretta and Cora got the personal ride on the back of the Reaper's horse.

Florian heard my thinking about ending the reign of the Queens. I had been so caught up in the joy of being taken far from that horrid cell, I had forgotten about him. I had known if I did manage to find my freedom, he was sure to take my absence as his roommate poorly.

Florian whispered to me as Mad Lucus worked on releasing the chain that bound my wrists, "Your Majesty, you kill that bitch or the other one and you cannot keep your promise to give me the Dungeon Masters and the King's physician as you swore to do. I don't deny this Haus needs no Queen, but before you do anything dumb, make sure to see you're a man of your word to those that deserve their reward."

I gasped and turned to stare at the bony Priceless. "Ja, I hear what you say. I apologize for leading you to think I would betray those that aid me. I will keep my vows to you brother. There is no need to fear."

Mad Lucus stopped his fiddling with my locks. "Huh? What is this you say Christian Victor? Who the fuck are you speaking to boy? You better not be planning to betray me, damn you," he growled out sounding quite irritated.

I flinched in fear that he would strike me for speaking without permission. "I said I won't betray you Master, and I mean this. I merely repeat what I already swore to you." I dropped my head to the bow quickly hoping that he wouldn't hear that private conversation between me and Florian any further. Yikes, Mad Lucus was reading my mind, you know.

Mad Lucus reached out and grabbed the crown by the bridle. "I think this crown has been squeezing your brains too tightly. How do I get this fucking thing off Gretta? I will not have him walking around on my leash wearing the signs of the office that belongs to me." He shook my head with vigor.

I whimpered in fear. "Give him the fucking key, Gretta. I don't want it. Lucus can have the crown, the Palace, and all that comes with being the Master of the Haus." I meant every Gott damned word of that too.

Mad Lucus stopped rocking my head when I said that. "I don't believe you were being spoken to, Christian Victor. You shut that mouth and mind your manners, or I put all the locks back where I found them right this second."

I let out another sound of terror. "Nein, don't leave me here. Please Master, I only say it to let you be the king. I am happy being the nothing. I beg of you to see me out of these chains and killed immediately. I give you no quarrel. There can be no danger of the broken jaw or loss of power if the Priceless is growing a tree, ja? What are you waiting for Gretta: I say I am willing to be put to the yard. Why are you standing there without calling the Guard? Are you deaf? This is no hallucination. I want to die. Just once can I not have what I ask for." I wailed as the tears of despair began to flow heavier than the drool that kept my chin and chest the wet mess.

Mad Lucus pulled my head toward him with anger breaking out in his expression. "I told you to shut up, Christian Victor. You speaking insanity without making a lick of sense. This stress of the Palace and obscenity you endure is causing your madness to peak I believe. You be still and calm this minute. We are not leaving until you can stop acting loony. I mean it." He stared at me with sternness to assure I heard his command.

Gretta laughed and applauded from the silver gate. "Ah, if only I had waited a few more days before throwing in my fortunes with you Lucus. The boy is cracked at long last. Well, a deal is a deal. I will allow you to take your prize from this hell hole, but you remember what is going to happen if he breaks any of the rules of our agreement. I would normally be pissed that the Priceless managed to squeak past my claws before they closed on him yet again. However, this time no matter what comes, I am the winner. If you cannot control him as you claim to be capable of doing then I get to end the boy once and for all. If you are the magic man then I share the power of the Haus with you in only one year. This little show of extreme misery from the Mad Maxx bastard is the icing on the cake. brother. Fuck, this has been the finest day of my young life. I thank you for the thrill of it Lucus."

I heard her cruel words roll through the bars onto the floor of that filthy cell. It caused me to shut down the begging for death for the moment. Anything that I could do to end her pleasure was my goal from that moment on. If I couldn't murder the FemDom outright then I decided I would do my best to torture her in anyway and in every way possible.

In fact, I made up the boy's mind my sole reason for being was to pay back every motherfucker that ever hurt the boy starting with the five brutes that showed brutality beyond imagination while I was the helpless prisoner. This was war.

Well, to be fair I was on the fence about this thinking. Mad Max wanted to end the boy's life for good. I (Christian) thought killing every fucking pervert in the Haus was the way to go. This disagreement about how best to proceed caused a great deal of wasted time as both of us fought to take possession of the wheel to see our desires fulfilled.

With both equally matched in strength – and Max and Mad Maxx unable to interfere without leaving Der Hund vulnerable to attack – there was not going to be a rapid resolution to this situation any time soon. Mad Lucus didn't know it, but his so-called prize was not going to be so easy to control as he had been before.

The Dominant noticed my sudden quieting. He waited a few moments to be sure I wasn't going to demonstrate further quarrel with his command. Once he was satisfied I was docile, he again requested information about removing that horrible Metal crown. Gretta growled out that she desired I be stuck for life in that damned thing but relented her refusal to see it off after cursing for several moments.

She reached into the bosom of her dress and took out a small set of keys. Like before she threw them into the cell stating that these would undo the locks of the bridle. Mad Lucus retrieved the set with a bit of irritation in his expression. I suppose he thought Gretta should do the honors of removing that complex restraining apparatus rather than leaving him to figure it out. It took at least fifteen minutes for the Mad Lucus to get me free of it. I admit the relief I felt at having that weight and tight band of the crown off after many weeks of the torture was heaven.

As he took the crown from my head Mad Lucus immediately retched covering his nose and mouth. "Oh, holy hell. The smell. Christ, Gretta. You forgot the boy had the stitches and wounds on his scalp. Did you never remove the threads or even bathe Christian Victor once during this filthy incarceration? Are you stupid? He could have died from infection fool." He kept his hands over his face to avoid the foul smell but crept closer to get a look at the damage caused by their neglect.

Gretta scoffed, "I wasn't aware the boy had such an injury, Lucus. I notice the little schizo never complained about it either. Oh well, he didn't die did he? No harm done."

Mad Lucus bellowed out in rage, "How the fuck could he say anything, Gretta? You kept the boy gagged. As it is he may die still. There is a serious skin infection visible, and his fucking hair is falling out. Gott damn it. It may never grow back if he survives. Shit, the stiches have grown into the flesh. This is a motherfucking nightmare. I don't care that it is the wee hours of the morning, call that asshole Noethan. Tell him to get to his clinic this minute. Christian Victor needs medical treatment now."

I heard that shit. "Nein, don't call that man. It is nothing. I will remove the stitches and use the alcohol on the wound. It will be okay, Master, I swear it. I don't need the doctor." I wrung my hands in terror at the idea of seeing that pervert ever again for any reason.

Mad Lucus reached into his suit pocket and took out the heavy chain leash and attached it to his collar. "Be still Christian. I won't tell you again. Come with me. You need treatment and you are going to get it. Stop this silliness at once. That is a directive." I whimpered as he hand signaled for me to stand and follow in silence.

I turned around and shot Florian a look of fear. He smiled back trying his best to assure me all was going to be okay. I did as Mad Lucus told me without further argument. Though I didn't want to go see the doctor, I couldn't stand the idea of staying there another minute. Gretta had slinked off down the hallway far ahead of us. I doubted she would call Doctor Noethan and I hoped she wouldn't, but there was only one thing that was for sure. I was leaving the cell, headed down the hallway in the right direction to see freedom.

I wrung my hands keeping my silence the entire trip to the doctor's office. All the while I was quietly thanking Cary and Matz for being the devoted friends when I had given up all hope. No matter what horrors that pervert forced on me in his office, at least I was finally above ground this time.

Mad Lucus and I had to wait for a bit outside the locked clinic for that foul doctor. I hadn't realized it was just after midnight when Gretta and my Master came to set me free. I guess they hoped to sneak me back to the fourth-floor apartment before any of the collars or other residents were up and about.

It made sense that Gretta wished to keep any eyes from seeing the sorry condition I was in after that month as her guest in the Mortar Palace. I was dangerously thin, haggard, dirty, beaten up and my clothing torn from the sexual assaults. It would surely have angered the service classes to riot if they were permitted to witness the dishonor, abuse and neglect heaped upon dare King.

There was no doubt I was more dead than alive as Lucus and me stood there waiting with impatience for the physician. I was quietly wringing my hands, trembling in both fear and weakness from my poor health.

Mad Lucus watched down the hallway for the appearance of Doctor Noethan but would steal looks at me once in a while. Each time his eyes set upon my pathetic flesh he would shake his head and grumble under his breath about the stupidity of the Silk Queen. I had to agree with him. If keeping me from expiring was the plan, she nearly dropped the ball. It was pretty obvious another week or two in those harsh conditions would have seen me find my peace at last.

The doctor came dragging down the hallway after making us wait nearly half an hour. He was yawning and rubbing his eyes when he approached Mad Lucus. I tucked myself behind my Master attempting to hide from the pervert. I didn't want my Master to be dishonored by my cowardly trembling. I couldn't believe I was about to have the panic attack from the fear of being spotted by that monster.

Doctor Noethan smiled weakly at Mad Lucus. "Ah hell, if I had been told it was you waiting for me to come to clinic I would have moved a bit faster, brother. I apologize for the wait. Gretta told me the patient was of no serious worth. Damn that woman She has a lot of gall to call one of your pedigree unimportant." H blew out his breath in frustration as he hurriedly began unlocking the clinic door.

Mad Lucus growled out with irritation in his tone. "I think she doesn't insult my linage in this matter. What she has done is demonstrate continued neglect of one of great importance. I can already see she is someone I will need to keep both eyes on."

The doctor stopped his task and shot Mad Lucus an expression of confusion "What? I don't follow you Lucus? She didn't tell me anything of this visit other than that I was to report to examine a situation that was of no real consequence. I have to ask, did you get a mild injury or perhaps have the stomachache?" He opened the door and motioned Mad Lucus to go inside.

Mad Lucus jerked on my leash with harshness. "The visit is not for me fool. I bring the Master of the Haus in for treatment of a festering injury of the scalp. Hurry the fuck up Anselm. I need to be getting the boy home before the residents awaken to see the rude condition of the Mortar King."

Doctor Noethan's mouth nearly hit the floor as he stammered out sounding afraid. "That is the Priceless hiding behind you Lucus. Holy shit! Are you out of your mind? He cannot be up here man. What if he manages to overpower you and make a run for it. I demand you take him back to his cell this minute. I go get the supplies to attend his injuries. Then I will come down to the Palace after you put him back under heavy restraints. He needs to be attended where there is no fear of anyone knowing of his poor health. How the hell did you gain permission to bring him up for treatment in the first place. This is insanity." He stared at me standing there wringing my hands behind Lucus as if he'd seen a ghost rather than the wreaked victim of his cruel perversions.

Mad Lucus reached out and grabbed the nasty doctor by his shirt collar. "You listen to me, you fucking pissant. I will not stand here and be questioned nor ordered around by a low life such as yourself. You get into the chop shop you call the clinic and pull out the tools of your trade. You are going to fix this horror show you caused by neglect.

You knew the boy had stitches that needed removal, asshole. You left them to rot in his head. If he is permanently scarred, that hair doesn't grow back or he dies, then I will see you murdered for this medical malpractice." He pushed the monster and he fell into the wall with a gasp of terror.

Mad Lucus dragged me behind him into the clinic heading for the first room in his sight. He stepped inside, flipped on the lights and ordered me to sit down on the exam bed to wait for the doctor. I wrung my hands faster and whimpered but did as he told me. I feared being taken back downstairs more than being handled by that pervert Noethan.

The truth is Mad Max nearly caused the boy to flee the room before I could strong arm the wheel in my favor. He was thinking of running as far as the boy could go. It was his hopes to incite the Guard to shoot us to death. I, on the other hand, saw value in savoring the fear that Noethan surely would feel the second he realized the boy was free. Even that man couldn't be foolish enough to think we wouldn't want to seek revenge for his forced abominations against us.

Doctor Noethan came into the room trying to appear the professional. I could see that he was trembling slightly. That made me feel a little better, but only some. I cringed at the thought of that disgusting creep touching me anywhere ever again, even on the boy's head.

He kept his eyes darting from me to Mad Lucus as he examined the infected wound. His breathing was shallow and ragged. I saw his nostrils contracting from the revolting smell that wafted from that neglected injury. Within a few moments he left my bedside and walked to his sink washing his hands with vigor.

He cleared his throat, keeping his back to the Mad Lucus but was still watching me with suspiciousness. “Well, this skin infection is severe. I will need to put the patient into a state of unconsciousness so I can remove the embedded stitches and the worst of the diseased flesh. I will clean out the entire area and leave it open to heal. This will create a large scar I am afraid, but dare is no other way to assure this opening is treated constantly. If I reclose it to minimize the physical damage, I risk the patient finding his grave with ease. It is far too close to the boy’s brain. As it is, it will take many weeks of cleansing, and a few rounds of harsh antibiotics to save his life.” He let out a worried sigh.

Mad Lucus shot me a look of terror. “What is this you say? That huge ugly spot will be left open. Nein, hair cannot grow there if you leave it to raise the heavy scar caused by lack of the stitching. Fuck that. I will not tolerate you marring the boy’s handsome looks. This was caused by your foul neglect, and you will repair him back to the way he was, or I swear you will find the grave, motherfucker.”

Doctor Noethan backed up with his eyes wide in terror. “I don’t think you are listening, Lucus. I tell you the boy is extremely ill. Look at him. He has lost at least thirty pounds, and his pallor is pale and grey. That smell is rotten flesh. If I don't remove the dead skin and treat with vigor the unaffected tissues below, the boy will die of gangrene."

I glared at that cocksucker with hatred. "You will not put me to sleep asshole nor touch me for your so-called healing. Master, I beg of you to let me die the honorable death. Gretta will see him put to the flames along with the Dungeon Masters for allowing the Mortar King to expire. This is my desire. To find my own peace while exterminating the most unworthy of continued existence in this Haus all at the same time."

Mad Lucus roared out in fury, "Shut up, Christian Victor. No more speaking of dying, I command it. As for you quack, I agree with my ward in only one respect. You shall not put him to sleep. I don't trust you as far as I can throw you. You give him a shot of the pain killer or sedatives, then get your ass to saving him. I warn you Anselm. Be praying that this damage you have allowed go unchecked doesn't result in the baldness or disgusting scar for life for Christian. If it does, be prepared to suffer beyond imagination for it. I also will be here through this entire procedure. I suspect I know why he is upset by your presence. I don't know what you were doing down there in the Mortar Palace that was of such distraction you forgot to attend your work on this patient to fullness, but I can use my imagination. I think perhaps if I press him in private he has quite the tale to share about the Kings physician's bedside manner, ja? For your sake, I hope I am merely watching the symptoms of schizophrenic paranoia in him and not the trauma fears I believe I am witness to. I do believe I made it clear you were never to sample my collar's artistic skills. Surely, you didn't disobey a Master's commands regarding his property. Not the honorable man such as yourself ja?" He crossed his arms and shot the doctor a wicked smile.

The doctor gasped and stole a nervous glance at me. "Nein, I wouldn't dare to abuse my position in such a dishonorable fashion, Lucus. I am offended you would even suggest such a revolting thing to me. If this boy were to say otherwise, I would have to remind you he suffers many hallucinations and delusions from his brain illness. I didn't neglect this wound on purpose. The Silk Queen bonded that metal crown on his head. I simply couldn't reach it to treat it. Ask her about this, and she will tell you that I begged many times to be permitted to attend the area. She wouldn't relent."

Mad Lucus scoffed then shot me a look of disbelief. "Is what the doctor says truth, Christian Victor? He says he never took advantage of my misused collar down below. All you need to say is he is the liar, and I will see him whipped and sent to the dungeon for his betrayal of my orders. You can see him punished for his crimes against me with only a word."

I turned my hateful glare to Mad Lucus. "There is no reason for your questioning what he tells you. He has stolen nothing from my Master." I was not about to let this asshole get the mild reprimand for the horror he put me through. Nor would I give Lucus the satisfaction of being the one to decide how best to see vengeance served. It was me that the man soiled.

That answer made Mad Lucus scratch his head in confusion and that perverted doctor smile. "See Lucus, there you have it. The King swears that I never take liberties with him other than in the capacity of treatment of his health. You can calm this anger and we can be friends again, ja?"

Mad Lucus snorted. "I find it very hard to believe you never molested Christian Victor when you had the free reign to do such a thing." He glared back at me appearing to be searching my eyes for the truth I hid from him.

Doctor Noethan chuckled. "My goodness Lucus. You must think me the beast to dare such obscenity to the helpless teenager. I admit I was interested when I thought it was offered freely by his Master, but I would never dare to rape anyone. Besides, you just heard him. He says your services were not stolen, so let this be the end of the matter. I can give him the shots of sedative and topical painkillers. We need to start this treatment with speed, or I think you have much more to worry with than your overactive imagination. The collars of this Haus will not be thrilled to see the boy looking so peaked, ja?" He smiled as Mad Lucus snorted again with barely restrained anger but nodded that he may proceed.

I endured that foul fucker shooting me up with his sedatives and other restraining medications for the last Gott damned time. It took him three hours to cud out the infection and remove his botched earlier treatment of the wound. When he finished I had a deep, open gash on the top of my head just above the now infamous facial scar that runs down the left side of my face thanks to asshole Gerard.

I sat there feeling the tingling in my head that indicated his painkillers were wearing off as he spoke to Mad Lucus. I listened as the quack gave strict cleansing instructions and bragged about the lack of smell since removing the rotten flesh.

I will tell you I sat there in silence glaring at him through the entire surgery. I ignored the pain, that painkiller was a joke, by focusing on the way I intended to see this man punished for what he had done to me. At least twice during the procedure that pervert dropped a cotton swab so he could have the excuse to retrieve it from the boy's lap. He was also much more hands on than necessary, often putting them on my shoulders or brushing across my chest. It took all I had to be still and not cower, flinch, or cringe.

I realized the doctor was testing me. He was unsure what to think about my lying in his favor to Mad Lucus like I had. I never can be sure of what went through his mind that early morning of my release. I would like to believe he thought me daft, and so terribly psychotic I didn't recall the horrors he forced on me with his buddies Tadeas and Sebastian.

It is the only thing that could explain why he and the dungeon Masters didn't pack up and run for the hills the second they realized I was the freeman. That or they were not afraid I would be willing to risk being put to the yard just to see them suffer for their crimes against me. Well, too bad for them, ja? Hahaha.

Mad Lucus examined Doctor Noethan's handiwork with an expression of revolt on his face. "It looks like someone carved him up like the turnip. This is fucking gross. You fix this."

Doctor Noethan crossed his arms and shot me an arrogant smile. "It has to be left like this for at least a few days. If you are unsatisfied with the way it heals I can cut a new wound in it and restitch it after the infection clears. If it bothers you so much put a bag over his head when you fuck him, Lucus. Not like you are that interested in seeing him from that angle when you enjoying his favors anyway." He chuckled with evil humor at his crass statement.

Mad Lucus trembled with inner fury. "Go fuck yourself, Anselm. You have no idea about what my interests are or are not with the boy." He snatched up my leash and demanded I leave the exam table and follow him in silence.

As I was nearly out of the room Doctor Noethan chimed out behind me. "You take care of yourself, Mad Maxx. It would break my heart to see all that hard work we do here this morning go to the dogs, ja?" I winced when he made that cruel statement but refused to demonstrate any other response over it. I wasn't going to give the bastard the satisfaction of knowing he got to me as he had.

Mad Lucus dragged me behind him moving like a man with his ass on fire. I knew he feared we would be spotted by my subjects. There was no doubt if that happened, rumors would then spread of my poor condition like the contagious virus through the halls. I thought it would serve Gretta right if such a thing did happen.

I didn't give my Master any lip about his rushing like the crazy man. I knew better. I was more than aware what I wanted didn't matter to anyone, nor did I believe it should. I had finally accepted, in that horrid Mortar Palace, I was the psychotic that was not worth the soiled clothing on my back.

We made it to the fourth-floor apartment that had been my once, but was no longer, home. He hurriedly unlocked the door and pulled me in after him. I was shocked to see him nearly falling to his knees the second the door was shut behind us. It was only then I realized he was in terror that he would fail to smuggle me to his home without being spotted.

You see, I didn't know at the time that Gretta had put in the contract any accusations of my being misused by the Silk Queen meant immediate incarceration for me back where I had come from, and exile for him. Had I been told I maybe would have been a little quicker in my step behind him but as usual no one said a thing to the psycho of the danger.

Once Mad Lucus had gotten his breath back, he was panting pretty hard you know, he turned to look at me standing there at the door. "Welcome home, Christian Victor. The place has not been the same without you. I dare say I missed you a great deal. Let's start this new chapter in our lives together by cleansing away the filth, foulness and Gott knows what from your flesh. Those clothes, or whatever they are, take them off. Leave them by the door. I don't want you dragging the stink of that dungeon across my clean carpets. Do it now. Remove everything, that is an order dammit." He tugged on the leash with force.

I nodded as I quickly removed my disheveled outfit. It was so ripped and filled with dirt the material often ripped before I could gracefully get it off the boy. Mad Lucus stood there watching with an expression of abhorrence as little by little each inch of the boy's dirty, bloody, bruised and cut flesh was exposed.

When the final article lay in the pile of rags next to me I wrung my hands in anxiety but kept my tongue still. I dropped my head low while he looked at my naked skin from head to toe. I could tell by his gasping under his breath he was not pleased by what he saw.

Mad Lucus stammered out after many minutes of silence between us. "All your bones show through the flesh. There are too many cuts and bruises to count, but at least they offer you a bit of color other than that horrid grey hue you sport. Did they ever feed you down there, Christian?"

I wrung my hands faster in fear. “They gave me the gruel in the morning sometimes, I think. I don’t remember Master. I apologize for my poor memory.”

He sighed loudly. “There is no reason to apologize Christian. I took you from those chains. I saw you were helpless to even ask for supper much less eat any of it. I was told you saw the dentist. Let me see the dentures.” He looked to the boy’s mouth with curiosity.

I shook my head with vigor. “I did see the dentist. He did the surgery to remove the nubs, but they confiscated my dentures, Master. Peter thought them too dangerous to allow me to keep them.”

Mad Lucus snarled. “You mean too much a danger for them. With those false teeth you may bite off anything they forced into your ravaged mouth. Say what you mean Christian and stop playing the polite submissive to your lover.”

I shot a surprised look at him. “Lover? I don’t understand you, Master. I thought you said I make you sick to your stomach and am not good enough for such a title. I am the low creature you have to bear, or you lose your crown.”

Mad Lucus nodded his head and rolled his eyes. “I said those mean things to see if you would show some fire. I was under the impression you only held your temper until you could be out of that terrible situation. Am I to believe that shit downstairs was no act? Nein, my Christian Victor is the slippery dragon of discreet. I am not buying this bullshit. Now that we are alone you can tell me why you lied about Anselm's taking advantage as well. Go ahead, tell me all about it, that is a directive."

I shrugged and dropped my gaze to the floor. "I don't know what you mean, Master. I deserved everything I got for being the insolent punk. I give you no further quarrel in whatever you ask. Do with me as you please, but I beg of you to never request any details about the last month again. All you need to know is I cannot verbalize the depth of my regret that I ever disobeyed my most wise and generous Master Lucus." I dropped to a kneel at his feet hoping that would be the end of his probing into things I didn't want to discuss. Mainly so he didn't get any perverted ideas, but also I didn't wish to relive them, ja?

Mad Lucus stood dare staring at me appearing most disturbed by my response then he breathed out. "Christ, you are at the bottom aren't you boy. This is both amazing to witness and pitiful at the same time. I didn't think it possible to bring the jaded Mad Maxx to the breaking point, but I will be damned if I am not seeing it with my very own eyes. Shit, well that's good. This relationship between us can move forward at long last. Come with me. I desire to scrub away all the grime. Maybe there is still the boy I love under all that wretchedness. I am ready to find out." he hand signaled for me to stand and follow him.

He ran a bath rather than asking me to shower. Mad Lucus explained that until my head wound healed I was not to get the area wet, so only tubs of water not the stream of it. I stood there wringing my hands in anxiety wondering if he intended to stick around to watch this humiliation of the cleansing as he had before the Palace.

I got that answer the second he turned off the tub facet, then quickly retrieved my enema tools. I groaned under my breath as I watched him preparing the bag for use. Like it or not this man intended to make sure all signs of my recent misuses were washed away from every nook and cranny.

He told me to assume the position for the enema treatment. I did my best to comply, but I suppose the trauma of all those sexual assaults had gotten to me. I was unable to maintain my cool as he started his personal aiding me to perform this ritual. He had to threaten to send me back to the Palace several times before I could calm down my kicking and screaming each time he came at me. It was not an easy task to hold still and endure his actions without restraints, let me tell you.

When that humiliation was over, which was a waste of time thanks to my lack of any food of worth for thirty days, he demanded I get into the tub of water. I held my breath and hoped the radiation would end my life with quickness. I had barely been home an hour and already I was thinking I couldn't handle another moment of this nightmare life, even above dungeon level.

I was forced to hold still as Mad Lucus scrubbed every square inch of the boy's flesh with liberal use of his fancy soaps. He cursed Gretta and Cora under his breath and called the Elders old bastards through the whole process. When he could find no more spots to scrub till the flesh nearly came off in the rag, he demanded I get out for the shaving.

I couldn't believe that shit. The man wouldn't allow me to attend my own fucking hair removal. I swear to Gott I was near mad by the time he got down taking every stitch of hair from my skin but that growing on my head. Bad enough he insisted on working the enema and didn't trust me to wash my own ass, but damn. This belief that I would cut myself up with my blade was pure insanity. Hell, if he was so worried why not leave the fucking hair. I am a man. Men are supposed to be hairy.

After all that horrid indignity I thought for sure I was ready to run screaming shoot me through the yard. However, Mad Lucus was not quite done with assuring my spirit was broken to the point of nearly unrepairable. He pulled that chain leash leading me back to the terrible bed with all the sexual positions carved into it.

He smiled at me as I stood there shivering in the cool air naked as the day I was born though cleaner and with less hair I believe. "It has been many a lonely night without my Christian in the bed to hold. I had the taste of your charms and I do confess I have dreamed of nothing else since then. I had to tie you up to get what you swore to me before that terrible day a month ago. Tell me, my heart. Do I need to put you in the chains this day too or will you comply with all my dark desires willingly?"

I shuddered with sickness rolling through my stomach, damned ants. "I told you I give you no quarrel, Master. I do beg you to grant the mercy of a few days for the healing before you request such favors. I am not in excellent shape.” I caste my eyes to the floor hoping he would grant the reprieve since I asked politely, you know.

Mad Lucus shook his head while crossing his arms. “Mercy denied Christian. I don’t care if you are sore any more than the brutes that caused it. I think you don’t answer my question. You going to do what you are told without being bonded or do I order you to the restraints?”

I winced as I looked at the chains welded to the headboard and back at the wrist cuffs. “Nein, I do as you say. I don’t desire to be bonded Master.”

He grinned with thrill in his expression. “You do anything I want without fighting me?”

I dropped my shoulders as hellish visions of my time in the Palace paraded across the wheelroom screen. “Ja, Master. I am your plaything. Tell me what you want and see the desire fulfilled without quarrel.” I thought with misery there was nothing the fucker could do any more disgusting than I already endured downstairs more than once.

Mad Lucus ordered me to his bed without hesitation after I said that. I endured his molestations, demands for the drawn out full oral services and eventual penetration intercourse. For the first time, he didn’t ask for anything truly out of the ordinary for any schwuler sexual encounter, except one. He demanded I pretend to enjoy the unwanted attentions.

I did all I could to follow his orders. Though I confess I completely failed at appearing the wanton lover to one I found utterly revolting. This man was not my Leo, nor was he even the Vampire of whom I had lots of experience feigning interest thanks to the fear of his killing me for many years. I couldn't pretend this nasty pervert was anything better than the men that paid for the services or that hideous Byron.

I ended up weeping like the damned novice when he demanded I yell out foul words of encouragement to his brutal thrusting. I could do nothing but drool and blubber while making a terrible mess of his sheets with all that fluid flowing from the boy's head.

My state of apparent distress did nothing to deter him from seeing his lust to completion. He simply told me to keep the racket down as he sought his orgasm without my cheering him on in his efforts.

When at last he finished with me, he rolled me to my back with an expression of anger on his face. I stared at him through the veils of tears terrified he would send me back to the Palace for not being capable of minding his commands. I was surprised when instead he grabbed a handkerchief from his nightstand and wiped the drool and tears from my face with furious vigor.

He then forced himself on the boy, kissing my mouth and molesting my parts with roughness. I struggled in his grip unable to keep down the panic, thinking he was going for seconds. My obvious disinterest in his lewd touching further infuriated the man.

He stopped manhandling me and pulled up from his brutal actions with fire in his eyes. “Stop this fighting me, Christian. I am sick to death of your refusing my advances..”

I whimpered with fresh tears breaking out. “Master, I don’t understand. I give you what you wanted. I didn’t argue. I didn’t refuse your requests.”

Mad Lucus scoffed. “Nein, you didn’t that is true Christian, but you were the mechanical sex doll. I could have that with any fucking silver that ever walked these hallways or draped across their Master’s bed. I desire you to want me, boy. Not merely endure me. I am your Regent, best friend, and lover. You and me will be together for life. I cannot stand the thought of sharing my deepest secrets, all my dreams and intimate moments with someone that obviously finds me disgusting.”

I looked away from his angered face. “I never misled you, Master. You ignored my telling you I didn’t want you as the lover. You put your collar on me anyway, then left me to die when I make the mistake no one told me could even be made. If that were not enough, you cut a secret deal with the one that saw me treated worse than the rodent to assure I can never be free of you or this Haus that I fucking hate. If I find you disgusting than be assured you earned that place, Master. I beg of you. End my life. You can have the Gott damned crown and throne. I already said I don't want it."

Mad Lucus reached out and grabbed my chin with harshness forcing me to look at him. "Christian Victor, it is time you learn the facts of life boy. This disease you have assures you have no life other than one of chronic despair and pain. Unless someone can find love for you despite the pitfalls of it. I apologize I am not the one you were hoping would find the heart for you. That said, I want you to realize that like it or not, I do love you as you should be loved, boy. Not for what you can give me in power, money or even sexual thrill. I love you because there is no one else I have ever known as alive or amazing as you are. If you had no crown and were not the Priceless of Legend I would still think of as no one but my Christian Victor. However, you are those things so many without such care for you as the human being seek to hold you there hostage. You need real protection, supervision and guidance in the scary, confusing world inside you head boy. You have no idea how terribly ill you are. One day, I pray you will remember all I tell you tonight and come to understand it with peace. If you never do, then it is too bad for the Mad Lucus. I cannot just abandon you to be ripped apart by the jackals of this fucking Haus. My love for you is as much a curse for me as the schizophrenia is for you. I don't have a choice any more than you do, my spatz. So, you will keep faking that you desire me until you no longer remember it is a lie. I assure you, in time, this will be as easy as breathing." He let go of my head.

I nodded as the weeping jag threatened to overtaking me. “As you say, Master. I beg the mercy of releasing me for the call of nature and a quick clean up please?”

He groaned as he nodded. “I just bathed you to spotless boy. You can use the bathroom but hurry back. I am tired and we both could use a little rest before I start trying to fatten you back up, ja?”

I rolled from his grip and hit the floor nearly sprinting for the bathroom. I got inside and made my water while watching to see if he was watching me. I noticed he had turned to the nightstand and was preoccupied with digging through the drawer seeking something. I finished my business and crept to the medicine cabinet above the sink. I spotted the bottles of pills Doctor Noethan gave to him for the treatments of my wound. I recalled one of them was the pain killer, though I didn’t know which one.

I feared Mad Lucus would turn back around and see me rifling through the pills. Without hesitation I choose one of the bottles and removed the cap with speed. I poured all the pills into my palm and popped them into my mouth like the candy. I turned on the water facet as if washing the boy’s hands and quickly cupped a few handfuls to wash all the medication down my throat. Mad Lucus yelled for me to move my ass just as I swallowed the last of the stolen pills.

I rushed back into the bedroom sure that this was going to be the last time I would go to sleep. I had read the painkillers make the overdosed go to the permanent slumber, you know. Well, they do. If you take the right fucking prescription that is. A large amount of the antibiotics though, they can kill you too if you can keep them from coming up.

Needless to say, I barely god back into the bed when the boy's stomach began to lurch wildly with sickness. I laid there turning green in the gills as Mad Lucus told me he was bounding me for the sleep until he was sure I had finished the acute cycle of my brain disease. I watched him with acidic belching starting to force its way out of my mouth.

Mad Lucus noticed my sudden change in color. "Christian? What the fuck. You are pale as the ghost boy. What the hell is the matter?"

I barely sat up when the first wave of projectile vomiting struck with force. Mad Lucus yelled in angry surprise as I fell from the bed to my knees helpless to stop the outflow of stomach acid and undigested pills.

Mad Lucus saw the cause of my tummy troubles rolling across the floor. He let out a horrible roar and ran for the bathroom while I continued to spew the evidence of the suicide attempt onto the carpet by the bed. I heard him cursing loudly and the sound of an empty pill bottle being tossed across the bathroom. He had quickly discovered what I had done without needing to torture it out of me.

In a few more moments, Mad Lucus returned to the bed. He lifted my uncontrollably wrenching flesh from his floor and dragged me to the commode. I had mostly emptied what was left of my chewed up stomach. The ants did nasty work of it, you know. I laid my head on the seat moaning in the agony of that stupid move I had made. Damn, I am an idiot.

Mad Lucus leaned down next to me and pushed a bottle of liquid at my face. "Here Christian, drink this, hurry up. It will stop this terror." I took it from his trembling hands willing to try anything to end this hellish experience.

I drank it down and felt better for a second. Then with sudden violence I began to vomit with more force than before. I wailed in agony as my guts threatened to come up with each reflexive movement of my digestion in reverse. I begged for Mad Lucus to end my pain by killing me at once.

He leaned down close to my red, tear strewn face and said, "You let that syrup of Ipecac do its job boy. You cannot fight off this opponent that you can be sure of. You have to purge all that poison from your system quickly or suffer the damage from your foolish behaviors."

I vomited air for several moments until I could at last pant out, "You give me the medication to make me barf. Why? I was doing it just fine without aid, Master. I am dying. Gott kill me." I wailed out as I began the next series of dry heaving.

When at last the urge to throw up ended and all the pills were safely out of the boy, Mad Lucus grabbed my upper arm dragging me from the commode. I was too weakened to stop him from doing anything he wanted to me. That barfing takes a lot out of a fellow, you know. He forced me onto the bed and bonded me by cuff to the chains on the headboard.

Once I was helpless to escape him he leaned down and glared at me. "You will have to sleep in here with the smell of that sour stomach of yours boy. I am going to the couch for my own rest far from the moron that tries to kill himself with antibiotics. I have had all I am going to take of your depressing attitude. You want to die? Then I tell you what. When I awaken I will release you. You will dress in the outfits I had made for you and leave this apartment without a leash or your protector Mad Lucus."

I gasped in shock at what he said, "Huh? You swear you will do that? You are not funning me, Master? You will see me free, wait, I go out the door and you call Gretta to take me back below, ja?"

He shook his head with a wicked smile. "I will do no such a thing. I will allow you a full twenty-four hours to run free of my influence. You go where you want. Do as you please. I ask no questions nor even think of you during this time. You can use this opportunity I grant you to jump from the banister or hell, go run through the yard till you find the honorable death at the end of the Guard's rifle."

That made me narrow my eyes in suspiciousness. "I don't understand Master. This is the head game you play with me, ja? You really expect me to believe you will turn a blind eye to my seeking my escape the only way granted to me? I am not the fool you think I am. What is the catch. I know you desire my crown. You cannot rule the Haus in place of the dead man."

Mad Lucus nodded and let out a long sigh. "Look Christian, I realize the risk I take letting you go in a few hours. Maybe you do seek your grave for truth. However, I am forever the betting man. For all these years I watch things happen in the halls and bet with myself of the outcomes. I told you once you, my heart, are the only creature that always seemed to beat my educated guesses even with the odds being severely unfavorable. I say to you, when I let you go from this apartment you can commit the suicide. It is likely that is what you will do, but I am willing to bed you won't. This time I think you will attend to something that needs to be done or you will never find your way back home."

I shrugged at that weird thing he said. "This was my home but not anymore. You stole it from me, Master. Gretta, she replaced it with the tomb. You are the loser if you think I will return to this apartment at the end of the twenty-four hours. I am happy to hear you grant me such a mercy, but I swore to never betray you again. So, I tell you the truth of it."

Mad Lucus chuckled at that. "You are adorably innocent for one so damned overused. I think that maybe is the problem. You take all the shit everyone ever poured on your head, and even when you level revenge you do it only because you are backed into the corner. Christian, you are blinded to your own reflection. You blame Christian Victor for the things others have done. Now you try to punish him for it with death. That makes no sense, boy. Turn that knife from your wrist and put it in the eyes of the criminal, not the victim, fool. Listen to me, when I let you go, take that time to seek out the vengeance on those that have earned it. I know whatever happened down there has killed the very thing that I found so attractive about you in the first place. That urge to survive at any cost lays in tatters at your feet. Well, my love, go out and take it back from the thieves that stole it from you. When you taste their blood and find it suits your palette, come back to me, your Mad Lucus. If you can find trust in the one that loves you, I assure you the reward will be the buffet of vengeance for all the wrongs that happen under this roof. I wish to have you at my side to aid me in seeing all of these monsters get what day have coming."

I shook my head feeling I may begin to weep again. "I don't want to kill anyone, Master. I don't care about the revenge. I just want to get out of this Haus. I desire to be the doctor to heal the sick. I want the Frau and children. I seek the green fields and baby lambs. That is my dream. I have enough nightmares without adding anymore."

Mad Lucus scoffed. "My love, Gretta, Cora, the Elders, and the Voters, hell and the collars, they will never let you leave. This is the truth of it. You have to accept that once and for all. Have you not had enough pain yet? How much more do you wish to endure? The nightmares you add from this moment forward are all on you. There is a way to end your suffering if only you could understand the things you thought you wanted are not in the cards. It may not be the life you wished, but it will be life Christian. In time, you maybe even find joy in it. Regardless, this must be your decision. I am through with forcing you to mind me as your Master. You leave my submissive but return to me as the Master of the Haus for real. Then I will be your Lord and you will be my King. You think on what I say to you. Get some rest. I see you in a few hours." With that he leaned down, kissed my forehead then left the room closing the door behind him.

I laid there for a bit thinking on the strange things he said to me. I didn't want to believe my dreams that had sustained me all those years were merely the fantasy. However, I couldn't deny the correctness in his assessment of my situation. I was never getting out of that Haus, not alive anyway.

Mad Lucus was right. I only had two choices. Kill myself or find a way to bring that fucking hell hole down from within. I fell into a fitful slumber with the visions of both homicide and suicide on my overburdened mind. This was going to be a true clash of the Titans. Mad Max (suicide route) vs. Christian (homicide path).

Mad Lucus came and gently woke me from sleep around five o'clock that afternoon. As he promised he unbonded me and handed me a black suit he had tailor made for me. Though thanks to my weight loss it was hanging on me like the potato sack. The breeches were black of superior quality as was the silk blouse. The long jacket was of the finest wool and not unlike the Vampire style Jonas tended to favor. Mad Lucus told me he stuck with what would be pleasing to both him and my Mann to try to keep the peace between them. Good luck with that.

On the right breast was a monogram of the Metal Crown and below it the family crest of Mad Lucus's royal line. He explained to me that since I was not wearing the trappings of my high office, this emblem would be the constant visual reminder to all that greeted me of my status as Master of the Haus and of course his own as my future regent. It seemed the trivial thing to me, but I pretended to be impressed to keep the crazy bastard from changing his mind about letting me go of his hold.

Ta my shock, the second I was dressed and looking dapper as possible given the sorry health I sported, he undid his leash. I almost fainted when he kissed my cheek turned around and went to the kitchenette bidding me good luck with my decision. He reminded me that he would be waiting for my return. Mad Lucus's final words that day were of his faith in me that I would do the right thing now that I was granted the freedom to do so.

I tell you I didn't let that apartment door hit me in the ass before I was out of there. Fuck him, I thought. I was never coming back to that pervert. I was free of the Palace and his leash at last. I had a full day to find a way to escape all of them. All I had to do is speak with Leo. I just knew once I told him of all the horror I endured and what the plans of Gretta and Lucus were, he would step in to help me slip out of a Haus.

I rushed up to the sixth floor practically floating up the stairs on the wings of hope. I ignored the throngs of silvers and blacks that gasped and fell to their knees all around me. The only thing I could see is the front door, and the green fields that hid behind them.

I banged on Leo's apartment door for many minutes without an answer. I was standing there wondering if I should kick the damned thing in to demand to know why he had abandoned me when I heard Der Makellos barking inside. That caused me to startle as the blood in my veins turned to ice.

I backed away trembling nearly busting out in tears when I spotted Kilian and Reece leaving the snake's haus. That was all I could stand. I took off like the jackrabbit back down the stairs nearly falling over every Gott damned collar that fell to their knees before me. I was headed to the fourth floor this time. If anyone could tell me what the fuck was going on with Leo, it was my beloved Jakob.

I arrived at his door sweating like the pot head during a piss test. I knocked for many minutes with the same results as happened above. No one was home. I couldn't believe my bad luck. I stood there unsure what to do as the anxiety began to rise within the boy. I paced the hallway wringing my hands unsure what to do next.

It was then I thought of my need to thank my Shadow King for his kindness, and I needed to find Birgit to rescues my Felicity. I took off in a sprint once more heading for the first floor at breakneck speeds. I ran down the hallway headed for the back stairwell half expecting Cary wouldn't be there like Jakob and Leo.

I gasped in thrill when I spotted him standing at the backdoor guarding it as usual. I ran to him like the grateful Frau greeting her sailor Mann after his return from years at sea. Cary was beyond joy to see me as well. Without thinking I fell into his embrace and ignored his wanton kissing of my mouth and pawing at my ailing flesh, at least for a few minutes.

Then I realized myself and pushed him off me with fury. "Christ, fiend. What do you take me for brother?" I punched him in the stomach, but he was ready for it, so the blow caused him only a loud groan rather than serious damage.

He held his abdomen and smiled at me with a dreamy gaze. "I take you for my honest lover, Christian Axel. Oh, my Gott, is it good to see you. I thought for sure I would never see you again other than those depressing views from the bars. How did you manage to get out? Gretta have a stroke and Jonas took over the post?"

I moaned in pain. "Don't I wish Cary. Nein, Matz's begging finally moved that pervert Lucus to step in. You don't want to know the deal he cut with that bitch to see me able to breath the dust of the hallways rather than the dirt below."

Cary nodded with a frown. "Lucus came thru. I suppose that is the best we could hope for. Roselina will be thrilled to hear her boyfriend is busted from prison. I think if you ask nicely she will let you give her one of your squirrely kids." He chuckled as he teased me.

I nodded. "Well, I was going to go see Birgit then Matz but realizing that lovely Frau is waiting on my couple. I surely cannot make her wait any longer after such a long absence. Tell you what Cary, you better pull a double tonight. I have been locked up a long time. I may need the whole night to satisfy that lusty woman of yours."

Cary reached out and popped me in the shoulder playfully. "Enough brother. You are starting to piss me off. The thought of you in another's arms makes me rage with murderous thinking. You belong to Cary and that is final."

I looked at my boots with sudden despair washing over me. "Is that so? Seems you are currently in need of taking the number lover. Tell me, do you mean it when you say thinking of another taking favor with me would enrage you to think of killing?"

Cary frowned and came closer, staring in shock finally noticing the open wound on my head. "You mean like ripping apart the fucker that did that to you? Ja, I mean what I said Christian Axel. Give your Cary a name and be assured that motherfucker finds his maker tonight."

I sniffed back the coming tears. "Uhm, I don't know who else to speak to Cary, but I have a problem that I cannot seem to fix. Something happened, you know below. I fear I cannot live with the dishonor of it. I have nowhere to turn brother. I have endured many foul things and always found a way to keep going. Not this time. If I don't find an answer soon, I am sure that I will throw myself from the banister to end the pain that won't go away." I felt my cheek turn wet with the first cold tear of utter degradation that was eating me alive from inside.

Cary saw the rain and came forward grabbing my arm and pulling me under the stairs out of sight of the residents. I fell into the weeping jag for many minutes as he held me tightly in his embrace. I felt so damned helpless and lost. Nothing could undo the damage caused by that birthday surprise. I let that calm patient Cary hold me as he carefully managed to get me to whisper to him of the driving force behind my breakdown.

The moment he got the details he let me go and turned quickly vomiting onto the floor, which to be honest didn't help me feel any better. He quickly got ahold of his gut reaction to my confession, then spent many moments assuring me this was not my fault. I could do nothing about the foul things those men did to me. Cary reminded me repeatedly as he spoke that I was chained and held down in a cell. They used tools to force the unnatural he said. Then finally he stated, anyone, even him, would have had to endure such perversions if they had been in that position like me.

When at last there was nothing else to say about it I found no relief by speaking of it. "Cary, brother, Mad Lucus told me that the only way I can find peace is to extract vengeance for the wrongs done to me. He said I am to stop spending my time playing the defensive and take up the habit of fighting back when not threatened, trapped or in danger. Do you think that is the answer to ending my torture over this dishonor?"

Cary shook his head and wiped his brow with a frown "My love, I will say this. The men that did that to you are monsters. Letting them walk around on the Earth is a criminal act. Now that they have the taste for such obscenity, do you really think they won't come back after you again? Maybe they do this horror to others. What they did to you is illegal in this Haus. I want you to think on that a moment. A Haus that turns the blind eye to the nightmares won't accept this perversion of which was forced upon you. There is a fucking reason for that taboo. It is beyond sick, even for this hell hole. I have to say Lucus is the wise man to encourage you to seek justice against these bastards. If you feel strong enough to do such a thing, then know your Shadow King is with you. I am even willing to bet that your men Almut and Hubertus will come to add muscle without our having to tell them why."

I nodded as I stared at his boots in a trance "Ja, I think you are speaking what I already know. Noethan, Tadeas and Sebastian must be destroyed. If you desire to be a part of this along with my men I won't say nein. However, I must ask you to allow me to do this with my own hands. I borrow only your strength, not your souls."

Cary nodded as he leaned in and nuzzled my cheek. "Then come on love. Let's go start the process of sending these creatures back to hell where they belong." We took off with speed from under the stairwell headed for the torture chamber to retrieve Almut and Hubertus.

We had no difficulty collecting the two of them. The second they saw me and Cary approaching they dropped everything. I was amazed that they followed us out of the chambers to the first floor without a single question nor quarrel. All I had to do is hand motion that I required their aid, and the men came running.

Almut, Cary and Hubertus went to collect our quarry while I went ahead to speak to the Guard. I had something very special in mind to pay these three men back for the cruel consideration they had paid to me. You must remember, Meine Liebe, equal service demands equal return. I knew just where to go to assure my appreciation for their special gift would not be misunderstood.

I had gone outside, I used the unguarded back door to leave. My sudden appearance in the yard immediately caught Iva, the Captain of the Guard, attention. I managed to keep him from shooting by yelling I wanted to make my deal with him to obtain something of his, not to try to run. He stood there giggling with great humor as he listened to my desires and what I could offer in return. It was the fastest agreement I had ever accepted. Turned out the only person hungrier for blood that early night than me was Ivan. Oh, and the fellows he was lending me for my dark task.

I was busy collecting all the items required for my blood sports when I spotted my men approaching. Each held one of the offenders in their strong grip. Noethan was struggling against Cary. Sebastian fought to escaping the huge Almut. Tadeas was subdued by the tough Hubertus.

All three of the men grew silent the second they saw me standing next to three wooden poles that Ivan and his men had quickly buried in the ground at my direction.

I nodded at Ivan. "The chains I requested, do you have them, or shall I send to the dungeon to get three sets, brother?"

The hairy Russian grinned as he shot thrilled looks at the now trembling prisoners. "Nein, your Majesty. Petrov has what you need. Ah, you pick a fine night for such exciting theater. I think their screams will be heard for many miles. Be sure to take your time. Me and the boys been desirous of a good show for many months. I hope you intend to savor the moment, da," he said in a thick accent.

I nodded as I shot a look of hate at the doctor and two Dungeon Masters. "You shall not be disappointed this night brother Ivan. There is a good reason many call me Der Brutale. Cary, Hubertus, Almut, strip those bitches to their naked flesh. Let's get this party started." My men grinned as they allowed a few Guard volunteers to aid them in undressing the perverts that struggled with all their worth. All of the Guard and my men had great fun tormenting the degenerates during this forced disrobing.

I watched with humor as the three of them begged without dignity that they be spared my wrath. I listened in stoic silence as Doctor Noethan assured his buddies that any moment someone from the Haus would come to their aid. He screamed out that torturing the Dominants and Haus staff in public, as I seemed prepared to do, was not legal. Their begging turned to cursing, then eventually, as they realized no one was coming as fast as they thought day would, wails of terror. I stood there quiet as the mouse waiting till all three men were helplessly chained to their poles.

The Guardsmen backed away, and I hand motioned my men to do the same. The Russians took off to a safe distance with the best view. While Hubertus, Almut and Cary stood to the left just beyond reach of the last of the three poles. I walked slowly in front of the bonded men. Doctor Noethen, then Sebastian and finally the prick Tadeas. Their yelling had gone silent as each tracked me with their eyes that were wide in fear.

I turned and walked back finally taking a place in front of the men where all three could plainly see and hear me, even if I whispered to them.

I shook my head as I looked to the slowly setting sun. “It is indeed a fine night. I guess you fellows have realized I am the freeman once more. I decided since I was denied the party to celebrate my rise to power. I should make up for that loss with only my closest friends to receive the invitations.”

Doctor Noethan whimpered, “You call us your closest friends, Mad Maxx. This is the truth of it you know. We all adore you. See only this morning I fixed your sickness and see you returned to health. Don’t you remember?”

I nodded with a snort,. “How could I forget you my beloved, Anselm? You know when I think on it I must admit I have much difficulty forgetting any of you boys. Every time I close my eyes, there you all are. I never forget the faces of my perverted lovers. No one is closer than those that can brag of their conquest of my sexual artistry, ja?" The three men started trembling as they realized that my words were indicating I was not happy to see them.

I chuckled when none of them felt the need to say anything to my observations of our honest friendship. "What is this? Do you fellows have the invisible ball gag holding you tongues to stillness? Well, you know as the daft psychotic, I understand sometimes there are things in the world only a special few can see. Who am I to deny you such delusions?" I reached into doctor's jacket and removed his preloaded sedations syringes. I gave each fellow a shot, to assure they didn't shock before I was through with them while I pay back the favor they granted me.

Sebastian yelled out as I shot him up trying to sound tough, though he was shaking like the freezing baby. "Mad Maxx, you let us go right this minute. I will remind you that we are the men of the Silk Queen. We did nothing wrong against you boy. We merely followed the orders of our betters. Now cut us loose and we will be on our way. You don't want trouble, do you? the Queen will be angry when she hears of this." I ignored him and gave Tadeas his sedative to complete that task.

I immediately stood in front of the three with fire blazing in my eyes as I whispered, "It is you that came looking for the trouble assholes. You were assigned to attend your King, not that fucking bitch Gretta. I am the Master of the Haus, boys. There is no one better than me. You did what you did because you loved it. Even without her say you would have beaten, tortured and raped me with vigor. That is okay. I want all of you to relax. I am only here to equal out the service imbalance caused by that pesky time I spent with you in the Palace. You see you boys brought me a special gift for my birthday. You really shouldn't have you know. I realize it is the thought that counts, but I didn't bother to get you a thing for your own. I now find myself in such an embarrassing situation. I am not a thief that takes service without returning the favor of it. You see I owe you boys your remembering me on my birthday, and I owe them too." I pointed off into the distance at the coming swarm of dark shadows.

All three of the men began to scream in terror as the approaching visitors came into their full view. I stood still in anxious silence as each took a place around me creating a semi-circle. I shot each one a frightened look while I counted them loudly to the sweet sounds of the frantic and terrified pleas of mercy from my three victims.

I finished my numbering the visitors and looked back at the railing men. "Exactly fifteen. It is only fair each of you have as many attend this party as you had for this worthless man, ja? Now don't get too attached. You cannot keep them. They are only yours for tonight. Oops, I mean you are theirs. You see this way I can pay you back for your service of perverted cruelty and at the same time service them for the unnatural they granted to me at your request. I bet you didn't know that is why they leveled me the Priceless. I can please all of my lovers at one time. All I need is a bit of chain, a knife, many lovers surrounding me, and a romantic night like this one. Alright, shall we begin? I do believe, if I recall correctly, you demanded I taste the unnatural. Let's start there." I walked over and punched Noethan in the mouth pulling out his tongue as far as it would stretch.

Can you believe it, Ivan was correct. As I cut out Noethan's tongue you could hear his screams for miles along with the excited barking and yipping as I thew it to my partners, the fifteen yards dogs for their dinner.

Chapter 44: Fifteen Dog Night

The Russian Guard jeered and laughed with thrill as Noethan screamed wildly from his torment. He and the two Dungeon Masters struggled so harshly in their chains, blood from the restraints cutting into them began to flow down their naked skin. The air filled with the smell of that crimson fluid. This scent caused the yard dogs around me, already excited from the taste of Noethan's severed tongue, to bark and beg with vigor for more.

It was at that moment, I almost lost my shit. The jeering of the Russian men, along with the barking, growling, and bumping of the yard dogs into the boy as they fought each other for the meat, threatened to set off a PTSD flashback reaction. I closed my eyes and put my hands over the boy's ears. I was desperately trying to block out the horrific images of my birthday night in the Palace cell.

I knew it was dangerous to use these animals that I was now extremely phobic of in an attempt at equal vengeance for what these men forced on me. However, it was a calculated risk I felt necessary to take. I truthfully believed the only way to cleanse my deep shame was to destroy all three of them with the very same weapons they had used on me. It was my thinking that if I saw the yard dogs giving the proper punishment to these abominations to humankind. I could once more find my affection for my beloved Der Makellos.

You must realize that what those animals did that night was not their fault. The yard dogs are not capable of the higher intelligence to do evil deeds with motive. That dishonorable gift is reserved exclusively for our species. The hounds had to mind their masters or find themselves beaten to death for it.

More than that, the canines are the prisoners to their natural instincts. These men used both weakness's in the animals against them and me. The way I wanted to see it they were as much the helpless victims of the twisted minds of these perverted men as your Master Maxx. To this day I still see it that way.

All that said, believing them innocent of the crimes didn't help to alleviate the terror rising within me. I was having a hell of a time enduring their presence all around me. It was too close to the nightmarish incident for me to do what needed to be done with stoic brutality.

Despite my discomfort, and panic, I managed to get ahold of myself. If I had not, I would have busted out screaming for mercy right along with the tormented prisoners. I took a deep breath and opened my eyes. The sight of seeing Noethan coughing and gagging on his own blood reminded me that I was not the helpless victim of this man anymore. I shook off the ice picks of terror flowing down my spine and approached Sebastian with my knife ready to do its work.

He saw me approaching and began to yell in terrified fury, "You motherfucking freak. You better think twice before you try cutting out my tongue. I assure you Greta will see far worse done to you than anything yet if you touch a hair on my head."

I stood there chuckling at his empty threats. "Ah, well you may be right, Sebastian. Gretta will want to see me back to the Palace for returning your kindness to me on my birthday. Then maybe she will try to have me degraded further than you boys already have done. However, I can assure you, she will have to hire fresh thugs to see her disgusting thrills met. You fellows have been officially relieved of your duties to the Master of the Haus. I do apologize, but these are tough times. I simply cannot afford the expenses you take out of my flesh, I mean pockets, nein. I had that correct. That is what you called me isn't it? Not King Maxx or his majesty but your sperm pocket, ja? You can correct me if I am mistaken. Many nights I spent with you forcing me to service your disgusting lusts are hazy in my memory, but not the one that matters. I seem to recall that Noethan started the party forcing me to taste the obscene and you, my brother, then personally filled me as the sperm pocket with your lust. Let's continue this celebration at that point shall we?" With that I reached down and grabbed his hodensack.

Sebastian let out a blood curdling wail as I used the knife to split open the flesh, following the natural seam that melded his scrotum together. Then with the quickness of the cat, I ripped the pinkish exposed testicles contained within the folds of skin out by their roots. I didn't even look behind me as I tossed them over my left shoulder to the thrilled hounds.

Sebastian screamed out nearly mad in pain, "You rotten sonofabitch. I am going to rip you apar with my bare hands when I get free. Do you hear me, Maxx? You are a dead man."

I leaned in close and whispered with malice in my tone. "Ja, you are correct. I am dead, brother, and when the sunrises you will be too." I walked over to the weeping, trembling Tadeas to finish off the first round of my belated birthday party.

He whimpered never taking his eyes off the slick blade in my hand. "Please Mad Maxx, I beg of you. Have mercy. I will do anything you want to see this debt repaid if you spare me."

I shook my head as I held up the knife for him to plainly see. "I do believe you steal the words from my own mouth there, Tadeas. I seem to recall making that very same statement on my birthday night. What was your response? Oh ja, I remember. You said I was going to love being the real bitch. I seem to recall you offered me the choice of which end I wanted disgraced by my suitors first. So, I am now granting you the same honor. Which shall it be? Hurry up and decide, Tadeas. Just as you pointed out to me, these fellows are growing impatient waiting to take their thrill with you."

Tadeas wailed out nearly incoherently, "Nein. Maxx, please don't do this. I beg of you."

I chuckled. "Ah, you finally understand, don't you? It is not so easy to decide when any response you give results in dishonoring of an important part of you. Tell you what Tadeas. Let's make this easy shall we? I will do what you did for me and make the choice in your place. Hmm, now what was it you decided? Oh, ja I remember. You told Sebastian I couldn't wait to give them both at the same time. You know what? That is actually the truth this time."

Tadeas shrieked as I forced open his mouth and pulled his tongue nearly off from my violent fury. I cud the tender flesh free with no effort. I held that slimy thing in my hand while grabbing his hodensack as I had Sebastian's before him. With the same ruthless motions, I removed his testicles from his scrotum sack. Then without ever taking my demon filled sight off his wailing face I threw all three amputated organs over my left shoulder to the eager hounds.

Insane laughter broke out of my mouth as all three men screamed wildly as they watched those dogs devour Tadeas' parts. The yard dogs were near madness from the thrill of fresh meat. It was a well-known fact around the Haus that the Guard that attended them made sure they were always hungry by underfeeding their wards. I had quickly become the hounds best friend by offering them this most unexpected dietary supplement.

I then turned to the shrieking men and announced loudly, I had to jell to be heard over their agonized wails. "I am going to take the break and allow you to rest a moment. A mercy you didn't grant me, I confess. However, if I intend to keep this party going all night like you fellows did for me, then I need to pace myself. Otherwise, I fear my guests of honor shall wear out from all the fun before the celebration comes to the proper conclusion at sunrise." With that I stepped over to briefly visit with my men standing to the left. They were looking damned confused over what they had just been witnessed and what they heard me saying to the victims.

As I approached, Cary blew out his breath his eyes wide in shock. "Holy hell Christian. I don't think I have ever seen anything so violent in my life. I assumed you would thud the fuckers and then maybe light them up with flames. Instead, you cut off their balls and threw them to the yard dogs? That is a bit much, don't you think?"

I glared at him barely containing my fury at his questioning me. "I will tell you only this once to keep your thoughts on this matter to your own counsel. If I desire criticism about how I hand out punishment you would not be the one I would permit to give it. You don't appreciate my handiwork, then go get out of my fucking sight, pussy."

Cary gasped as he dropped his head in a bow of shame. "Uhm, I apologize your Majesty. I forgot my place. I will say nothing more, I swear it. I thank you for the mercy you demonstrate to your unworthy servant."

I nodded with an expression of fury. "That's better. Forget yourself again and I will see you beaten to death for your poor memory skills. Do you hear me Cary?"

He nodded appearing emotionally injured and subdued. "As you wish, Master. I am yours to command."

I scoffed. “Are you now? Well, we can test that later. At the moment, you may have noticed, I am busy with those ahead of you in line. I will not stop till I fulfil my appetite for the dark pleasures. I tore my fury from the Shadow King to the other two standing there in shock at my unrestrained cruelty toward my Dark Bonded. Almut? Hubertus? Do you share in your brother’s complaints? Do you boys have anything to say about my behaviors? Just so you all know, I intend to cut these fuckers up piece by piece until the hounds are fat and useless from devouring their flesh. If you are against me in this decision, then I suggest you say it now. Breath a word about it later and I will see you whipped to death for daring to question my authority.” I glared at the two Torture Master black collars with irritation.

They shot each other a look of fear, then Almut shook his head. “Nein Master. Hubertus and I are your loyal men. We do what you ask and think only what you tell us to. We serve you without hesitation nor quarrel. Your will is our own.”

I chuckled with wickedness. “Is that so? I hope for your sake this are not lies you fellas voice to me Almut. If it be truth then I say finally someone around here says something of value to me. Let’s test your resolve to serve your King, shall we? I order both you to go inside the Haus and borrow a sharp butcher knife, one each. I am in poor health and will likely require a strong back to cut through bones at some point in this action. Get going and return quickly. I will call for you when I am ready for the help.” Neither man even wasted time nodding but took off with speed to mind my command. I noticed they both were grinning with thrill at what I told them I wished of them.

Th moment the Torture Masters were out of earshot Cary leaned closer and whispered, "Christian Axel, love. Please baby you are scaring me. I know you are upset by what happened below, but this extreme blood thirst is not a good thing. I am asking you nicely to kill them quickly and be done with it. You got your point across to them. You can be assured they will go to hell with an appreciation for the dishonor they caused you."

I reached out and snatched Cary up by his collar with aggression leaning into his face with fury. "How dare you tell me what to do. You are pushing your luck with me lover. If you know what is good for you then you will shut up. I am about to lose my temper with you Cary. I fucking mean it. You are to never speak to me common as you did in front of the men ever again. I must warn you Cary, my training Master Peter ordered his Dark Bonded Felix to cut out an eye for offending him. Want to find out what Mad Maxx der Brutale will command you to cut out for doing the same? I don't think you do brother. I am not as merciful a man as Peter is."

Cary trembled as he stared into my eyes and saw there was no soul in them. "What has happen to you, my heart? The man I love wouldn't speak to me like this. We are friends and lovers, brother, but you treat me like the barely tolerated servant. You sound like, well everyone else in this fucking hell hole. I thought you were different."

I chuckled as I pushed him back with strength near knocking him to his ass. "Are you trying to flatter me by calling me cruel as any Dominant in this Haus. Good move there, brother. I confess I was about ready to see you tied up next to these nothings to await your slaughter. You have managed to save your life by reminding me why I keep you around. I admit your humor is a comfort to me. Beware though, no one in this Haus is irreplaceable. Dare to piss me off again and maybe I decide laughter is better left to the comic strips."

Cary shook his head in disbelief. "Are you psychotic or something, Christian Axel? Did you not hear what I said to you? Have you forgotten that I love you and you love me? If this is an act you can drop it. No one can hear what we say to each other."

I sneered at him as I looked back at the loudly weeping victims bonded to their poles. "This is your mistake, fool. You didn't bother hearing me when I speaking with you Cary. Perhaps, you are the one in need of the medication for psychosis. You are severely out of touch with reality. I told you I am the straight man and didn't desire the lover status with you in this Bond. You held me hostage. You demanded that I agree to sex with you, or you'd withdraw your necessary aid to me. If you are treated cruelly by me with little regard for your feelings in the matter, be sure it is the equal service you receive for that you gave me. That said there is no need for you to fret, brother. You mind your manners, do as I tell you, and grant me all that you swore to me, and I will never deny you access to my artistic skills. As for my love, you will never have that because you don't give me yours. You say I am like these monsters that reside in this Haus. Nein, you are far more their honest reflection in both meaning and action. You traded my honest affection for you as my brother to demand the right to fuck me just like everyone else in my life has always done. The way I see it, love is a word all you motherfuckers throw around but have no understanding of its meaning. Now if you are through acting the little whiny bitch in a fantasy romance with the Master of the Haus, I have these other unwanted lovers needs to attend. Don't look so sad Cary. I will be on my knees sucking your cock and enduring your mount to your satisfaction anytime you ask me to. I would think you thrilled that your sex toy is out of the locked drawer at last." I didn't bother to give him a chance to respond taking off back to continue the torturing of my abusers the moment I was done telling him what I really thought of him. Ja, I know seems cold, but I will say I have the right to say with honesty how his demanding I allow him to fuck me made me feel about him.

I went right back into the gruesome action of cutting pieces from the three monsters. This time, I removed Noethan's sex organs, Sebastian's tongue and Tadeas's pinky finger. With each slice of the men, I could feel a tiny sliver of my humanity hacked away with it.

A cold, emptiness filled the boy's chest. The world around me lost its luster and even the howls of the excited Russian's that cheered on my brutal actions seemed like a distant unimportant background noise. Everything seemed unreal to me, as the darkness of the night seemed to reach into the boy and become a part of him.

The truth was, though I didn't know it at the time, I was losing the ability to feel empathy for my fellow human beings. I had always managed to hold on to the hope not everyone was like the men and women in the Haus that heaped abuse, rape and cruelty upon my head. In these moments, I could no longer believe that. I had come to the conclusion that the entire world was a brutal place. Survival without any kind of truthful joy or hope is all I had really ever known.

For the first time, I honestly thought there was no such thing as love, kindness, or mercy. All that was just like that bullshit Peter told me when I was twelve that breaking my metal would bring me freedom. Lies he told to me to keep me subdued for their cruel thrills.

I understood at last the only reason everyone didn't do what these revolting men had done was because of fear of reprisal either by the law or by the survivors of their cruel behaviors. I knew that if given the chance humankind would basically destroy each other just for the selfish thrill of it. I was beyond fury as I came to grip these hard learned lessons.

As I cut off tiny pieces of the men's flesh I mumbled to myself angrily, "There never was no fucking green fields. The baby lambs are only created to kill for the Dominant's supper. Christian Axel you are not the Priceless. You are not the Collar King, Mortar King nor Master of the Haus. You my moronic friend are the fucking idiot beast that got everything he deserved. The cursed are only here as the entertainment for the blessed. Learn your place, boy. You don't like it? Then too bad for you." I confess, I suppose I am the ignorant fool not to have made these discoveries sooner.

You'd think I would have been a bit further on this learning curve with all I had already endured. Since I could remember I had been bent over something so others could crawl on top of me to use me for their fun. After they finished with emptying their baser urges into me, they used me as the step stool to climb higher to the sky. Begging them to leave me be or grant me any mercy fell on deaf ears. They had been telling me repeatedly of how I was too ill to know what was best for me. I needed aid to attend my daily functioning because of my inability to understand reality. Until then I had never bothered to listen to them.

Well, they had tried to teach me that being the schizophrenic means being raped and tortured. It is the only way for me to prove I was of some use to society. I was too hardheaded to accept that was the only kind of life I could hope for. Yet, the evidence that they were correct had piled all the way to my ears at long last.

Behind the screams of my victims, I could hear my Masters and rapists telling me their cruel sport with my flesh was for my own good or the only thing of value I could provide dem. I listened within the wheelroom as each man repeated how much of a burden I created for them. All said I was lucky they even bothered to lower themselves to care for my disabled ass. I owed them that very thing for all their troubles you know.

Well, Meine Liebe, I decided that if there really was such a thing as the emotion of love without dark motive, I had never found a shred of evidence of it. I had thought I felt it for others (Leo, Ryker, Annette, Jakob) but I had not received the equal service of it back from any of them. I couldn't even find gentle tolerance from most. More often than not, I tended to elicit pure hatred, with the worst of it coming from my own fucking parents.

I listened to the shrieks, howls and screams of the perverted men slowly dying by my blade and found no peace in it. The humiliation that drove my knife was not magically cleansing my soul as Mad Lucus said it would. Nor did their flowing blood wash away the memory of the nightmare as Cary told me it should.

The honest truth is I could find no joy in the revenge against them. No matter how deep I cut into them I was not able to undo the horrors of that obscenity as it replayed in repeat every time I closed my eyes. All that gruesome scene of vengeance was managing to do was deepen my belief that I was unworthy of life. I believe if I were honest with myself, a nasty creature like me should be joining them in a grave with haste.

Ta add insult to injury I began to think of how I thought no woman would want the overused catamite for her Mann. Now that I couldn't forget that I had been used in such an unnatural and abominable fashion, I lost all faith that any respectable Frau was in my future. How could any girl want the disgusting creature that was called the Mad Maxx to pass on his genes through children with her? Nein,

I knew I wouldn't want to touch me if I had been any female. I assumed I could accurately guess the minds of the fairer sex since I had always been treated like one of their gender.

The thought of endless nights trapped in the hairy arms of the man, enduring unthrilling and painful sex acts that made me feel like trash filled my mind to near madness. It was just something I couldn't face. The hope of a Frau was dashed forever and that was the only thing that had kept me sane through all those horrid sexual assaults. With that Noethan, Sebastian and Tadeas opening my eyes to the threat that there were far worst fates than being raped by a man, I really was coming apart at the seams.

On top of that, it had been made painfully clear to me that at any moment, with Gretta and Cora gunning for me, I could find myself helplessly chained in the Palace again. Then other fellows like these could give me more birthday surprises.

I began to wonder what exactly this Mad Lucus expected me to do when he gave me that advice to strike before anyone had the chance to hurt me? Did he expect me to kill everyone in the Haus to assure I was protected from future abominations, rapes and torturing? That was not only stupid to expect but surely impossible to do. I didn't have a weapon with amazing firing capacity nor the ability to nail all the door shut before setting the Haus into a deadly blaze.

All this shit weighed down my cracked minds as I systematically whittled away at Sebastian, Tadeas and

Noethan with my knife. I cut off just the superficial flesh or small pieces, hour after hour, to assure all would live till the sun rose.

I didn't wish to do such a brutal thing, but I had suffered the agonies of their twisted games an entire night. I had to make sure they experienced that same fate with the entire Haus being aware of my cruelty. This was a sure way of teaching as many as possible a lesson about fooling with the Mad Maxx. No one would quickly forget the sounds of those dying men's screaming anytime soon. I noticed, no resident, not ever the Queens, dared to come out. I could see many at the windows watching the show with pure terror in their expressions which seem to ask me to stop my punishment of the three.

I watched the eyes of Noethan, Sebastian and Tadeas, searching the faces of the audience, seeking with desperation for a champion among them. It caused me a bit of bitter thrill when I saw the light of hope for a savior leave there eyes after the first three hours had passed and no one came to their rescue. Just as they never came to mine.

I asked them several times if they were enjoying the endless torment. Of course they couldn't answer me without their tongues. I didn't need to hear their answer. I knew they did what I had done: pray for the sun to rise to end the pain. I made sure that they found true empathy for all they had done to me, while assuring that they would never get the chance to do it again, to me or anyone else.

In fact, everything I did to them was a spin on something they had forced me to endure while hopelessly restrained. I made sure to parrot all their behaviors from that night. When they screamed I answered with laughing. I granted no mercy but instead encouraged extreme pain while jeering, making fun, and even pissing on them when I needed to make the water. I wish I could say this made me feel vindicated. That would be a lie. It made me feel like a pervert, because Meine Liebe what I did to them was an abomination. That old saying an eye for an eye sounds good on paper but beware my little one. The second you try to get the equal justice to the crime, you become the criminal.

I was not completely depraved despite being beyond disgusting as I killed them slow. The two things I was not willing to replicate in return service was the photographing and forced orgasms through use of the prostrate milking machine. I was simply not perverted enough for that shit. These fellows, however, didn't have such limits. These photos of my disgrace were of no small matter. I realized if I didn't find a way to destroy any evidence of that horror, I was in so much trouble, even the grave couldn't grant me peace from it.

I quietly approached my Dungeon Masters and pulled them to the side right after I had chop off the fellows fingers and toes. I ordered them to go to each man's apartment and rifle around. I told them they were to tear the apartments apart if necessary, till they found every single roll of unexposed film or any photos that may have me in them.

I gave Almut and Hubertus strict orders of death to never breath a word of whatever they may see in the photos. Once they had the items, they were to find me at Cary's haus before the morning hour of nine. I told them both that showing up without what I asked for would result in them joining the sorry three in hell by sundown.

You see, I couldn't allow the rumor of what had occurred in the dungeon to get out among the population. I knew that being the helpless victim would not save me if others knew of the atrocity I had suffered. Mad Lucus in particular would likely remove his gold collar in pure disgust. He would never tolerate the embarrassment of being with someone as deeply soiled as I now could claim. If I wanted to survive even another day, I was aware I would have no choice but to return to him. His turning me out of his protection meant Gretta would have an excuse to send me back to the Palace, this time for good.

As midnight came and went, I still had not made up my mind on the idea of simply ending my agony through suicide versus joining Mad Lucus in his bid to see the Haus toppled. All I was sure of was that no matter what I decided, life or death for the Mad Maxx, I didn't want my legacy to include being remembered as the unwilling victim of such a revolting perversion.

In fact, Cary informed me that the abomination I suffered was so reviled by the residents, anyone caught engaging in it willingly, remember willingly is the key here, would be put to death immediately. No one was except from this most severe of all punishments regardless of their status as Dominant (even the Voters, Elders and Thrones) or submissive.

Realizing that Sebastian, Tadeas and Noethan couldn't have done what they had without Gretta's blessing caused the hate for the woman to rise to even higher heights than before. I was unsure if maybe it had not even been her own suggestion made in her desperation to see me broken once and for all.

Regardless of the Silk Queen's place as the mastermind or merely the eager approver of the birthday nightmare surprise, I knew the next person I would be visiting with my wrath, before jumping off any banisters, was that disgusting bitch. I desired to see her tortured for her part in the mess. There was no way I was leaving to join Mad Lucus in the fourth-floor apartment or to find my grave, whichever I decided, before I had my vengeance on her too.

I knew I had to hit the ground running the second I had finished off the three offenders. I only had till six the next evening to tie up all my loose ends or find my grave. Then I knew Mad Lucus would come looking to collect what he believed was his, alive or dead. Thank goodness I had the loyal aid of my men Almut and Hubertus.

There help in collecting all the shameful evidence of that crime against me was essential. It was perhaps the most important part of my plan in exacting revenge on the Queens for her part in that horrid birthday surprise. If the boys were successful, and I moved with swiftness against

Gretta, I thought I may even be lucky enough to have a little time to consider if I was going to kill myself or choose Mad Lucus's offer.

As the wee hours of the morning passed, I found the boy's flesh growing weary. My health was quite poor from the intense starvation and raging infections within me. It would turn out that the infection in my head was only one of the sicknesses that I had picked up in the Palace filth.

The very incident that caused me to be torturing three men in the dim light of the Guards bon fires had also left illness deep inside my tissues. Not only is what they did beyond repugnant to common decency, it is inherently dangerous. Crossing the species like they had can and does spread infection, parasites and potentially deadly viruses.

I found this out the hard way. I had been most unfortunate to have picked up a strong bacterium that dug deep into my immune system. It would take almost a month of heavy antibiotics to see me returned to baseline health because of it. It was why I was losing so much weight and taking on the hue of greyish skin that had frightened Mad Lucus.

The only thing that I can say about this extra nightmare in an already hellish situation is that the pills given to me for the head wound, thankfully worked there magic on this non-human illness too. I cannot stress how terrible things would have gone for me, if further investigation into how I acquired this particular sickness had happened. I wouldn't have been capable of hiding the truth of its origin nor denying the incident that introduced it into my blood stream to Mad Lucus or anyone that found out about it.

One last result of this obscenity was when I found out I had the sickness by accident a week or so later. It made one thing quite clear to dumbass Master Maxx. Gretta had known that I was at serious risk of death by her approving the act that caused it. This means, she had tried to do more than break my spirit by permitting this cruelty. She intended to see me dead in the most dishonorable, slow, painful way possible. That bitch.

Anyway, as I was saying, as the hours ticked away and the morning dew began to grace the yard flora and fauna, your Master Maxx began to weaken. With only an hour and a half left to sunrise, the tortured men were barely much more than the head and torsos of what used to be human beings. I had cut away their noses, ears, fingers, lips, eyelids, toes, feet, kneecaps, hands, manhood, and most of their ass cheeks too.

They barely squeaked as my blade made a fresh slice off their trunks. All three had screamed to hoarseness as they had caused me to do many times in the Palace cell. I had Cary break into Noethan's office to find smelling salts when Tadeas kept trying to escape his fate by passing out. I wasn't going to be so unkind as to let him miss out on all the fun. He and his brother monsters had made sure I found no such mercy during all their twisted sports with me, you know. Fair is only fair, ja?

By this time the yard dogs had settled down from their earlier excitement. They still gobbled up each chunk of bloody meat I threw their way, but most had found their worst hunger pains sated. The bunch of them had started behaving as the gentleman to his canine brothers. I noticed they had started taking turns seeking the meal.

It appeared to be based upon each hounds place in their pack hierarchy as to which fellow got to enjoy the next morsel thrown their way. If I had not been so damned frightened of them, I likely would have found it of interest to study that seemingly mannerly behavior they demonstrated.

The calm, well organized way the yard dogs approached the situation as time wore on was in direct reverse to that of their human counterparts, the Russian Guard. They had been rather subdued and quietly watched the torturing in the beginning. I saw them passing around a bottle or two of the vodka from the start.

As the hour grew late, they began to build bon fires so they could easy view the carnage and there relief shift arrived not long after that. Instead of Ivan and his day men going to their homes for the night, they stayed to enjoy the show.

The second shift increased their number and the number of bottles of vodka. It didn't take long for the fifty or more Russia's to become the loud, boisterous, cheering mass of spectators.

I could hear them betting with each other on everything from which yard dog would take the next bite, to where I was going to make my next cut. Many times, the group of them broke out into native songs and the chanting of, "Mad Maxx der Brutale, Master of the Haus. Long live the King."

All the hairy bastards were soaked with alcohol by this time, except their Captain, Ivan. He never took his steel colored eyes off me, nor joined in his boy's revelry one time. I could understand why he was chosen to lead these brutes in their tasks of guarding the Haus residents and keeping the hostages like me from escaping from them. He was one cool, calm customer. Nothing seemed to cause him to forget his rank or duties no matter what the temptations offered him.

I staggered a bit from the weariness that had started to overtake my flesh as I approached the near dead Sebastian for another cud. Ivan noticed this subtle sign of my growing weakness. To my utter shock he got up from his seat centered among his men and rushed forward.

He grabbed me as I tripped over my own boots catching me before I fell to the ground while holding that blood slicked knife, damn that would have been bad. "Hey there, Mad Maxx, you better look where you are going there. In the dark it is easy for a man to stumble and seem the fool, da," he said in his thick accent while winking at me in humor.

I nodded. "I thank you for the mercy of your aid, Ivan. I will remember your wise counsel in the matter. Don't let my clumsiness detour you from enjoying the theater. We still have an hour to go before the final curtain call." I chuckled and wiped the sweat from my brow.

Ivan then leaned in and whispered where no one but the two of us could hear his words, "Mad Maxx, I think you will not last another hour. You are not at your best. Allow me to finish this torturing and I will let you do the honor of stilling their hearts when you are ready to see it done."

I shook my head and whispered back, "I thank you for the offer, Ivan. I mean no offense when I say to you this is my responsibility. I cannot expect another to take such a burden."

Ivan chuckled as he shot a look at the messes that once were men on the poles. "You don't understand, my brother. This thing I offer to do is my pleasure, not a work task. I would consider it an honor if you would grant me your permission to taste their blood with my blade, your Majesty."

I narrowed my eyes at him. "Ivan, you and I have known each other since your bullet found its way into my leg years ago. In all my time in this hell hole it is your rifle that has blocked my escape from the shit that incited my fury on these men tonight. Give me one good, damned reason why I should grant any honor other than my own blade in the throat to the man that has tried to murder me how many times now?"

Ivan smiled with thrill and rubbed his dark beard with his humongous hands. "Ah, you drive the hard bargain Mad Maxx. I confess I have always secretly admired your courage and definitely enjoyed that short work you made of the pigs Olaf and Vilber. Great show by the way. I am a huge fan of your work. So, tell you what Sire, you allow me this thrill I request, and I will makes sure you can have full access to the entire Haus yard without fear of harassment from my men or me from this day forward. Do we have a deal?"

I glared at him. "Hell, nein, I let you kill the motherfuckers if you and your men turn your heads while I walk away. I swear I never come back here again."

He laughed hard when I said that. "You know better, your Majesty. I cannot do as you ask. If I allow you to escaping the yard then the local authority's put the bullet in your head for me, and that bitch Cora puts one in Ivan's head for his neglect of duty. The best I can offer is your taste of the sunlight and short acreage of freedom from the darkness in the Haus halls. Don't be the fool, Sire. Take my most generous offer and be grateful for the mercy of it. You may never have another chance to obtain my favorable deal with you again."

I sighed and dropped my eyes to the ground. "Ja, that is truth you speak. There is no reason for me to deny it is a fine agreement you put forth to me. These bastards are so far gone by now, they cannot tell the identity of the man that wields the knife. I accept your generosity with gratitude, but I must warn you to remember, I deliver the fatal blows at sunrise."

The big Russian nodded as he pulled a huge hunting knife from his heavy belt. "No worries, Sire. I am the skilled surgeon. I will make each strike count but leave the winning blow for the Master of the Haus. Stand back your Majesty. I don't want you injured by accident while I get to my dark business, ja?" I nodded and backed away to take a place next to Cary that who was sitting on the ground to the left of the boisterous Russian guardsmen.

Cary watched me approach, then sit down next to him with a look of hurt in his expression. "Christian Axel, I been thinking about the harsh words you said to me earlier tonight. I uhm, well, there was a bit too much truth to them. I was so caught up in becoming your lover I didn't hear your when you said nein to me. I guess I thought, well to be honest, I don't know what the fuck I was thinking." He looked at the ground appearing shamed.

I groaned and rubbed my temples to try to stave off a coming headache. "I can answer that for you. You were thinking only of Cary. Like so many before you, you believed that somehow forcing me to endure your intimacy would cause me to change my mind about my innate gender sexual preference. Well, too bad for you that you cannot make the gay man straight or the straight man gay, brother."

Cary nodded as tears began to well up in his eyes. "So, that is the way of things then. I am Dark Bonded with a man that hates me and the Shadow King that many want to assassinate. Boy, did I fuck up. I suppose I am cursed to never know the romantic love I dreamed of since long as I can remember."

I chuckled bitterly. "That makes two of us, brother. I already told you I would have giving anything to Dark Bond with that beauty you call Frau and lock you out of your own bedroom. That will never happen, of that you can be sure. Nein, Cary, you and me don't shared this silly vision you have of the romantic lover. However, if you show me kindness, loyalty, honesty, and be gentle in your handling of my flesh, be assured you have the loyal, fair sex partner that will not deny you your thrills to full satisfaction."

Cary's head nearly snapped off he turned it at me with such suddenness. "What? After you tell me you don't desire to be in my loving arms, you add that you'll do it anyway as a return in service. Do you really expect me to overlook the coldness of this arrangement? How am to find thrill in knowing you allow me to fuck you because it is your duty? It will be brutal for me knowing you hate every second of my touching. That is not how it is supposed to be in the sex act. That is, well, unnatural."

I scoffed at him with a coldness in my expression. "Exactly Cary. That is what I have endured all my life, and now so shall you. Let me see if I can recall how this discussion goes, it has been awhile since I had one like it. Oh ja. I say to you that if you find disgust in the way our intimacy is nothing more than a release for you and a burden for me there is an answer. You will nod and appear eager to hear how we can resolve this sadness. I then tell you to keep your cock in your pants and out of me. Instead, we can be the greatest of friends and closer than brothers with honest love between us. You will scoff at my suggestion and tell me that if I really loved you then I would let you fuck me and yell hell ja Cary, I love you so much now that you showed me how good sex is with a man. Well, tell me. Am I close or did I miss a step in this bullshit manipulation you are about to try on me? Look brother, I stopped buying into the lies that sex is equal to love long ago. You throw an emotional fit over this shit you were told on the front end, but I have been down this road many times with others before you. You will demand to couple with me, regardless of how I feel about you or what you do to me. I won't give you any quarrel, so stop trying to start a fight you already have won. You can drop the dog and pony show meant to guilt me over not being in love with you. I am not going to fall for it."

Cary's eyes blazed with anger. "Ah, you would know all about that kind of show, wouldn't you Christian Axel? I mean I knew you have the impressive list of lovers long before I got my turn with you but damn, this latest you have added to those skill is impressive. I wonder, do I need to invest in the condoms for safety's sake or have you gotten all the wild sex business out of your system?"

I glared at him with sudden hatred over his purposefully cruel words. "Ja maybe you should get the boxes of prophylactics and perhaps a board to tie to your ass, so you don't fall in when you fuck me. I wouldn't want my lover soiled by accidently touching my tainted overused flesh. Glad you are finally seeing this relationship you insisted on having with me. I play the disgusting whore and you are the snotty client that thinks himself better than the worthless creature he lowers himself to fuck."

Cary nodded with an angered frown. "You are a such a sonofabitch, Christian. I will have you know if anyone knew what you told me happened down in the Palace they would never want to touch you again. I tell you I love you so much even that knowledge doesn't change my desire for you, and you throw it into my face. You dare to say I am no better than these criminals that have misused you in every way possible. Well, you can go fuck yourself Christian. Cary doesn't have to put up with insults like that from you or any other man. You don't want me touching you? Good, because you have nothing to worry about. After what I know about you I find so fucking disgusting I couldn't get it up if I drank as much vodka as the Guard is drinking tonight," he yelled into my face as the tears broke loose and flowed down his cheeks.

I sat there calm as the dark skies above us "That is the best news I have heard in years. If only you actually meant it, then I could die a happy man."

Cary spit into my face and took to his feet in full fury. "I do mean it you revolting cocksucker. Go ahead Christian. Order the Guard to restrain me too, so you can cut me up and feed me to your real lovers."

Now that was uncalled for. “I think you better go home Cary before you say something I will make you regret. I see you in a few hours. You can count on the fact that I am fully prepared to pay you back for the kindnesses you showed me in my darkest hours. You may wish to ask Roselina to be absent from your home so we can have the mercy of a little privacy.” I wiped his spittle from the boy’s face with my coat sleeve as I said that with a cold tone.

Cary shook his head wildly in disbelief. “Are you deaf, Christian? I said I don’t want you anymore. You are no longer welcome in my home or in my bed.”

I nodded as I chuckled. “Sure, I heard you Cary. I heard Ryker too. and Peter, Jonas, Leo, Roland, Matz. Oh, I heard it too many times to list. We don’t have all day to argue over nothing, you know. You all say the same thing when you don’t think you are getting your way. However, this time you waste your breath. You are going to have your way, fool, just like all the rest of them. I will be there at your house just after sunrise. I predict you open the door and then demand I get into your bed. I suggest you go get a shower while you still have the time. I don’t feel like offering the bath service this morning and I cannot stand giving the oral services to a smelly lover. See you soon, brother.” I watched as Cary growled till he turned red in the face, then turned and stormed off headed back to his Haus just like I told him to do.

I stood up slowly feeling a bit faint and walked back over to see how Ivan was progressing at his game. I stopped to watch his work just beyond the reach of the patiently awaiting yard dogs. Ivan certainly did seem to be enjoying himself to the hilt. His men had become the unruly mob of yelling, jeering creatines howling for blood.

Ivan was standing by what was left of Noethan. "What is that boys? I cannot hear you. Which shall it be? His nipples? How about a nice hunk of his bicep? Nein? Perhaps you desire I cut off his chin?" His men shouted out the names of the spots they desired to see removed over each other till the words they said were nearly impossible to understand.

The Captain of the Guard put his hand up to his ear signaling he desired to hear them better. "This is never going to do fellas. If you cannot agree among you of your honest wishes, then I will have no choice but to pass this one over and moved to the next without a single stroke of my knife."

I crossed my arms and shouted out. "Remove his eyes, brother Ivan. The man refused to use them in this life. I don't think he should be permitted to keep them for the next."

Ivan put up his hand demanding silence from his wayward men. "Ah, now there is a suggestion I can sink my knife into. You boys pay attention to the Master of the Haus, Mad Maxx. This man could teach all you a thing or two about brutality most sublime." Ivan smiled at me with glee then turned around with gracefulness and dug both Noethan's peepers from his skull.

The nearly dead doctor wailed with unearthly sounds from his tongueless mouth. The Russians applauded vigorously while Ivan did a sweeping dance step as he tossed the freed eyeballs to the awaiting animals. I confess the gruesome scene of the bloody head and torsos twisting, jerking and contorting against their restrains to the poles was something right out of a horror show. It felt as if I had fallen into an Edward Munch surreal scream painting.

I found myself break into a sweat of terror as I repeated under my breath, “This isn’t real. This cannot be happing. Please make this stop.” But this was not a hallucination any more than what the men that suffered this fate had done to deserve it.

I cannot express how grateful I was to notice a sudden lessening in the poor lighting. With great thrill I spun my head all around watching as all around me the shadows fled back to their daytime hiding places. Sunrise had come at last.

I maintained my distance and silence for another few moments as the rays of the daylight peeked over the distant horizon. Ivan removed both of Sebastian’s nipples and threw them to the dogs with a loud yip of victory. It was time to end this game. I finally felt pretty confident that the three brutes had earned the right to their deaths.

Without a word I stepped forward blocking Ivan from approaching the gurgling Tadeas. He stopped his approached and his smile melted to a frown. I pointed off into the distance at the sign that the time had come for everyone to sober up and get back to work. The all-night party was over.

Ivan nodded as he pulled a handkerchief from his jacket to whip his blade clean. “Do you need to borrow my knife Sire, or you have a better plan in mind?”

I shook my head. “May I ask Petrov to loan me his machete for a moment? I swore the heads of these men to a friend. It will take a strong, sharp blade to separate the empty heads from their useless hearts.”

Petrov staggered forward and happily gave the large knife meant for the hacking to me without asking for favor or promise. I bowed my head as I took it from the helpful guardsmen. Ivan backed away with his wicked smile returning across his hairy face.

I approached Noethan and began chopping at his neck. It took a couple of blows before the man finally stopped wriggling in a death dance. His head rolled off the shoulders, hitting the wet ground with a sick sounding thud. I didn’t hesitate as I moved on and did the same to Sebastian, and then finally the scumbag Tadeas. I had managed to behead all three in less than six minutes.

The Russians called out a command to the yard dogs in their native tongue. I watched with nervousness as each canine trotted off into the distance, headed back to their hound cottage to sleep off their feast. The second the last dog was out of sight, I felt immediate relief. I had not realized the extent of how frightened of those animals I had truly become.

Ivan ordered his men to put out the fires and clean up their messes in the yard. I walked over to each severed head, picking it up by the hair. I wore no expression on my face but inside I was glad that nightmare was over for good. These men would never hurt anyone again. That was worth at least a bit of solace even if it couldn't purge what has already been done by them.

A couple of the Guardsmen nearly sent me on a sprint of fear as they approached from behind me carrying shovels. I let out a yelp and backed away holding on with dear life the heads I had collected from the corpses.

Ivan came towards the retreating boy with a humored expression on his face "Whoa there, your Majesty. What are you doing picking up those nasty bits of these cadavers? Let my men bury this trash. I am sure you have far better things to attend. Like maybe a nap or perhaps seeing to that payment you promise me and my men for our aid in this serious matter?"

I shook my head and frowned. "I have no issue with your brutes burying the remains of these wicked men but their heads I already told you I swore to grant to another. As for your payment, I am a man of my word. I will return to you before the hour of six tonight ready to see our deal is paid in full." I dropped my gaze hoping he wouldn't see the pain that I held in over this forced situation.

He chuckled. "I have heard it said you are not one to shirk your duties when there is an agreement at stake. I confess I have fantasized what it would be like to have you at my side as I engaged in the forbidden things. This we did together tonight was better than I could have ever imagined it to be. I need not say how excited I am to see this thrill deepened by your arrival with the payment for it. I think that ecstasy will rival the revelry of this night. Don't forget, you must see to all the men's needs not just Ivan's."

I nodded with an irritated scoff. "I recall the details of our haggling, Ivan. Though I still don't think it fair I have to attend all your men when only a handful or less did anything of worth rather than get drunk. How many of you motherfuckers are there anyway?"

Ivan snorted with humor. "Fifty=four. Shit, what are you bitching about Mad Maxx? For you this should be a piece of cake. Why a fellow with that experienced tongue of yours should be capable of doing this without even breaking a sweat."

I glared at him. "Experience won't matter in this case. There is only so much one man can do you know. You expect me to take care of you and fifty-three more brutes without a single wink of rest tonight. I will be the walking dead before this the afternoon sees this sunset."

Ivan startled me with a friendly slap on my back. "I know you too well, Mad Maxx. You will manage to get the impossible done despite your fatigue. I have total faith in your legendary skills."

I snorted and took off for the Haus as I shouted back at the laughing Captain of the Guard, "Well, just don't shoot me when I come back to see all you later. Do not forget to bring plenty of lube. I don't believe I can recall a time when I was in for a rougher fucking and mind you I had five Elder Masters at one time." My grumbling about his clearly unfair deal with me caused Ivan and all the Guardsmen to break into loud laughter as I hauled ass to the back door entry of the Haus.

When I opened it, people took off like scared jackrabbits in every direction. The black and silvers and a few of the Dominants, ja you read that right, fell into a kneel. They all trembled on their knees while the rest of the Dominants backed to the wall dropping their heads into a reverent bow. I stopped briefly in the hallway staring in amazement at this odd behavior.

I was going to ask one of the kneeling Dominants from the fourth floor about it until I realized what was likely causing them to act that way. Not every day you see the Master of the Haus strolling into the backdoor carrying three severed heads by the hair (two of them high ranking Dominants and the Doctor, an outside staffer).

I supposed the sight of it made everyone a bit nervous they maybe were next on my list. It was something they should be concerned about too. I certainly had a very long list of people I desired to see feeding a tree. I decided to let it go. I had a lot to do still and my time to get it all done was running out fast.

I hauled ass down the dungeon stairwell, nearly knocking several black and silver collars down them. It wasn't because of me rushing nor did my touching them to topple any either. The main reason many nearly fell was because of their insisting to kneel to their King even when the conditions made such honoring behaviors dangerous.

When I arrived at the bottom of the stairs, I went right to the dungeon gate under them that led to the Palace. I took the keys I had snatched from the late Sebastian's coat. As I unlocked it and walked inside, I wondered why no one, not even the powerful Gretta, had come outside to put a halt to the punishment. I had simply assumed the second I began to cut up her men, she would come out to demand my arrest and interment back into this Palace hell.

The smell of that musty place immediately set my hair on edge. I almost took off back the way I came. I didn't know if I had the guts to face that nightmarish cell even if I did have the key to it. The sound of Florian singing to himself down the long Palace hallway gave me enough courage to do what I had promised him I would do. I never break a promise. I wasn't going to start with the only friend I believed I really had, the Priceless Florian.

Florian let out a loud gasp of thrill as he saw me approaching the silver gate. "It's you. I knew you wouldn't leave me to suffer alone as I have done for almost two hundred years. Come in brother. I have so much gossip to catch you up on."

I chuckled as I used the keys to get inside with him. "Well, you can be assured my brother you are alone no more. I bring you three buddies to keep you company till the end of time."

He squealed in joy when his eyes caught the sight of the three heads in my hands. "Oh, my Gott. You shouldn't have, Mad Maxx. They are exactly who I asked for. Brother, you are the best. Wait, I thought you swore to give me two doctors, the Dungeon Masters and a bit extra. Where are the rest of them? Did you leave them in the Ritual room, and this is the prank?"

I rolled my eyes. "Christ man, give me a minute to collect you the full set brother. You'd think with all these years attending the court, you would have a little patience at having to endure a few more days without everything you want. I promise I will get you all the company you can stand brother." I tossed the heads like bowling balls across the cell floor into the Mortar Throne.

Florian smiled with excitement. "Oh, ja? So where are you headed right now? Do you have a moment to stay and chat with me like we did in the old days when we were the roommates?"

I shook my head as I turned with a wicked chuckle. "Not this time old pal. I am off to tie up a loose end through repayment, then I am going to see the Queen bitch herself."

Florian gasped appearing horrified. "The Queen? You must be out of your mind, brother. The only thing bothering with that woman is going to be that she will see your head join these other fools at my feet. You escaped this place. Take my wise advice and go back to your apartment and leave the Silk spider woman to her own business."

I laughed harder. “You worry far too much Florian. For your information I have a sure plan that even that slippery spider kind not overcome with her power and charms. If she tried, maybe I call my new friends the Guard to come shoot her.”

Florian shook his head still appearing unsure of my airtight plan. “Oh, so now you claim to have the Guard doing your bidding, do you? The Guard don’t work for free, idiot. How much are day costing you for this aid you think they would give you to answer you calling them.”

I shrugged. “Well, I go to see Cary next. He came to help me when no one else wood. I owe him my affection. Then I am seeking Birgit and Viviana for my Felicity and to reward them for their kindness. After that I plan to march up to Gretta’s fifth floor apartment and give her a piece of my mind while taking a chunk out of hers. The Guard is last on my list that needs return of services from the Mad Maxx today.”

Florian giggled. “What you returning to them in service there, Master? I happen to know you only have one thing of value to trade with any of these nothings.”

I shot a look of hate at him for daring to say that to me. “Fuck you, Florian. I am not that perverted to allow a hairy Russa to coerce me into their mount. Give me a little more credit than that will you.”

He scoffed with disbelief. “Is that so? Well after what I saw down here, I beg to differ that you are not the perverted. That is the single thing about you that is true.

However, I will bite. If you didn't use your assets to seduce Ivan on your side, where did you get enough money to pay off that brute?"

I cut my eyes to him with demons rising within. "You can call me the Mad Robin Hood Florian. I intend to rob the rich to pay the poor. I promised Ivan and his all his men a ten percent pay raise if they were willing to back my metal crown."

Florian nearly fell off the throne when he heard that. "What? How the fuck are you intending to do that insanity brother? This plan I got to hear."

I kicked the metal gate with my boot as I sneered at him. "I assure you brother, when I am done ripping apart Gretta and that dog Cora of hers, they will be more than happy to see that Ivan and his boys get their funding. I warned the Silk Queen right after she tricked me into her bed before I busted my collar that I would demonstrate for her why they level me Priceless. Well brother, I am ready to give her the full show. I am going to ask you nicely. Do not lecture me about keeping my murderous rage and thirst for revenge out of the realm of the sovereign leaders of the Haus. I have made up my mind that these are the last few hours of Mad Maxx. After I finish paying up what is owed to Cary, Birgit, Viviana, Cora, Gretta, Ivan and his Guardsmen, I am leaping from the fourth-floor banister. I simply cannot live as I have always afraid of the next raping or beating and I cannot stomach the monster I must become to avoid that fate. I am never getting out that front door, Florian. It was all a damned lie. They were never going to let me go free no matter what I do. No frau, no children, not for me, the cursed Mad Maxx der Brutale. I would rather be dead then be one of them. I thank you for the mercy you show me by being my devoted friend. It has been a pleasure, brother. Enjoy the throne and your new men. Goodbye forever. I walked with briskness headed back the way I had come while feeling genuinely happy for the first time in my life. I was going to be free at last. All I had to do is finish the game I never wanted to play in the first place. I had a little less than twelve hours before my window of opportunity closed. There was no time to waste and so many loose ends left to tie up before turning myself over to the reaper.

Chapter 45: Darkness Rises

I trotted up the dungeon stairwell with a bit of a spring in my step. It should have seemed strange to me that the joy I felt was because I had decided to commit suicide. The thought that maybe I should speak to someone about my self-destructive wishes never occurred to me.

All I knew was now that I had made the choice to die, I felt light as the feather. The heavy burdens of shame and guilt that had been piling up on my shoulders since ignorantly accepting Peter's collar were finally gone. I cannot tell you how wonderful I believed it to be that after a few more hours, no one could hurt me anymore. No more beatings, thuddings, cuttings, cruel words, brutal raping and no more putting up with special services with the man for good.

I began to hum a little tune to myself as if I didn't have a care in the world. I ignored the Haus residents that screamed, fell to their knees and trembled the second I crossed their path. I realized I was covered in blood and all of them had heard the wailing of my torture victims for the last eight hours. I knew that is why all them were freaking out like they were. I had always hated the idea of everyone thinking poorly of me. This time, it didn't bother me even the least bit.

Truth is nothing mattered to me anymore. I wasn't even afraid that Gretta or Cora would send brutes to see me arrested for killing her men. I had made up my mind I was never going back to that fucking Palace cell, nor was I willing to be Mad Lucus's bitch for a lifetime either. Nein. Good luck trying to get the corpse to fulfil their perverted pleasures. Mad Maxx was finished with that shit.

I won't lie. It really felt great to be great to be through with that stupid struggling to survive. I'd only had terror and pain to look forward to day after day and year after year. I traveled in a slow stride headed for the Haus back door. I wondered to myself why it had taken me so fucking long to give up the war I could never win. It seemed to me if I had known how magnificent giving up could feel I sure as shit would have done it much sooner.

I approached the back exit of the Haus with speed. The relief door guard for Cary stood there staring at me with a fearful expression. The moment I was close enough to hear him I saw him back up onto the door and put his hand on his weapon with nervousness.

I halted my march and glared at him full of demons. "Move motherfucker or I will move you."

The man shook his head as he sputtered out in a terrified tone, "I cannot let you pass, Mad Maxx. Please forgive me but it is by order of the Voter Peter I block you from leaving this Haus."

I nodded as I growled back. "Voter Peter you say. And exactly who is that cocksucker to forbid the Master of the Haus anything? I think you forget the identity of the one that says move aside. I repeat this one more time and I will make you sorry for your insolence, you little nothing."

The door guard shot a worried look at the emblem of the Metal crown and Lucus's crest on my coat. "Uh, I apologize your Majesty. I am the fool. I wasn't thinking. Allow me to get this open for you. I beg your forgiveness for the oversight." He turned and held it open backing as far as possible from me in case I decided to retaliate for his daring to question me.

I said nothing as I stormed out never bothering to look back. I made a beeline right for Cary's shoddy cottage. I watched as all the black collars that were strolling around doing their Haus chores run as fast as they could in the other direction. The second they saw me I must have been a sight. Thin, haggard, pale, bloody, and full of hate. No one appeared willing to mess with me that morning. Good thing too. I was in no mood to be fooled with. Hahaha.

I knocked on the door and Roselina answered with quickness. "Ah, your Majesty. I am thrilled you have come to visit with your unworthy servants this fine day. Can I get you some coffee perhaps," said the lovely woman as she bowed with grace motioning me to come inside.

I went in nodding. "Ja. Coffee and breakfast would be great, Roselina. I think you should take the baby and go to the Great Hall to enjoy both. Tell the attendants the Master of the Haus grants you permission to sit at a fine table among your betters. I am sending you for this reward for being one of the only bright spots in my shitty life. If they give you any trouble let them know I only fed half the yard dogs. I am more than happy to see all the animals filled to stupid."

Roselina's eyes went with in surprise und thrill. "Eat at the Great Hall with the Dominants? Me? Oh, my Gott. I will go get the baby and Cary right this moment. Don't you desire to join us, Sire? You are so thin. My Lord, please you could certainly use a healthy meal or five."

I stared at her pretty face with lust rising in the boy's heart. Okay, maybe the feeling was a bit lower but let's keep it clean, ja? "You are most kind to think of me, my lady, but I will get something later. For now, I say to take the baby, but leave Cary. I have things to discuss with my Dark Bonded. He will join you soon. You go get started and wait for him."

Roselina nodded as she jump as if startled. "Oh, oh, I understand I apologize for not, uhm, I go get the baby right now. Thank you for the generosity, Master. I am deeply grateful for the mercy of it." She blushed, then rushed off to retrieve her child nearly tripping over her feet as she ran.

I chuckled under my breath that the girl acted with such embarrassment over this expected situation. She was aware that Cary demanded the special services in our bond. I guess she had not considered that fucking under the back stairwell was not the safest place to pay Cary for his services to me. If I was to see to his demands, I needed somewhere the prying eyes couldn't tell the wagging tongues that Cary was in violation of the law, ja?

Roselina came back out of the back room of that hovel almost as fast as she left for it. In her hands she carried their little girl and on her face a guarded smile. I nodded at her trying to appear friendly, but I could see that something in her expression indicated there was about to be trouble. I was not that surprised. Cary and I had been in a bit of a disagreement earlier. I realized the little bitch obviously was still pouting. Told you, he is a pussy.

I watched Roselina leave the Haus and stood there wondering if I should stand there or go kick Cary's ass for wasting time I didn't have. It was at that moment that a sullen Cary came out of the back room and stormed to the kitchen table. He pulled out a chair and threw himself down into it crossing his arms as he got comfy. The whole time he never took his angry eyes off me.

After a few moments of silence passed between us I finally scoffed. "You know I am getting tired of this game you play Cary. I come here in good faith to see your lust satisfied as we agreed, and you play the martyr still. Either make your move to fuck me or let me get on with my pressing business. Damn you, make up your fucking mind. I don't have all day to coddle your hurt feelings."

Cary snorted. "You come here and act the cold whore. Then expect me to want to fuck you. Holy hell you are crazy as they say you are. I am not turned on by your frozen offer, that I can assure you."

I shook my head in disbelief then looked at him with seriousness. "Oh, you aren't? Well forgive me, lover. I didn't realize myself. I forgot to grab my sexy outfit and high heels this morning. It is no excuse, but I was a bit distracted by all the screams of the dying and all. Tell you what stud. You tell me what you need to find your interest and old Maxx here will do it. What's it going to be? A bit of a strip tease? Perverted suggestions? Letting you rub on me? Name your poison, Cary. I am all yours."

Cary glared at me with venom pouring out of his expression. "I think maybe it is not you that should be taking the steps to turn on his lover. Perhaps it is me that should be trying to do the things that turn you on. Now let me see. What would the whore Mad Maxx find of thrill? Gosh you are so fucking experienced I am sure there is nothing I can do to bring you to a place of ecstasy. Oh wait. I know. Bark, bark, bark, bark. There you go lover. That do it for you? Go ahead and get into that bitch dog position. I can growl too if that would work better for you…" He didn't get the chance to finish that sentence.

I rushed over and punched him in the face so hard he fell from the chair to the floor. "You sonofabitch. I've had enough of your bullshit. First you want to fuck me when I say nein. Then you don't when I say ja. I understand you are the fickle bastard that sees me as the whore. That's fine with me but I will be Gott damned if I am going to stand here and tolerate your insults for offering with honesty to meet the conditions of our agreement, motherfucker. You knew what I was when you bonded with me, asshole."

Cary grabbed his jaw and slowly got back to his feet. "Nein, I thought you were the overused victim, but I think you are actually a fucking willing perverted freak." He pushed me in the chest nearly knocking me over followed quickly by a right hook to the side of my face.

I shook off the blow and ran at him. I plowed into his chest sending both of us into the wall. Cary grabbed me around the throat while I pounded my fists into his stomach with vigor. I hit him with solidness into his diaphragm breaking his choke hold. He fell to his knees, and I kicked him in the face sending him sprawling onto the floor.

I stood there gasping for air. He was squeezing the air out of me, you know. "Well, I may be the perverted freak, but you are the moody bitch that cannot decide what the fuck he wants. You don't want to fuck me anymore that is great news for me. I am happy to leave you the wanton man without release at my expense, Cary. One less nightmare I have to endure of that you can be sure." I started to head for the door, but Cary reached out with suddenness grabbing my ankle.

I tripped and fell onto the floor as he got on all fours and leapt on me. "You call sleeping with me a nightmare? Oh, well I can understand that you nasty motherfucker. I am the wrong species for you to find sexy. What's wrong, not enough fur for you, ja?" He grabbed the back of my hair and pounded my forehead into the ground nearly knocking me the fuck out.

I rolled away limply gasping and failing as he got to his feet. "Cary, stop it, I mean it. This shit you say is neither fair nor correct and you know it. Why are you doing this? I don't understand." I panted out as I tried to get up but found the world spinning too fast to gain a footing.

Cary staggered toward me with an expression of fury on his face. “I thought you said you been through this before with others before me, Mad Maxx. You think you know everything don’t you? I have news for you brother, just because you are not picky about who, what or how many you fuck doesn’t mean you know shit about the emotions that go with it. I tell you I love you and you treat me like a Goddamned fiend for it. You say you don’t love me back and never will. I cannot undo this bond. Everyone in this Haus knows I am the Shadow King. I am stuck with whatever you deign to grant me. Well fuck you, Maxx. I am not going to let you treat me less than the yard go. You claim that shit was against your will but after what I saw last night, seems to Cary you have more concern for the canines than for me. I noticed you gave them what they really want but tell me I have to be satisfied with less. I don’t fucking think so.” He jumped on me grabbing my throat once again.

I grabbed his wrists as I sputtered, “Please be merciful lover. Make this quick. Snap my neck and send me to my peace. I beg of you. Kill me.”

Cary’s eyes went wide as the fury left them and sudden shock se in. “What? Christian, you don’t mean that. Fight me you bastard. I will release you but not before I whip your ass for breaking my heart and crushing my dreams of our love.”

I groaned with the increasing headache pains. “I do mean it, Cary. End my suffering. If you love me for true you would do it. If that is not good enough for you then do it because your King commands it. I don't want to live like this. Nein, I cannot live like this anymore. I beg of you to show me the mercy no one else ever has."

Cary's hold weakened allowing for me to breath, but he didn't get off me. He is a heavy bastard. "Oh, my Gott. What have I done? Christian, baby, I didn't mean any of that mean shit I said. I was hurt and wanted to hurt you back. I know what happened was not your fault. You are not a perverted freak, nor the overused whore. Please hear me love. I am the sonofabitch to injure one already in such agony. Can you ever forgive me?" He began to sob like a big kid.

I nodded in his grip. "Sure can. All you need do is squeeze a little longer. You bring me peace and I swear I forgive you anything you want to call or accuse me of."

Cary shook his head wildly. "Nein, I am not going to kill you, baby. I love you, Gott dammit. Hear what I am saying to you. You are my world. I cannot bear to be without you for the rest of my days." With that he let go of my throat and grabbed the sides of my head.

I gasped for air as he leaned down and began to kiss me with eagerness. He pinned me with his weight and held my head still for his tongue bathing with his hands. I tried to push him off, but he held on tighter and increased his frenzy of adoration.

I let out a groan of discontent and closed my eyes the second I felt his erection pushing into my stomach through his clothing. It had become clear I was going to be proven right about my earlier prediction. The man was demonstrating obvious behaviors that I had managed to do the thing needed to gain interest in his couple with me, show vulnerability. Who knew that would be his aphrodisiac? Well, shit, I am the unlucky bastard, ja?

I stopped fighting his sloppy forced kissing. Despite my urge to try to escaping him, I held still as he pawed and fumbled trying to rip open my shirt. Eventually he managed to get his hands where he wanted them and soon after he went for my breeches. I said nothing but reached down to aid him in his attempts to gain access to what I swore to grant without quarrel to him.

I winced and held my breath when I saw him spit into his hand. I looked about the room wildly hoping to spot a bottle of lube or anything that would make this a bit less rough. Like most everything in my life to that point, not even fucking butter was laying out in view. I gripped the sides of his upper arms to brace as he lifted my waist up to greet his mount from the lover's position.

I let out a wail as he moaned in thrill the second he entered me. I held on to his arms for dear life as the wanton Cary began a strong, rapid thrusting. He acted as if he hadn't had intercourse in years. I did my best to be compliant, but I admit I did yell out several time and once even exclaimed that he needed to be less rough. He didn't listen. The man was deeper in his thrill pleasure world than in me.

I did as I always did back then. I endured this uncomfortable sex act with feigned lack of disgust that I actually felt about it. When the pain got too much to bear without losing my mind. I told him to try changing the position. That didn't help a bit.

A couple of times he did stop his couple to pull me into heavy kissing. I didn't bitch because it gave me a moment of rest from the worst of the pain. I used that time to try to recover my resolve. The rest of the time I continually wailed hoping the sound would slow him down. It didn't, since like everyone else he thought the noise meant I was enjoying what he was doing. He's an idiot.

That morning nothing I did would alleviate the ache of this unnatural act. I really needed a few days off to heal and recover from the horror of the last many weeks of sexual torturing. Too bad for the Mad Maxx. Days off from the job as the human pin cushion were a luxury I didn't get, nor do I get often now whenever I return to the Haus. Oh well, sucks to be me or you. *Master Maxx sighed and kissed the top of my head.*

I had hoped Cary would find his apex with rapidness. What I had forgotten is the man had a wife unlike my other lovers, also known as rapists. Not sure on Cary. Roselina didn't neglect her Mann's needs. That was indeed an unlucky break for me. I ended up having to suffer through a long, drawn out sexual session with my Dark Bonded at the worst time possible in my young life.

With each passing moment of being held tightly in the sweating, panting, moaning arms of my Dark Bonded, I felt more disheartened than I even knew possible. I was beginning to think I didn't have the strength to stand up to the Queens, nor did I want to seek out Birgit and Viviana.

I thought maybe Felicity was safer left to these kindly women's care. Why the hell would she want to be with the revolting Mad Maxx anyway? I wondered if maybe my hands were so soiled with vulgarity I would ruin her fur if I dared to touch her. Nein, my beautiful little lamb deserved better than what this revolting man could grant her. Or that's what I decided that morning anyway.

It took all the strength I had left not to demonstrate extra relief when Cary finally reached his fucking orgasm. I was unhappy that I would not be seeking my grave free of the trappings of this unnatural intercourse. Yet at least the seed that would disgrace my remains would be that of one I didn't despise. Cary was the rude bastard to say the nasty things he had to me, but he wasn't truly a cruel man. Just a misguided one.

Cary let out his yell at apex and then dropped down on top of me. I winced and squirmed under his spent mount trying to escape the barrage of grateful kisses he heaped on the boy's mouth. He ignored my honest protests and continued this cuddling with a glazed look of satisfaction in his expression. When his annoying behavior of adoration didn't cease after several moments I lost my temper with him.

I pushed on him with all my might trying to roll him from his finished union with me. “Get off, you heavy bastard. You got your service, now let me up from this dirty floor. Christ, I am not your fucking Frau, Cary. I am the mad. I don’t need your snuggles to assure me you’re still interested in me despite your lust being sated. I have shit to do, Gott dammit. You are wasting my time.”

Cary gasped as he tried to lean in and kiss again. I turned my head to block his attempts to quiet my lips with his own. “Christian baby, you have not found your release yet. Allow me to take care of that and we both will be the happy men.”

I snapped my head back and bellowed in anger as he began fondling my manhood. “Get your fucking hands off my cock, Cary. I am not interested in you like you are in me. I tell you that for the last time. You want to see me the happy man, go get that beautiful wife of yours. I let her touch me anywhere that wants to, twice. Otherwise, I think you are paid up for your services to me. Let me up this minute or I will break your fucking skull, motherfucker.”

Cary smiled at me with wickedness. “There you go speaking sexy to me again, Christian. Keep that up and I will demand a second trip to paradise. I know you are trying to be polite, but I swear I don’t mind seeing to your needs too, my heart. It would be my thrill in fact. I heard your cries of enjoyment during our love making. You say you are not into this sex with the man, but your sensual sounds during my mount says otherwise.” He quickly leaned down and force his tongue into my mouth,

I yelled into his slobbering maw and pushed on him angrily till he backed off. “You’re a Gott damned idiot, Cary. Those were not cries of passion coming out of my mouth, you brute. I was yelling like that because you were hurting me. Damn, do I feel sorry for Roselina if you cannot tell the fucking difference between sounds of joy and screams of pain.”

Cary frowned and got off me while offering his hand to help me from the ground, thank Gott. “Oh, holy hell. I apologize Christian. I just assumed that, well I mean you have been doing this for, uhm, a long time. I didn’t think it would still hurt as the seasoned bottom. I confess I am new to this business of same gendered sex. You need to tell me if I am causing you discomfort, lover. I cannot read your mind you know. I want it to feel good for you too.”

I took his hand and pulled to my feet seeking out my breeches that Cary had tossed across the room in his thrill. “If you want to aid me in finding pleasure, then stop fucking me, Cary. Otherwise, I will give you some advice I suggest you remember the next time you couple with the male lover. My backside is not a Gott damned hole in the ground you can just plow without care. It was not made for this penetration business no matter what you insane people think. You continue to treat your male playthings as if they possess the magical female organ designed for that nasty shit, then you will break your toys for good. Oh, and before I forget to say it, I demand a fucking bottle of lube. That spitting shit is not only nasty it doesn’t work, Gott dammit. You touch another bottom male without it and maybe they will kill you for the agony you cause from the dry fuck bullshit.” I angrily pulled on my pants glaring at the blushing Cary that was staring at the floor readjusting his own clothing.

Cary whimpered then shrugged. “I apologize for that oversight, Christian. I am used to intercourse with Roselina. The woman doesn’t need that kind of aid.”

I nodded widely. “Uhm, ja. That is because nature build her sex organ for your cock, idiot. My inability to produce simple comfort for the penetration intercourse and lack of it resulting in the production of children means something, Cary. I don’t possess the fine qualities of the vagina for a reason. Despite that we share the same parts, you insist to misuse me in your dark thrill. It makes absolutely no sense to me. You have that gorgeous female to attend you in every way, yet you are chasing after the inferior quality substitute from me? What I wouldn’t give to be you. If the tables were turned I wouldn’t have met you. Do you know why? I would be spending my life in bed with Roselina fucking her till my cock fell off. She would control me with her female wiles, and I assure you I would thank her daily for the mercy of it. The only time the idea of a male would ever cross my mind would be when I game names to the many sons she would honor me with. This sex between same genders is unnatural and sick.”

Cary was about to yell something to rebut my statement when a vigorous knocking began at the door. He shot me a frightened look. I shrugged back at him as if I had no idea who it could be demanding his attentions so early in the morning. I may have seemed the stoic as he rushed to answer but deep down I assumed it was Gretta's men come calling for the Mortar King' blood.

Me and the Shadow King let out a relieved sigh in unison when Almut and Hubertus walked in as he opened the door. I saw Almut carried a huge manila envelope in his hands and Hubertus was without baggage of any kind. I frowned and approached the duo thinking they had failed to do as I ordered. Almut and Hubertus immediately bowed their heads in reverence to me.

Almut held out that envelop in his hands. "Sire, Hubertus and I did as you demanded. All three homes and the medical clinic were searched with care. No film or photos were found. However, there was this item with your name clearly written across it in Doctor Noethan's penmanship. I found a camera with this, and it has been smashed and buried without witness."

I narrowed my eyes. "What? I told you to bring me anything that could take the photo along with any picture you maybe find. This envelop and the assurance that a machine I never get to see is how you follow my commands? Idiots. I should have you disemboweled for insolence." I backhanded the fuck out of the huge Almut. He nearly fell to his ass from the surprise and force of it too. I was the grouchy one, ja?

Almut fell to his knees trembling in terror. "Please Master Maxx forgive this unworthy servant. I take you this moment to prove the camera is no more. I swear to you no photos of you, or negatives, were spotted despite our vigorous searching." He again tried to push the envelope at me.

I snatched it from his hand this time and growled out. "I warned you both what would happen if you returned without the things I know existed in those brutes possession. Cary. You go tell Ivan I need two more poles put down. Looks like I have to do the bar-b-que in the heat of the fucking day." I sneered at the two trembling torture Masters as they shivered and shot each other looks of terror.

I opened the manila sleeve marked "Mad Maxx die Brutale" and reached inside. Within a moment I was staring at a handful of photographs. I need not tell you who or what the subject matter of those pictures were. Hubertus and Almut had done their job to perfection. All the evidence of that abominable night was now in my possession. Best of all, neither of my men, which had not been made aware of the secret, had seen a single one thanks to their being held in that envelope. The story of my revolting seventeenth birthday in the palace was corralled once and for all.

Only me, Noethen, Sebastian and Tadeas had truthful knowledge of what happened that night. I had stilled their tongues that could tell the truthful tale and held the only witness to the crime in my hand. Cary and Gretta were the loose ends left to this dishonor, but I was about to settle the score with one of them. I knew it was not in the others best interest to breath a word of the horrors he had been told of during a weak moment. Other than trying to insult me with his inside knowledge that is, that asshole.

I winced as I glanced at the shameful photos. “Ah, you may rise Almut. It appears you have shown no insolence to your Master after all. I will see you both rewarded not punished for this perfect service you have provided. Tell me only one thing before I grant you the desires you asking in repayment from your King.”

Almut let out his breath with relief and stood up shooting a big smile at his brother Hubertus. “We answer with honesty any question you ask and thank you for the mercy of your generosity.”

I nodded as I dropped the offensive pictures back into the cover of the envelope. “Did either of you look into this folder?”

Hubertus shook his head wildly. “Hell nein, Master. You told us to stay blind to the things we were seeking. Whatever is in there was not for our eyes to witness.” Almut nodded his approval of what his brother black collar claimed.

I blew out my breath and handed the envelope to the worried looking Cary. “I think you boys and me will get along famously you keep this excellent work up. Finer men I couldn’t asking for. Name your pleasure and your Master will see that it is fulfilled to your satisfaction.”

The King’s men grinned with thrill as Almut bowed his head in politeness to speak their wishes. “Me and

Hubertus have the Fraus and kinder that live like pigs in the cottages. Would it be too much to request the mercy of a week in the Haus among the empty third floor apartments for a holiday from our impoverished surroundings?"

I scoffed. "Nein, it would not be too expensive a request to give from your King for the loyal service you have given to him. In fact, I was going to ask Cary why the fuck my Shadow King and his family don't obey my orders. I told him and Roselina to pack up and see the Black Collar Mistress for assignment to the finest available for a man of his status. I will give him till the end of the day to complete my command or see himself punished severely for disobedience. I add that you two shall do the same. I grant you Almut and you Hubertus a permanent place on the third floor in the spare apartments assigned to the black collars of high favor. I think it wise to have my guardsmen as the protective neighbors of their vulnerable Shadow King and his family, ja?"

All three men nearly fainted when I said the words every black collar prays for all their lives. They had all been uniformly blessed with a life within the luxurious walls of that vile Haus. None would know the sadness of dirt floors and freezing winters for all their lives now that the Mortar King granted them a lifetime pass, which is my right as Master of the Haus.

For a moment they stared at each other in seeming disbelief, then I nearly ran face first into the wall in a wild flight when Hubertus let out a loud yippee of joy. His two black collar brothers joined him in the sounds of celebration. I stood there panting and holding my chest from that panic moment as they all fell to their knees thanking me profusely.

I listened to the silly verbalizations of their extreme gratitude for a moment then raised my hand for silence. “Enough of this. You are hurting my ears with all of you trying to stick your tongue in them I know you are grateful, and I say you earned your right to live like men, not animals the moment you had that fucking black collar forced around your necks by the Dungeon Masters. Get off your knees, idiots. I don’t have time for this useless crap. I have place to be, people to visit, and you all have plenty of packing to do. Moving is the bitch, ja?”

The men stole glances of surprise at my lack of interest in their kissing my ass, but they took to their feet. Cary chuckled as he loudly agreed moving was a pain and the Torture Masters joked about pulling back muscles having to haul their meager possessions up three flights of stairs. I allowed them to thrill for a bit, then I quickly dismissed Almut and Hubertus to attend their duties. The moment day were out the door, I looked back to Cary demanding the envelope back.

Cary frowned as he handed it to me. “Is this what I think it is, love?”

I nodded. “Ja, that nightmare is real brother. I have the evidence here in my hands to prove it.” I looked at the thing with disgust in my expression.

The Shadow King focused his eyes to the envelope. "I will start a fire in the hearth, love. You throw that shit into the flames. The perverts are dead, and with this horror burned to a crisp you can put the whole thing into the past. In time, maybe even forget it ever happened, ja?" He headed for the shoddy stone fire pit to start the preparation for the inferno.

I watched him build the fire as if in a trance. "Ja, we destroy this, and no one can ever prove such perversion occurred. However, I will never escaping the nightmares of it, brother. I keep one photo for a task I have to attend to today, but the other ones need to be sent to hell where they belong."

Cary stopped his task and shot me a look of concern. "You are keeping a photo of that humiliation? Why? That is madness Christian. You cannot risk someone finding it. I beg of you allow me to burn all of them."

I shook my head still feeling as if hypnotized. "I need it for a task I tell you, then I swear I destroy it immediately after I finish using it to my advantage. There is one other that is aware of what happened down there besides you, me and the criminals I killed. The photo I choose will be my weapon to keep their silence without having to repeat last night's blood bath."

Cary gasped. "Oh shit. Another knows of this dishonor. That is not good Christian. Okay, I don't dare to question your good judgement on this. I pray you can keep his fucking mouth shut lover. If he were to ever wag his tongue, well I say no more. Grab the one you want to keep and give me the rest. The fire is the readied gate. Let's send those pictures to hell where they belong."

I nodded and took a deep breath. "Give me a moment. I have to select the correct pose for this thing I must do shortly." I trembled as I pulled all the pictures out and looked upon my shame.

Cary's expression softened to one of pity. "Baby, let me do this for you. It is not healthy to endure seeing the horrific sights of what they did. I am worried it may set off deep grieving in you."

I snapped my gaze to him with the boy's eyes filling with fury. "That's funny. You didn't have issue with traumatizing me with your cruel words before you fucked me Cary. You mind your Gott damned business and let me handle my own dishonors. You are the last motherfucker I would allow to see the nightmare I hold in my hands. Maybe the truthful sights added to the secret I stupidly trusted you with would lend more clout to that verbal abuse you seem so fucking fond of, ja?"

Cary looked to the floor in shame. "Ah, you have me dead to rights on this one. I was a complete bastard to you. I confess to the fault and beg your forgiveness that I surely don't deserve. If you hate me forever I can honestly say that's fair. I earned it. I did say things I shouldn't have dared utter to you in my anger, Christian. You are my beloved and I had no business to be so cruel to the one I love."

I scoffed. "Even if you spoke with honest anger, you said things you should have never said to anyone Cary no matter who they are to you. How can I trust you when every time I turn around you spout the things that could see me disgraced for eternity? Don't you realize that if I am sent to the flames for such abomination you throw away your own life and that of your family too? The only way you can be assured a life without poverty or torment is if I live or die with my honor intact. I warn you. If you feel the need to insult me stick to the less harsh truths of my revolting existence. I tell you there is no limit to the trash you could honestly claim me to have done. Leave the obscene and unnatural thing you know of to silence."

Cary nodded as I took another deep breath to brace for the horror of my task at hand. I looked over the horrific images feeling I may burst into tears any moment. I could smell, taste, hear, see and feel each photo. I cannot explain how that is possible only that it is. The madness that took over that night threatened to blind me to reason once more.

Luckily, I found the photo that I had been hoping existed among the lot of them. The second I spotted it, I crammed it into my breeches pocket and stuffed the hellish rest back into the envelop.

I tossed it at Cary still sitting by his raging fire. "Burn them. Do not leave until every last one is fine grey dust, brother. I agree that you don't deserve my forgiveness for the mean things you said to me, but today is you lucky day. I grant you the thing you certainly haven't earned. I swear I leave you without malice for anything that has been said or transpired between us. In fact, Cary, I can say I was wrong when I said I will never love you. I do love you. As my brother and maybe someday when you think of me, you will find that was enough to bring you happiness. I see you in a better time and place. I thank you for your honest service and true friendship. When you finish here, go join Roselina for breakfast in the Great Hall. Send her home to pack and go see the Black Collar Mistress for your improved living assignment. Tonight take that beautiful wife into your arms and make love to her in my name. Be assured I will be there with you no longer envious of your lucky place in that gorgeous woman's heart." Cary threw the envelop into the flames as an expression of frightened concern came over his face.

I was nearly out the door when he called out, "Wait Christian. I don't like the way you are speaking. Something is off about it. I think you need to talk about the grief you surely suffer, my love. Please come by later today to visit with me about it, ja? Or come by the back door tomorrow perhaps? I am happy to listen to whatever you need to say to ease your burdens. That is what a Dark Bonded lover does."

I chuckled as I headed out of his hovel. "Is it? I told you I bonded to you for that pistol you wear around your waist Cary. I must say you have wielded it with deadly accuracy. The only problem is you aimed the wrong weapon and pulled the trigger to overkill. You didn't have to use such deadly force. The quarry was already mortally wounded brother. Oh well, my decision to Dark Bond with you is one of millions of classic examples of my rash, idiotic reasons for anything I do. The jokes are on the Mad Maxx but this time I refuse to continue playing the role of the fool. If only, never mind. Make sure you treat Roselina right, that is a directive Cary." With that I took off out the door without looking back.

Honestly, that was the last opportunity anyone, including me, had to stop the coming train wreak I call my life. I marched across the yard headed for the back entry of the Haus resolved to do two things. Put the Queens in their place and take a dive off the fourth-floor banister immediately after that.

There was nothing keeping me from seeking my peace in this way. I had given Felicity a loving home though Birgit didn't know it, I had no friends, family, or even a home to go back to. Everything that a heart holds dear was either stolen or never existed for me in the first fucking place. I didn't even have something simple like dignity or honor left thanks to the fiends around me.

I finally looked around to find dare wasn't a damned thing left to tie me to this life. That morning, I found the rudder to my ship broken the fuck off. I admit I had become completely adrift in a violent inner tempest on the ocean of hopelessness. I knew it was only a matter of time before the gale winds of self-loathing blew me into the barrier reef of failure.

What I am trying to say is that I didn't want to wait for the horrific ending that Gretta, Cora, Peter, Jonas, Mad Lucus or a score of others had likely planned for me. Nein,

I decided that despite my total lack of control of anything in the boy's short, worthless life, I was going to be the Master of how it would end.

Had Cary realized the big trouble I was in, or Leo answered his door the night before, or even Jakob, maybe things could have been different. As it was, I was left to wallow in my deep despair, and complete loss of interest in continuing the to believe that my life situation was ever going to improve.

Ja, I had come to the end of my rope. That made me vulnerable to anyone's whim willing to throw me the life preserver. Too bad that I was trapped within the Haus walls when the serious depression I was suffering became deadly. You are aware that the chances I would get the much needed psychological assistance from a good heart were nil. Well, if that is what you were thinking then let me say Meine Liebe you would be correct.

You see, my heart, I had bottomed out for the second time in my life. That means I was helpless to defend the boy's will from hijacking by anyone trained in the skills of grooming. That is when someone with dark motives spends much time training, conditioning, and preparing a person to become their possession. Often the groomer will build trust and break down all the boundaries of the one being groomed. Over time, the offender will isolate, use severe threats, and lead the brainwashed victim to believe the groomer is the only person on Earth that will love, save or care for them. This is the actual way that the children collared either silver or black are slowly turned from the normal to the life-long submissive.

Peter had begun this process on me at the age of twelve. That bastard had almost finished the job when I bottomed out the first time. He would have completed this cruelty had Ryker not interfered with his carefully laid plans. That confusion of my bonding to the wrong person undid all the efforts Peter had made to get me to the point of no return without his aid.

My father was making a second run to finish the job he started when he was tricked into tossing my collar by Jonas. Jonas intended to take for himself what Peter had started but Gretta blocked him. She did that by forcing the Vampire to share me with his Elder brothers. It is impossible to correctly groom someone unless there is only a single voice shouting the commands in the victim's ear as Price Ryker had proven only the year before. Jonas, of course failed, and I broke my metal.

When I returned from Heslach, Peter made a third attempt to hijack me by mislabeling his underhanded attempts to groom as the Dominant training. Jonas and Kilian were doing their damnest to force me to my knees as well, but as you recall I saw their bullshit too clearly to fall for it.

Mad Lucus was the latest in the constant attacks on my free will by the monsters that surrounded me. I had almost fallen under his spell but at the last minute the psychotic break came on. I was literally saved by the instability caused by the madness.

This time, I would not escape the results of the expert groomer. We get ahead of ourselves, but the identity of the bastard that would show up to save your worthless Master from himself is unfortunate. He was the one that would manage to do the unthinkable. His taking possession of my will would be almost as easy as stomping the dying insect under a big man's boots. I would like to think it was pure luck of the draw that he was there to catch me during my hardest fall, but that is not realistic. I have always believed somehow that motherfucker had managed to view all my movements that day, then laid in wait for the inevitable.

I admit it could have been far worse, but let me say, upon reflection it was still almost as bad as it could get. Yikes! I am sure you think you are aware of the way this story is about to go, but I am willing to bet you are dead wrong. I know this, because to this day, I am still unsure how exactly this secret nightmare became the truth of my long term brutality.

If I had to pick a spot in my long story to say this is where the boy Christian Axel was exiled from the mind, it would have to be here. The moment I stormed up the stairs to the fifth floor to confront Gretta I essentially sealed that gentle boy's doom. I was so full of hate, fury, and shame, I was a dead man walking. The perfect target for the hunter of the easy prey.

The stress of confronting the woman that had all the power of the Haus at her fingers caused chaos to breakout in the wheelroom. I white knuckled the wheel with the added strength of Mad Max and his bonded Max. The three of us grunted and broke into wails of agony as the walls began to shatter all around us from the panic rising within. I watched Mad Maxx throw himself over the sleeping Der Hund in a futile effort to protect our core from our coming apart at the seams.

I shot Mad Max a look of terror as I saw the electrical storm begin to build within the boy's brain. "Brother, it is no use. Abort this mission and help me guide the boy over the banister before the stress seizure or catatonic stupor sets upon him."

Mad Max shook his head as he moaned out from the lurching of the wheel in his hands. "Nein, Christian we must see to the loose ends first. Die with honor is the only way to assure the safety of Cary, Almut, Hubertus, and Felicity. We die now, then they find that fucking photo on us. We will be the disgrace, and all those involved with us will be destroyed."

I wailed as a sudden strike from the lightening made connection with my head. "Fuck them. When has anyone ever cared for us, Mad Max. Let them rot, Gott dammit. Besides neither of us is strong enough to hold off the shutdown. They will find the photo on us dead or in the fucking seizure, fool. I for one would rather be where we never awaken to face the humiliation of it."

Der Hund let out a loud scream and came off the floor tossing the weak Mad Maxx across the room. “What the fuck is going on. I take a quick nape and you idiots let the killer shattering to happen. Gott damn you both.” The Core tried to come at me and Mad Max, but a sudden quake sent him back to his ass before he reached us.

Mad Max trembled in terror at the sight of Der Hund’s fury at us. “Oh shit, we are doomed, brother. Der Hund is going to shatter us both for this. Okay, I help you send the boy to the banister. May as well send the whole lot of us to hell, ja?”

I chuckled with bitterness. “Now you talking, brother. Here, grip tighter. Max I may hate you but right now I must beg your aid in this. It will take all three of us to see this plan to the end.”

Max smiled at me with that goofy grin of his. “Why Christian, how can a man say nein when asked to do something so important with such politeness.” He came forward and did the forbidden. He took the wheel adding his strength to me and Mad Max’s grip.

Der Hund saw this abomination and let out an unearthly shriek. “Nein, the soul must never touch the wheel. Oh, my Gott. This is a horror.” He dropped to his face on the floor and covered his head with his hands as if preparing for an explosion.

At that moment there was a sonic boom in the brain. I turned my head to seek the cause of such an incredible loud noise. Mad Max and Max did the same. Just then a bolt of lightning bigger than I had ever seen in all my days made a direct hit onto the wheel.

The three of us were struck by proxy by the electrical charge. We were held helpless, dancing wildly from the shock as the force squeezed us together. The unfathomable heat liquified our borders until there was no distinction between me, Mad Max or Max's persons. The fast cooling that followed prevented any of us from escaping his ailing brother.

As the smoke from that bullseye strike cleared, the three shards formally known as Mad Max, Max and Christian had become the Mad Maxx die Brutale. We had been basically melted into a single shard that was old and angry as Christian, as well as strong and sadistic as Mad Max. To make this abomination as bad as it could get, the powerful soul Max was trapped between us.

Der Hund sat there on the floor staring at the Maxx Brutale shard in disbelief. "You fucking fools. You disobeyed my commands and allowed Max to run the wheel. The boy is lost for good, and it didn't even take the Gott damned shattering to do it. You listen to me, assholes. Finish that shit with Gretta, then you take the boy and send him right to hell where he belongs. Do it before the thing you have become gets the chance to hurt anyone. I have endured many horrors in my life, but I swear to all that is holy I will never stand to become like the perverts that disfigured me in the first place. Do you hear me? End this travesty with quickness or I will end it for you."

I glared at him through my fire filled eyes. "I do intend to end this boy but not because you say I must. You can go fuck yourself, pussy. You couldn't take the isolation, so you lay that burden on Christian. Dur Hund is the little girl that couldn't handle the backhands either. Nein, he left that task to Mad Max. Well, you lose your soul, and it took the broken to reach into the ether to retrieve it. Why don't you go find that whore Maximillian and apologize to him for leaving him to suffer in your place? Der Hund, you are not fit to be the General. We don't want you here telling us what to do when you never been in the battle. Get out and don't come back. You are no longer welcome."

Mad Maxx that had been thrown free of the melding let out a loud gasp. "Nein, you cannot do that. Der Hund is the core, fools. If he leave us we have no guidance for the real world. The boy will be lost forever in the confusion of the fantasy nothing."

Der Hund glared back at us and crossed his arms in defiance. "I am not leaving, and you cannot make me, motherfucker. You are powerful. I can see that. But even combined you are no match for my strength."

A high pitched voice called out from behind Mad Maxx from the shadows. "That may be true, but with my will added to theirs you are finished Der Hund. I agree with them. You are useless and lazy. You leave us to do the dirty work, then we have earned the right to run the boy without your interference." Maximillian stepped out into the light of the wheelroom with a wicked smile on his face. He was awake at last.

Der Hund jumped to his feet and backed away in terror never taking his eyes off Maximillian. "You will be sorry, boys. You have no experience with the brutal world. Without me, the boy will suffer and so will everyone around him. That is not what we wanted"

Maximillian giggled into his hand. "You mean that is not what you wanted, Der Hund. As for me, Christian and Mad Max, we couldn't give less of a fuck. You hold us back from doing what should be done with your empathy, visions of love and belief in the green fields. Well guess what, asshole. Look around you. The only green we are ever going to see is the mold on the Palace walls. Get the fuck out. Leave now or suffer with us for change, coward."

Der Hund let out another terrible wail just as the vortex of the nothing opened up within. He shot us all a look of pity then ran straight for it. We stood there without expression nor emotion while our Core shard leapt into its center. He spun for a moment, then with a flash was gone, lost in the world beyond our reach for what we thought would be forever.

I looked at the stoic Maximillian and the trembling Mad Maxx. "Alone at last, brothers. Der Hund gives us orders no more. We are finally free of a Master. What shall we do first?"

Maximillian smiled at me with his own fire rising in his eyes. "Finish that business with Gretta, Mad Maxx die Brutale, then end this fucking bullshit once and for all."

I nodded as I shot a smile back at him. "I can see we are going to get along just fine brother Maximillian. What about you Mad Maxx? This is no longer the monarchy you know. You get to vote. What is your pleasure?"

Mad Maxx backed away appearing quite frightened of the rest of us. "Uhm, I think we need to find Leo, Jakob or maybe Cary? I think we are in trouble and death is not the answer to all our troubles. We need to speaking of our desperation to someone we can trust before we do anything rash."

Maximillian broke out into wild laughter, and I joined him as I said, "You are the intelligence shard? You have got to be funning. That was the dumbest thing I have ever heard. Talk to someone we can trust? There is not an honest heart in this Haus fool. The three names you give are possible. Really? Leo the child molester. Jakob abandoned us. Cary, bark, bark, bark. Damn. If I had the time for such comedy then I surely would desire to see the rest of your standup act, brother. However, we are late. You stay back there, and Maximillian will keep an eye on that traitor. You watch how the men handle their own difficulties you little whiny bitch.." With that I took back up the wheel.

I got off the floor looking around me with a bit of confusion as to where I was located or how I had come to be there. It was then I recalled the sensation of that oncoming seizure. By seventeen, I had a lot of experience with the brain spasms.

In a panic at being in public while helplessly suffering the trance dance, I had gotten off the stairs on the third floor. I was able to quickly hide myself in a rarely used hallway and wait out my brain's electrical malfunctions. It was a stroke of luck that no one had spotted me unconscious during the rebooting nor run into me while I fought my way back to rational thinking.

I shook off the deep fatigue while rubbing the soreness from my tense muscles. I waited a few more moments to be sure the danger of a second seizure passed. I could hear the residents of the third floor in the distance yapping and going about their daily lives as I stood silently behind a fancy sitting table display against the hallway wall.

I decided I was strong enough to finish the journey I had started. I limped down the abandoned corridor and returned to the stairwell without incident or witness of worth, or so I thought. The blacks, silvers and Dominants all fell to their knees, or bowed if above submissive level, as I moved with speed to the fifth floor. I hoped that bitch was home. I really didn't feel generous enough to wait any longer for the things I had longed to say to her for years.

It was no small bit of providence that the Silk Queen did answer her door almost the second I knocked. The expression on her face when she opened up and saw me there was, well Priceless.

She gasped and grabbed her chest in fear. I had caught her off guard before she could remember to pull that whole badass act, you know. "Uhm, Mad Maxx. This is a surprise.

Is your Master Lucus with you? Or do you have a message for me from him perhaps? If so be quick about it. I am busy with other things."

I interrupted her with a sneer. "I have no Master you bitch, and you know it. Open this fucking door and let me in or I will kick it in. I doubt whatever bullshit you are doing in there is as important as the what I have come to see you do."

Gretta's eyes narrowed as she attempted to appear insulted, though I could see the fear in them. "You forget your place, Mad Maxx. I don't speak to psychotics. You get the fuck back to Mad Lucus or I will have the Guard haul you back below for your insolence." She tried to close the door, but I kicked it knocking it back into her face with a thud.

I growled in fury as I pushed my way past the stunned woman. "It is you that forgets your place, Gretta. I am the Master of this Haus, and you are my servant. As for being psychotic, you better pray I am not or you are in a lot of trouble, ja?" I chuckled as I went to her loveseat and plopped down as if I were the familiar visitor to her apartment.

Gretta held her forehead groaning under her breath from the smack she had received. "What the hell is this all about, Mad Maxx? Is Lucus using you to try to frighten me? Well, you can march right back down to the fourth floor and tell that bastard I will not be threatened. I can see him exiled and you returned to the dirty cell for this attempt to renegotiate or whatever this bullshit you pull on me is."

I scoffed. "You don't listen too well bitch. I told you Lucus is not aware that I am here. No one is, that I can assure you. I have personally called this little meeting between us to see a few demands of my are not trifled with by the sorry likes of you. I have a personal reason for seeking revenge on you Gretta. You will sit down in that chair and take what you have coming, or I swear I will show no mercy in making sure you beat me to the floor from the banister railing."

Gretta dropped her hand from her bruised head staring at me in disbelief. "How dare you threaten me. I am going to call the Guard this minute. You have signed your death warrant, boy. I don't care how damned daft you are I am not putting up with this bullshit from the likes of you."

I chuckled as she rushed to her phone to call the Guard. "I wouldn't do that if I were you, honey. I don't think you will enjoy explaining to Ivan, the Elders and Voters what Henner was doing in the Palace the night of June 2nd? I on the other hand won't mind telling them the entire story since I was helpless to tell your buddy nein when he made his advances toward me. That will not go well for you or for Henner, will it? Isn't the punishment for such perversions death by burning? You can correct me if I am mistaken but be careful arguing with me about this sensitive subject. I am most painfully aware that I am not misidentifying one of my five offenders or his owner."

Gretta glared at me with hatred. “I refuse to admit that I understand a thing you are saying to me Mad Maxx, but if I were, then I would caution you such allegations against the Queen will never stick. Not when it comes from the mouth of the loon that hallucinates shit. You foolishly killed the only three that could possibly back your untruthful accusation. I do believe you have come here to shake me down in error. Leave this moment and maybe I forget it happened.”

I let out my breath. “Ah, you speaking of Sebastian, Tadeas and Noethan? I wasn’t aware you had already heard of their demise. They had the most unfortunate accident. It was a real tragedy I am told.”

Gretta put her hands on her hips in defiance. “How could I not hear you, idiot. I swear half the Haus showed up at my door to complain to me of all the screaming they did all night long. You kept the Haus awake and frightened with your insane revenge on those poor men. I could have you sent to the Palace for that alone and no one would question me for doing it.”

I nodded with wickedness rising in my eyes. “Ja, you could, but you don’t. Isn’t that interesting? Maybe that is because you hoped I would tie up all the loose ends you leave laying around in your efforts to bring Lucus to your table. Well, that does sound like an intelligent move on your part. Send the insane Mortar King to still the tongues of the men that did the bidding of the Silk Queen, but in order for you to desire their silence, there had to be a secret you feared they would talk about. I wonder what it was you feared they may say to others that warranted you wishing them dead?"

Gretta snorted. "Guess we shall never know for sure, will we? You killed them. I heard the rumor you cut their tongues out. Not easy for the dead men to tell tales much less the dying ones without that organ."

I chuckled with evil humor as I reached into my pocket to retrieve the photo. "You are not the least bit curious to know how I traced their foul behaviors back to you Gretta?"

She tossed her hair back trying to appear irritated instead of the curious that she really was. "I have no idea what you are spouting, I told you this already. Look you got your fucking vengeance on the men that misused you during your reign in the Mortar Palace. I think it in your best interest to return to your Master. Mind your manners, do as you are told, and there will be no reason for you to worry about anymore straw beds or bridled crowns, ja?"

I forced myself to stare at that photo I held despite everything in me wishing I could run away screaming from it. "I am not worried about your raising a hand toward me ever again Gretta. You are right in that I gained revenge on the men, and that they cannot speak of the abomination they forced on me no more. However, turned out that saying a picture is worth a thousand words is very true. You see I knew you owned a German Shepard that went by the name Henner. Leo, he walks Der Makellos now, but back when I was the boy that was my job. I met your hound just a bit before I broke that bat collar. He is a beautiful animal, one you must be quite proud of. The boastful owner of such a champion dog adorned his neck with a special collar. Ah, let's see, silver with the bone charm that has his name etched on one side. On the other is the name of his honored Mistress Gretta written in the rhinestones, that sound about right? A stunning and unforgettable piece of canine jewelry. I often fantasized of getting my own hound such finery when I became the doctor. That was all fantasy though, even the doctor part. I can see that now, just like I couldn't miss that collar from my boyhood memory on the hound of yours when he was among the party goers at my birthday party. I got many opportunities to get the close look at it. There was no doubt that was your Henner enjoying my party favors along with a few of his more common buddies. Funny, I don't know how he managed to gain the invite to the festivities without his Mistress granting permission for him to attend, ja? Do you want to hear something even more confusing? I also see the fancy collar Henner wears on the hound in this photo I hold in my hand. It is a remarkable work of art your man Noethan created here. He managed to capture the true horror of what it is like to be tied down and raped by dogs." I held the photo up to the light pretending to examine it while ignoring the expression of pure horror that came over Gretta's face.

She gasped. "What you just said is an act that is strictly forbidden in this Haus. If you dare to claim such obscenity you will be burned at the stake and your name disgraced for all time, Mad Maxx."

I looked up feigning a curious startle. “It is forbidden in this Haus, you say. Oh my, well, that is a surprise Gretta because I not only seem to recall it happening, but I have the photographic proof of it right here. And other less interesting pictures of this so called taboo safely hidden away from the prying eyes. I actually jest with you. I am aware that it is illegal, but I do seem to recall the punishment is reserved for the offenders not the victims.”

Gretta scoffed. “Well fool photos or not, you have put the men responsible to a far worse death than burning at the stake for their crimes against you. The only thing those photos can do for you now is assure that your disgraced as the tainted and will see you trapped within that Palace below, and that is where you will end up if you dare to show anyone a single one. You surely are aware Lucus’s royal snobbery will not tolerate having the scum like you in his bed after that rumor gets out.” She chuckled thinking herself clever.

I nodded as I dropped my gaze to the floor in fake shame. “Ah, ja. You sure have me there, Gretta. Lucus would be disgusted if he knew. Maybe he would even want to murder all those involved in ending his bid for the regent to the Mortar King? I mean, I killed three of them, but then there is that pesky question about what the fuck Henner was doing there that night. You don’t think he or others might think you had any involvement in this heinous act, do you?”

Gretta frowned. “I don’t believe you Mad Maxx. Henner is not viewable in that photograph. Noethan was an idiot, but he wasn’t that stupid.”

I chuckled even harder as I turned the picture around so she could see it clearly but kept it in my possession you can be assured. “He wasn’t? Then you are saying you ordered he take all those pictures of the crime that could tie you to your part in that dark deed? Nein. I don’t think you did tell him he could document this obscenity, Gretta. I think he and the perverts did this revolting addition to that nightmare you ordered all on their own. Noethan kept the souvenir of all the fun he had at my expense so he could enjoy my torment repeatedly in private for years to come. He didn’t know you cut that secret deal with Lucus, nor that the two of you would set me loose to shut his mouth for you. Guess he is painfully aware of your betrayal now though, ja?” I winked at her with malice.

Gretta walked to her chair and sat down slowly appearing to finally understand the gravity of her weak position. “Okay, Mad Maxx. Let’s pretend you are correct on everything you say, and I am not confessing that you are, mind you. If it were true, then I suppose I would be interested to hear your demands to see that photo disappear, and your tongue hold the secret of your disgrace. Go ahead and enlighten me. I am attentive. Maybe we can work something out as partners, ja?”

My eyes went wide as if in shock, though I was mocking her. “You mean you and me are bargaining? Ah, you are far too generous Gretta to consider the desires of the fucking Master of the Haus. You misunderstand your position in this situation. I am your better whether you like it or not. You sent your brutes to harass, abuse, and rape me in that cell. Now you try to pretend like you have choice in this matter. Hell, nein. You will do what I tell you, all of it, or I will hand this little piece of artwork and all the other ones I have over to Claus, Cora and Jonas. When they are done with you, Henner will get to know you better than you allowed him to know me. You understand me bitch? I warn you, say another insolent word to me, and see if I don't keep my promise to see you dead."

Gretta trembled as she shook her head and dropped her gaze to the floor. "As you say. I am listening."

I scoffed. "As you say, what? I cannot hear you Gretta.."

She swallowed hard then sneered as she said with an expression of disgust on her face, "As you say, Master. I am listening and thank you for the mercy of it."

I nodded as I chuckled hollowly. "Well now,, that is better. You dare to address me common again bitch, I will make the believer out of you. Now, on to my commands, servant. You will pack up your shit and move out immediately this very day. I am giving your fine apartment free of charge to my Mistress attendants Birgit and Viviana. They are to receive free lodging and food for all the rest of their days. You are to pay for it from your own pocket if any additional expenses come up. Next, you will see that my men, Almut, Hubertus and the Shadow King Cary along with their families received the finest third floor apartments for life. Next, you will go to Cora and tell her you are approving a ten percent raise for Ivan and his men. You intended to trap me in the bed of a man that I despise with all my being, so I am returning the favor to you, sweetheart. You will move up to the sixth floor closer to your ex-lover Cora. That way you will be stuck having to see her everyday as she heads down to the main Haus or Great Hall. Let's see how you like being cornered by a stalker."

Gretta's eyes went wide in shock. "What the fuck. Look I have no problem seeing that your men, the Shadow King, and the Guard receive what you demand. I, however, refuse to turn over my Haus to the low brow likes of Dungeon Mistresses and move to the sixth floor. Besides there are no vacancies. Do you expect me to kick an Elder over the banister so I can have his apartment?"

I nodded with my eyes shining in diabolical humor. "Ja, which is exactly what I expect you to do, Gretta. What I demand is not negotiable. It is to be put in writing and I won't leave this apartment nor take away the threat of this photo till it is filed. You will pack your shit and go upstairs. Kilian is to be demoted to Voter and one more thing, he is to be taken to the Palace and locked up as I was. Almut and Hubertus are to collect a vat of battery acid. Kilian will be restrained in the weights to the wall while my men throw that acid into his face. He will be held for three days before any medical treatment is granted him. During that three days, I demand a pair of earphones that play a song in constant repeat be taped to his ears so he cannot remove them. His brother Reece is to be arrested, held in the pit for one month without food, then burned at the stake and buried in an unmarked grave. Do you understand me Gretta? You better get to writing all this shit down or I will bid you adieu for good."

Gretta sat there appearing in a trance as she nodded. "Uhm, okay, ja. I go get the contract." She got up and began to walk off staggering a bit like someone had knocked her in the head with a mallet.

I called out to her sounding furious. "Okay what, Gretta. I cannot hear you."

She turned and shot me a look of hatred that thrilled me to the bone. "Okay, Master. I go get the contract and see you will done at once." With that she took off.

She returned in record time. I was surprised at her lack of further quarrel as she carefully recorded all my demands. I sat there watching her every move feeling nothing inside. I suppose she was shocked I had not asked for a single thing for myself other than revenge on the Altergotts and her by proxy. I really thought I would have some kind of strong emotion about finally getting truthful justice over something horrible that had been done to me, but I guess when that fusion of our shards happened we lost the ability to care about anything, even ourselves. Gretta handed the contract signed in our blood to the fifth floor black collar attendant. He took off with speed for the Hall of Records. I stood up taking a final look at the woman that had helped ruin my life. I hand signaled her to kneel. She did it and the look of indignation on her face as she dropped to her knees before me was worth the extra moments of the inner pain I felt at my continued existence. I left her there with instructions to get packing bitch as I rushed down the stairs tearing up that horrific photos into a thousand pieces. The time had come at last. I leaned over the railing taking deep breaths, bracing for the leap. I confess nothing had ever seemed as glorious nor inviting as the banister that morning except maybe the view I was sure to enjoy all the way down.

Chapter 46: To Protect and Defend

I stood there peering over that banister on the fourth floor trying to find a single excuse to not take the leap. I could hear the voice of my long dead buddy Ryker in the boy's ears. I recalled him saying many that found themselves in the silver collar that was obtained by the wrong gender preference had found their freedom from the nightmare like this. Jumping from the railing in the suicide was considered in the Haus as the honorable death for those without hope for a better day.

I felt the fool for buying into Peter's, Jonas's and even Leo's lies that breaking my collar would see me the freeman. I should have taken this route the moment Peter cut me loose of his ropes that horrid morning I was officially the broken in Priceless pleasure submissive. If I had done the right thing rather than fighting for a false dream, I wouldn't be finding my grave in the most revolting of conditions. A Dominant and Master of the Haus that wasn't even permitted the lover of his choice. My life had been the pathetic waste of time there was no longer any doubt.

I closed my eyes and put my arms behind the boy's back. This was to assure I didn't embarrass myself as I went over by struggling in the last moment with second thoughts. Nothing would be more horrible in my mind than watching Mad Maxx die Brutale flailing his arms trying to fly like a clown. I know it sounds silly, but I didn't want the witnesses to my last moments to chuckle at such useless antics.

That radio DJ announced loudly across the airwaves of my impending demise. "Hey, attention everyone. Is it the bird? Nein. Is it the plane? Nope. It is the idiot Mad Maxx about to take the dive without the wings. Look out below. That boy is going to finally do something of worth, it is about fucking time."

I scoffed at that rude thing he said, "Shut the fuck up, DJ. I want you to know I fucked your father and your brother too. I would have fucked your mother and sisters but even the Mad Maxx has some standards. Yikes, they look like yaks but with more hair on their faces. Do you hear me, bastard?" I began to laugh insanely at my insulting that dumb ass guy the never stops speaking. *Master Maxx grabbed his temples and sighed as if in pain.*

I watched the residents rushing about their business below me. I was waiting for the path to the floor below to clear of human obstructions. I mean I didn't want to accidently land on someone like Kilian had done to Byron that day Jonas threw him off the third floor. Wait, I guess that was Kilian's suitcase, but you know what I am saying, ja? I was sure my frame, though thin and worn, could kill even the biggest brute from the velocity of my decent. With the bad luck I had always known, likely I would end up crushing some poor little silver child.

It took several moments before I saw my opportunity to leap. I leaned forward allowing the weight of the top of me to engage with the force of gravity's natural attraction. I bent my knees to destabilize the sureness of my boots firm grip on the floor. I intended to go over the railing headfirst like the swan dive. That way I could be sure a quick death from the snapped neck.

I teetered there like the playground equipment enjoying what I thought was the last few breaths of life. I let out the yell and pushed forward with vigor from my sliding feet. I was going over the side almost in the slow motion. I forced my arms to stay clasped behind me as my head took a sharp turn downward, but something was wrong. I was suspended there as if frozen in time not moving forward nor pulling back.

I opened my eyes full of confusion and shock. It was impossible that I was not already dead by seconds. I was staring at the ground below. Somehow, I had managed to become stuck to the metal barrier. It had to be a hallucination or maybe my breeches were caught on a nail holding me back from the fall. I wriggled with all my strength trying to break that hold the prevented me from reaching my goal of the grave.

I flinched and my blood went cold when I head a man's voice yell out from behind me, "Stop struggling, Maxx. What the fuck are you doing? Holy hell, man. You almost fell. Hold still and I will help you back to safety. Oh, my Gott, what if I had not come by when I did? I cannot even imagine how close you came to being the yard fertilizer. How did you even manage to get like this? Did you slip on something?"

I heard the voice but for the life of me couldn't place the identity of it. "Let go of me, you motherfucker. Who the fuck do you think you are to touch the Master of the Haus? I will see you whipped for it. Back off, I mean it. That is a directive."

The male voice deepened then echoed as he responded, "Nein, you can see me whipped if you want, Maxx. I don't care. If I let you go, you will fall, Gott dammit. Is that what you want? To be the worm food? I don't believe you will injure the man that saves you from the potentially deadly accident. Now help me, you stubborn bastard. You are too heavy for me to hold like this for long."

I nodded and yelled out wildly, "Ja, the worm food. I do want that. Sign me up for it. Let me go. I can fly, you know. Watch me." I thrashed with vigor against the hold of my would be savior.

The man wailed out in terror, his voice distorting in my panicked ears to that of a mechanical device. "Oh, my Gott. Help me. Someone help. Mad Maxx is having a fit. He thinks he can fly. Please mercy, anyone. I cannot hold him. He is going to be killed."

I laughed manically as I felt the boy's flesh slipping slightly further down the outer side of the banister. "Help, help me. The Priceless is going to die. Hahaha. Yell all you want, fucker. No one is coming. Don't you know that no one cares, fool. Look at them. Ants, fire, dogs, humans, they are all the same. I won't do this anymore, you bastard. You cannot keep me here. There is no other way out. I am escaping their lust. I prefer the dust. See, I am going to be the freeman at last."

The voice really began to become terrified when I said that shit. "Maxx, please listen to me. I care. I beg of you, don't do this. Stop this fighting and let me help you. If you do, I swear to Gott we can speak about this trouble you are having. Suicide is not the answer, brother."

I was able to recognize at this moment the man had a weak hold around the boy's waist. "Fuck you. Don't call me your brother. I have no family. I never liked you much and you are not my kin. You are nothing but a worthless gossiping DJ."

The man gasped as his grip slipped a bit more. I was almost too far gone to be saved at this point. "DJ? What the fuck is wrong with you, Maxx? It is me, your buddy Matz, not this fellow you call the DJ. We are brothers, remember? Oh Christ, will someone please help me. Mad Maxx has fucking lost his mind for true."

That name busted through the psychotic hallucination with force. "Matz? What are you doing here?"

Matz groaned as he tried to tighten his hold on me. "I don't think that matters right this minute, Maxx. There is far more important things happening now. I ask again, stop struggling. I cannot hold up against your strength."

I shook my head to clear it of the strange feeling that I was floating away. "Ja, okay Matz. I don't know what I am doing. I am lost. Help me please. Can you help me escape the Haus? I don't want to live like this anymore."

Matz snorted as he battled to maintain. "Ja, sure Maxx. Anything you say buddy. All you got to do is grab that railing and hold on. I can then let go and seeking help to get you back to safety."

I nodded. "If I take the railing you promise to help me get out of here? No lies, Matz. They are going to take me back to the Palace. I would rather be dead."

Matz sighed loudly. "If that is what you want, Maxx. I swear to you I will help you get out of here. Now grab the banister please. I am begging you brother. I don't want to see you die."

I unclasped my hands and took hold of the fancy patterned metal guard under the railing. This immediately stabilized the boy from the deadly rocking back and forth. I heard Matz let out his breath in relief, but he didn't let go his death grip on my waist.

He pulled hard but I didn't budge. "Okay Maxx, now put down your feet and pull back to this side. You are almost there brother. Where the fuck is your Master Lucus? Why is he allowing you to run wild without supervision in the hallways in the first place?"

Well, that was it. Matz almost had me back to Earth. Then he went and opened his big, fat mouth about that pervert Lucus. I let go of the metal guard and reached to my waist punching his hands to try to get him to release me.

Matz screamed in sudden shock. “Maxx, nein. Maxx, what are you doing? Stop this..”

It was at this moment I felt strong hands clap the boy’s shoulders. I watched in confused silence as the world spun wildly. I was flying but not downward as I wanted. Somehow Matz had managed to hurl me back from that banister with great force. The fourth floor wall stopped my helpless tumbling through the air. I slid down it, till I was half sitting, half laying on the fancy carpet. I found I couldn’t move from the spot I landed. I had been severely stunned from that collision.

In front of my baffled eyes stood the huge Voter Byron smiling at me. The skinny Matz was behind him wearing an expression of concern and fear. I tried to say something, but the words seemed to be stuck in my throat. All I could do is stare at the men as if in a deep trance.

Matz came forward and Byron put up his hand to block his reaching me. “You back the fuck up, Matz. Maxx is upset. Give him space to breathe a minute will you? Can you tell me what the fuck is going on,” said the brute.

Matz shook his head in disbelief. “I think I just thwarted the Mortar King from trying to end his own life Honorable Byron. I saw him headed this way earlier. I hadn’t visited with him in a long while and was seeking an audience. I wanted to check on his welfare, you know. Well, I found him trying to leap from the banister. I swear to you, I didn't have anything to do with whatever caused him to be as you find him. I would never harm a hair on my King's head. You can be assured I didn't try to push him off the railing if that is what you are thinking."

Byron sneered at Matz then said in a sarcastic tone. "Oh, you are innocent of anything that may have caused this unfortunate situation. If you expect me to believe that then you are trying to play old Byron here for the fool. You maybe didn't chuck him with your hands, but there is no doubt that your actions are among those within his heart that drives him over this edge."

Matz glared with fury rising. "You have a lot of nerve pointing that fat finger at anyone, especially me dishonorable Byron. I will have you know Maxx is my ex-lover. I loved with that man for months. During our time together he told me about the horrors you inflicted upon him when he was the helpless little boy. The only difference between you and me is I was punished by your buddies for trying to do what you actually did. I confess I have not always treated Maxx with the respect he deserves. However, I can say with certainty I regret the pain I cause him and not a day goes by that I don't wish I could take all the evil I did to him back. My mistakes nearly cost me the greatest friendship I could have dared to dream to possess. I will never repeat the errors of mistaken that gentle soul as someone that is only here to fulfill my selfish desires. Matz learned his lessons well. Can you say the same honored brother? I bet not."

Byron scoffed. “You speak pretty words that are as empty as that head of yours. Where did you learn to use your tongue like that Matz? I know. You polished Roland’s cock enough to work out the rough spots, ja? Well, you waste that fancy skill you’ve been taught on one that knows better. Tell me something Matz, did you try to saving Maxx because he is your truthful buddy or because the Priceless flesh won’t be worth anything but to the blow flies when he is the corpse? Humm, I wonder. How will you pay that rent without that sweet ass of his?”

Matz nearly choked on his own spit when the Voter indicated he somehow knew of our secret business, not that I had been working as the whore in a while by that time. “Huh? I don’t have any idea what you are speaking about honored Voter. Maxx doesn’t pay my rent to get me to fuck him. I cannot believe you would go so far to insult the King by even hinting that he would have to pay anyone to be invited to his bed. Shit, many in this Haus would happily risk death to have him merely look their direction much less taste his legendary artistry.”

Byron shot a knowing smile at me with wickedness in his expression. “You twist my words with purpose Matz, and you know it. I just said the very thing you did, only with the proper manners. Tell me Mad Maxx, what does Matz charge the clients to sample your legend? Enough to afford him that fine apartment on the third floor there is no doubt, but I look upon the one doing all the work. I see no improvements in your life my boy. Seems to me that Maxx takes all the pain while Matz enjoys all the gains, ja?” He searched my face for the answer to his dangerously loaded question.

I dropped my gaze to the floor trying to shaken off that nasty head blow to the wall. “I fear I don’t understand your line of inquiry any more than my brother Matz does Byron. You are not making any sense.”

Byron snorted then crossed his arms as he looked from Matz to me with humored smugness. “Ah, of course. What was I thinking? The use of guarded discretion is wise when the penalty for such a criminal act is severe. You boys need not worry about your old buddy Byron. The secret of your illegal prostitution ring is safe with me.”

Matz let out a gasp as I shot him a look of fear. “Prostitution ring? What the hell? Is that what you think of Maxx and me? Nein, never. Whoever told you such a lie should be whipped to death for spreading such false rumors. My continued interest in the Mortar King is of the honest kind only. Maxx and me are past lovers, nothing more and nothing less. Forgive me for saying this but you are the vile creature to suggest otherwise.” He crossed his arms feigning indignation and did a fantastic job at it too I may add.

The Voter nodded still smiling with diabolical thrill. “Well, you are right to correct me for such a grievous error in my accusations, Matz. I didn’t mean to say prostitution ring at all. That would indicate that you were working other whores in your stable. Nein, that is indeed wrong. You only have the Mad Maxx enduring the perverts’ interests to get the money for your supper, ja? I will say shame on you Matz. Mad Maxx is the helpless schizophrenic, and you swoop in taking advantage of his weakened position almost the second he arrives back from the hellish Heslach. Wow, and you call yourself his ex-lover and buddy? Shit, I wouldn't even call you a decent human being."

I opened my mouth to dispute this horrible thing he said, but sadly truthful one. I found once again the words hung in my throat. I sat there trembling in pure horror at this dangerous man that had tormented me since I was still the submissive had found out about the whoring business. Matz stared at me as if confounded. He didn't know what to say any more than I did. Neither of us knew who told Byron or how much he even knew of the dishonorable and illegal things we had been doing.

Matz broke the silence with a loud scoff. "I told you whoever is wagging their tongue with falsehoods against the Mortar King best beware of it. I can assure you Mad Maxx is not one to sit back and let such lies go unpunished. Now, I thank you for the aid in getting him out of the dangerous situation, but I think Maxx and I have it from here. We don't desire to keep you from the important things I am sure you are about honored Byron." He made another move to approaching me still sitting in the floor where I landed.

Byron turned around with the speed of a bullet and punched Matz right into the face. The skinny Dominant staggered backward and fell to his ass. He had been knocked to stupid in a single blow by the huge Voter. I let out a yell of pure panic as the brute turned back around and leaned down grabbing me under the arms.

Byron grinned into my face in an eerie attempt to appear friendly, “Hush Maxx. I am not going to hurt you I swear it on my honor, love. Be still and I will get you out of here before the news of this little mistake you made trying to leap to your doom reaches Lucus’s ears. Surely you don’t want to hang around till that ugly motherfucker comes to see you punished for it, or do you? All you need to do is say the word. If you don’t want my help hiding you out from that rat bastard then I swear I will let you go and move on without quarrel.”

I tried to swallow but my mouth had gone dry from fear. “What are you going to make me pay for your help, Byron? I think maybe I am better off accepting Lucus’s punishment rather than making a deal to give you a reward for anything you do for me.” I tried to stand only to find my legs too weak from fatigue and that blow to hold my weight. With big old Byron standing there holding my waist like he was, I was not able to get up. Well, that was some scary shit trust me.

Byron frowned with seriousness. “I would be upset by what you accuse me of, but I realize there is complete truth in what you say from our past dealings. That said, I beg your mercy and forgiveness for the stupidity I have always demonstrated when dealing with you. I also swear that if you let me help you this moment I do it for free. I won’t ask you for anything other than your saying you can find it in your heart to let the troubles between us be the forgotten memory."

I narrowed my eyes with suspiciousness. "I don't understand what you are saying Byron. Speak plain brute."

He scoffed. "I said that if you can say that you forgive all the stupid, brutal, and cruel things I have done in the past to you while you were helpless then I will not only help you escape Lucus's wrath over this suicide attempt but will swear to never again repeat the gross errors that I ask release from this moment. I throw myself upon your mercy and beg to be given the second chance to be your true friend, not your worst nightmare."

I shook my head in complete shock. "You really expect me to believe this bullshit you spew, Byron? You rape me, beat me and ignore every Gott damned time I said nein. Now you think I magically trust you to do anything other than drag me off to some dark place to take your thrill against my will again. No doubt you will repeatedly do exactly what you have in the past until your lust is sated and my soul is crushed. Shit, man, you must think me the hopeless psychotic if you thought I would buy what you are trying to sell, you bastard."

Byron nodded and suddenly appeared saddened. "Ja, I wouldn't believe me either if I were you. However, the way I see it you really have no other reasonable choice but to take my offer of asylum. I can assure you, stay here and they will send you back below. Allow me to take you with me. This way there is at least the chance I am telling the truth, ja?"

I shuddered with disgust at the idea of voluntarily going anywhere with Byron other than to his execution. My ears suddenly perked as I noticed our tussling had drawn a bit of a curious crowd. I could hear the voices of onlookers calling out to each other. They were demanding someone notify Mad Lucus his collar had been attacked at the worst or was possibly having the fit.

I shot a look of worry at Matz. He was still sitting against the banister guard appearing in a daze. My pimp was most definitely out of commission, at least for the moment. I watched a black collar rushing off toward Mad Lucus's apartment to alert that bastard of the troubles they all assumed they were watching between me, Matz and Byron. The window of opportunity for escaping detection was fast closing.

I dropped my sight back to my lap as is sighed in defeat. "Okay, I will go with you Byron. I ask you to be gentle if you do intend to break your promise to refrain from molesting me. I am not in good health. I swear I give you no reason to beat on me, but I also beg you to be honorable by taking no advantage of one that is helpless to stop you."

Byron smiled with happiness as he lifted me to my feet by the waist. "You do me a favor that I sure as hell have never earned. There is no fucking way I would ever betray your trust for that reason alone." He put my arm around his huge shoulders and quickly dragged me along after him heading for the stairwell.

I was told by Matz later that Mad Lucus did indeed come to the scene of that botched suicide attempt. He was quite angered to find no sign of his Christian Victor throwing a psychotic fit. The only one there was a nearly unconscious Matz with a fast swelling black eye.

The angry Mad Lucus demanded to know what the hell was going on that caused such a ruckus that he was stirred from his daily routine. Matz, unsure of what Byron's game was, decided it was best to lie to the man rather than risk the Voter spilling his discovery to Lucus's vengeful ears.

He told Mad Lucus that he and I were visiting peacefully when Matz nearly had the fatal accident. He claimed he, not me, nearly fell from the fourth-floor banister acting the silly fool by hanging too far over it. Matz then finished the lie by saying it took both Byron, who was happening by and heard my calls for help, and me to pull him to safety.

He explained that the physical stress of that near miss had caused me faintness. Byron had then escorted me down to the Haus door to get some air. Matz assured Mad Lucus all was well, and I had managed to shake off the incident as I tended to do. This explanation appeared to satisfy the pervert as he never to this day questioned me about the particulars of the things that happened that afternoon.

In reality, Byron escorted me up to the fifth floor and managed to slip me into his apartment without a single witness to his hijacking. I admit I was more than a little afraid of the man, but at that moment too depressed to care about what his truthful intention were. I assumed he was going to drag me to his bedroom, take what he wanted as usual then threaten me with telling Lucus or Gretta of that prostitution stuff to keep me coming back for more of his raping. That is not quite the way it went though, to my surprise.

Byron gently aided me to his couch and sat me down without touching me in any inappropriate way. I sat there in cautious silence as the big brute ran to his kitchenette saying he was fetching me something cool to drink. I was still too weak to move fast enough to escape his clutches, so I decided to just endure whatever foul shit was really up his sleeve.

The Voter returned with a glass of soda and a bowl of soup. He sat them down in front of me and then took a seat across his living room facing me. I didn't know what to make of this odd behavior he was demonstrating. I had never been with this man alone or otherwise, where he was not doing his damnedest to paw, fawn or fondle me in some way. I have to confess, his purposeful hands off distancing was a much appreciated change of pace.

He leaned back into his overly stuffed recliner with a small smile. "There you go Maxx. I swear I never see you look so thin in all the time I have known you. That soup is from the can but good. I know you cannot chew the sausage or sandwich though I think either would be better to see you gain weight. You must be hungry brother. Eat it please? I swear to you, I only just opened that can. You heard the can opener, ja?"

I nodded. "Ja, I heard you open the can. It is rude to refuse such mannerly offers and waste the food. I thank you for the mercy of this meal, but I swear to you I am not hungry. Maybe another time."

Byron frowned appearing concerned. "Not hungry you say? I think there is far more than the lack of interest in food going on with you these days, Maxx. May I ask. Why did you try to kill yourself only a few moments ago?"

I scoffed as I shot him an angry glare. "You need to hear that answer? Really, Byron? I thought you indicated we have a long history of knowing the other. You tell me something. If you were the Priceless, how long would it have taken you to leap to your death?"

Byron chuckled with bitterness and shook his head. "Fair enough, Maxx. However, I say to you Byron is not the fucking powerhouse that you are my boy. I couldn't have handled half of what you already have before the age of thirteen. Yet, that is the pussy Byron speaking. Why after all that you have already overcome do you choose now to do this horrible thing?"

I shrugged. "Because it is too late to do it yesterday and I don't want to wait for tomorrow."

Byron slapped his knee and laughed heartily. "Ah, so simple yet so complex. Very clever answer, Maxx. That really doesn't tell me a thing about the deep motives that drove you to this at last. Listen, whatever you want to tell me about your difficulties I can swear to you it won't go further than this room. I know you don't believe me when I say I want nothing more from you than to help. The way I see it if you are bound for the grave then you really have nothing to lose unburdening your soul of its hurts, ja?"

I scoffed. "You make the assumption I have a soul Byron. Maybe once I did but you are one of the fellows that helped to fuck it away. I see no reason to fill the air with meaningless words that will do nothing to change my mind. I want to escape this hell hole, and death is the only door that was ever there. I thank you for not allowing Mad Lucus the chance to stop me from doing what I must do. I don't mean to demonstrate further bad manners to your thus far generous hospitality. However, If you would be so kind to hurry up and get to whatever nasty shit you intend to do to me, I would be most grateful for the mercy of it. I have to be dead by six tonight."

Byron stared at me appearing mildly humored by my unabashed honesty. "I told you I would not force myself on you Maxx if you would forgive me for all I have already done. Can I assume you will keep your end if I do my own?"

I snorted. "Sure, Byron. I don't even recall what it is you did. You never took liberties that were not granted you by right. I am the idiot that agreed to that fucking closet contract with you and the brute Friedrick. You merely took what was offered. I don't blame you for being the opportunist. I should have thought on that ill designed contract a bit more rather than rushing into something with fear clouding my good senses. As for what happened below, Well, you didn't break the laws there either. The coronation ritual for the Mortar King is not of your design. That visit you gave to me. You didn't whip me when you could have. The favor you take was your right by Gretta's direction. Again, can't blame you for taking what you could get legally from me. I don't seem to recall you once pulling me in some dark hallway to take your lust out completely against my will and law."

Byron appeared surprised by what I said. "Seriously Maxx? Am I having the hallucinations? Are you actually going to sit there and say with complete honesty I had the right to fuck you even though you obviously didn't want me too? Holy hell. What the fuck. Are you degrading yourself over that whole yard dog business downstairs?"

I nearly fainted when he said that. "Excuse me? What did you just say? I, uhm, what? Yard dogs? Damn Byron are you okay? You are speaking crazy." I stammered out feeling my ears burn with shame.

He took a deep breath and looked at his boots in what appeared to be honest regret. "Forget it Maxx. I know all about that nasty shit Tadeas, Sebastian, Noethan and that bitch Gretta did to you down there. At least now I understand why they locked me up to keep me from seeing you anymore. They didn't want to feel my wrath when I found out what abominations they were really up to."

I felt the tears starting to well but thankfully none fell down the boy's cheeks. "Who told you? I swear it wasn't my fault, Byron. They tied me down. I tried to get away. I didn't even know what they were doing. I go this minute to end my life. The four that caused this are punished. I am honorable. I swear it. I will show you." I staggered to my feet and began heading for the door fighting both the swoon of dizziness and the threatening tears of shame.

Byron rushed from his seat and tackled me to the floor before I could reach the door. I crumpled up under him. He pinned me to the spot. I struggled best I could but found I was helpless to break free of his immense weight. He rolled me to my back and held my head still by grabbing both sides of the boy's head. I panted in fear of the man as he gazed deep into my eyes with pity in his expression.

Byron took a deep breath then said, "Maxx, you are right. This was not your fault. You are the victim not the criminal. The dishonor of it belongs to those that breath no more. I think I finally understand what it is that drives you to do something that nothing before this managed to do. Tell me Maxx, are you trying to kill yourself because you think your soiled so deeply no one can love you because of it?"

I felt the tears breaking loose as I nodded. "Ja, Byron. Who would want the disgusting whore you hold in your hands? Not unless they never found out about that dishonorable shit that happened. How can I face the world acting like I am not what I am? Nein. I thought maybe no one ever discovers the truth of it but you sure did. Sooner or later more will hear of it, no doubt. Then what? I am disgraced in more than just my own head. The society will shun me, and I will find no friends, lover or family other than the perverts that are into that kind of abomination. Even if I could hide it forever from everyone else I will always know what they did and what I did. I cannot make the memory of it stop tormenting me. Then I am told I never get to leave this place Byron. Not ever. I cannot have the frau and children, and what woman would want me anyway? They will eventually put me back below and maybe the will do worse than yard dogs next time. Listen to me please. If you ever had any real feelings for me, then kill me like you offered to do that day in the Palace. I swear I give you anything you want right this minute without quarrel if you show this mercy to me. I beg of you brother. I don't want to live like this anymore." I fell into the weeping jag deeper and more despaired than ever I had felt before.

Byron sighed loudly then pulled me to his chest with force. He wrapped his arms around my waist to hold me there even if I attempted to struggle free. I didn't bother. I didn't care what he did to me as long as it included his breaking my fucking neck when he was finished with it.

For many minutes he cradled me like that. He said nothing but did rub my back gently from time to time. At one point he dropped his head down and leaned his face into my neck and shoulder like a mother would do to calm a distressed kid. Other than that, he never touched me with inappropriateness, nor did he take advantage of my broken spirit in any way.

When the tears finally began to slow a bit, he rubbed the back of the boy's head with softness. "Get it all out, Maxx. We can take as long as you need. When you feel strong enough, I would like to say something to you that I think you need to hear."

I groaned in abject misery. "Say whatever you want Byron. Then take my offer. You can have me anyway you like long as after you end this horror I call my life once and for all."

Byron shook his head and sighed loudly again. "Nein, I refuse your offer Maxx. I won't kill you no matter how much you beg nor for anything you have to offer. I have told you for years I love you and I mean that. I don't feel this way for you for the power you wield. It was not the sex with you that makes me crazy with desire to possess you for all my life. It is because there is no other on Earth more giving or honest than the Mad Maxx. I was the fool to believe you would bother to look at me the way I do you. I swear I am the stupid man no longer. I finally realize, if you try to bully such an emotion from another you do nothing but kill the very thing you want so bad. Listen to me Maxx. No matter what you think of yourself I swear to Gott a more beautiful or innocent person doesn't exist than the one I hold in my arms this minute. I should have been satisfied that I could call you my friend rather than the evil I did. I cannot undo it any more than you can erase that horrible thing those men forced on you below. So, if the moron Byron can change his plans and find a new dream despite his mistakes surely the unbreakable Priceless can do the same. I want to make a deal with you Maxx that for a change is stacked in your favor."

I wailed out in anguish. "I don't want to make any more fucking deals with anyone, Byron. I want this horrible pain inside me to end. I want peace and quiet. I want to go where no one can hurt me anymore. Are you listening? Or are you still only a fool."

Byron chuckled at that. "Ja, I am the fool if you think I am going to just step aside and allow you to make a huge mistake without hearing me out. Now, I don't desire to injure you anymore than you already have been. I beg of you to be still. If what I say doesn't change your mind, then I will let you go. I will not end your life for you Maxx, but I swear to all that is holy I won't try to stop you from finding the peace you have no doubt earned a thousand times already."

I moaned in frustration. "You remind me of my place, Byron. A thousand times? Maybe more. Fine. I am not strong enough to fight you. Say what you must then let me go. I am so very tired."

He nodded. "Ja, I can only imagine how fatigued you are Maxx. I thank you in advance for giving me this chance to sway you to hold on a little longer. First, I think part of your problem is there is nowhere for you to find sanctuary or privacy. You need rest from the stresses of your hard life like anyone does at a labor job. Lucus has taken over that gift Rolf gave to you. I know you have no money without selling your skills to the perverts that have no restriction on the evil they are willing to do. So, I offer you my spare room here in this haus. You tell no one of it, and I give you a key. Anytime you need to be alone, come and find it in your own room free of charge. You can even decorate it anyway you like. It will be your private domain and I will defend it as if it were my own domicile."

I growled out in irritation. "Sure Byron. I run to that spare room you guard like your own home because it fucking is your place, fool. And you give me worse that what I flee from. Do you take me for stupid?"

Byron laughed till he choked. "I earned that distrustful accusation, Maxx. However, I swear it on my honor. When you are in that spare room, the door closed, no one on Earth will be allowed to touch or speak to you. I will guard the door with my own life."

I snorted. "Okay say I believe what you promise, which I fucking don't, you think having a fucking room to catch a breather in is going to change my mind Byron? You waste my time. Six is coming, Gott dammit. I think you distract me with worthless words to help those looking to clad themselves in the flesh of the Master of the Haus."

Byron let out his breath. "Will you let me finish dammit. I know your problems are far too big to be contained in a sometime sanctuary. I am also prepared to offer you my honest service to protect and defend your honor and life. You need significant aid to prevent the sneak attacks you have fallen victim to so many times. That will never end thanks to neglect and cruel games unless you have someone in secret to end the shit before it starts. You can be assured from this day forward, any enemy of Mad Maxx is also my own. I am going to do whatever I must to see you are never held down and raped by men, women, yard dogs or other shit again. I give my oath in blood to give up my life if necessary to see you are not violated against your will. You will never be alone in your battle with the beasts of this Haus Maxx. Your brother Byron will always have your back."

I scoffed now feeling fury rising in my chest at his words. "Oh? You are ready to do that, are you? Well, who is going to protect me from you, Byron? Prayer, track lessons, and an expensive pair of running shoes perhaps?"

Byron began to laugh again. "Damn, you are a fucking funny guy Maxx. I wonder why I never noticed that about you before. The more I get to know you the more I realize how amazing you truly are."

I pushed back away from his chest. "Hard to spot humor when there is nothing comical about our situations together, ja?" I glared at him noticing he still hadn't let me out of his embrace.

Byron stopped his chuckle and took on an expression of seriousness. "Once more I say I deserved what you say. I offer no quarrel. I said I have been a shit and I have been. You are right when you say I never broke the rules to take what I desired from you. However, I did take without empathy for your situation. So, be rude all you like. Say what you must. Like that guilt you carry over that bullshit that was not your fault, better to have it outside in anger than inside with self-hate."

I nodded. "Finally, you say something that makes sense, asshole. Ja, I hate you."

Byron smiled with bitterness. "That's fair. Just know I don't hate you Maxx. I am willing to do what it takes, for as long as it takes, to win your trust and eventually at least know you like me maybe a little?"

I snorted "Your natural life span won't be long enough for that to happen, Byron, and honestly the fucking universe will be the distant memory by the time I call you a true friend."

Byron sighed. "Maybe. Yet it is the chance I am willing to take Maxx. I have one more thing to offer you in my bid to see you give up this idea of killing yourself."

I shot a look of anger at his arms still holding me in a hug. "Looks like I am all ears, buddy."

Byron chuckled. "You are fucking hilarious, I swear to Gott. What a most unexpected treat. Okay I saved the best of this offer for last. I have been thinking lately this Haus of perversion is part of my problems in finding a truthful loving relationship. Like you, all I ever wanted was someone to call my own to come home after the long day and find them smiling in thrill at seeing me. Anyway, my father left most of his fortune to my older brother and sent me here to be out of the way of his showboating with only enough cash to survive in this economy. My mother never agreed with the way he split the fortune. She and I were always close. Well sadly she passed away earlier this year. My grief over the loss was deep but my beloved mother speaking of her love for me from beyond the grave. I found out she left me the trust fund large enough to see me out of these nightmare halls for the rest of my life."

I shot a look of surprise at Byron. "Well now, that is the best news I have heard in a while. When are you leaving? Want me to help you pack? Shit, I am most happy to take a moment to see you leave out that front door brother. Nice of you to share your good luck at gaining the only thing I ever wanted. Wow, this is really low of you Byron. You are going hold me hostage in your lap as you brag of this to one that failed to even see the parking lot without a fucking leash on him like a dog. Tell me, are you getting a hard on torturing me with your stories of how great it is going to be for you? You are one huge asshole you know."

Byron grabbed the back of my head with sudden anger that flashed in his eyes. "I said be still and hear me out Maxx. I am trying to explain my offer if you will shut the fuck up."

I stared at him coldly. "I was wondering when the Byron I know was going to join this party. Sure brother. Go ahead with you words. I am listening. Not like I have the choice as usual."

Byron appeared to realize his rash outburst as he let go of me with an apologetic expression. "Shit, sorry about that

Maxx. I get a little testy when it comes to speaking about my mother. I uhm, well, I told you she and I were close. This thing she has done for me is a miracle I never thought was possible. The wonderful woman left me enough cash to see me comfortable on the outside, but there is an excess of it that would allow me to take care of another. I suppose she assumed I would need it for my frau and eventual children."

I chuckled. "I thought you said you and your mother were close Byron. I happen to personally know you are the schwuler. There isn't going to be any fucking wife and kids for you."

Byron groaned. "You misunderstand Maxx. I am not the schwuler. I am the bisexual. I find women sexy too. I just haven't found the right one, is all. Until I do, I was thinking maybe you would want to come with me? I could give you a place to stay, food, and help you get the car and job. Just think, you would be out of this Haus for good, and I could have the buddy to keep me company."

I stared to him wide eyed. "You want me to move out of the Haus with you to be your lover?"

Byron shook his head and looked at the floor. "Nein, well ja, I mean I want to take care of you Maxx. Your being the lover or merely the companion is up to you. I would offer to be your guardian and making sure no one takes advantage of you outside the walls. I protect and defend you inside then I do the same when we are the freemen? What do you think of that?"

I shook my head barely able to whisper. "I don't know what to think about what you are saying, Byron. I mean, how can you get me out without Jonas dragging me back. Or shit any of dem. That Vampire has the guardianship and Peter the contract. You are trying to fuck with my head, ja?"

The Voter grabbed my head again to force me to stare at him, but this time was gentle about it. "Nein, listen to me Maxx. Look, my mother's money is tied up at this moment. I cannot leave until the estate is released. I can get a lawyer to wrestle those guardianship papers from Jonas with ease the second you are out of the minority. That is next June, ja? When you are legally the man you can come to court with me and testify that you want to live with me instead of Jonas. I will fund the transfer and see to your every need if you say ja."

I almost fainted at that information as I whispered in disbelief, "But the Haus, they won't let me go Byron. Lucus told me I am the Master of the Haus. They will never let the King go."

Byron chuckled. "Ja, Lucus is right. They won't want to let you go. However, the real reason they hold you is because of Jonas. He holds your papers and therefore controls where you can go outside this Haus. Inside it Lucus and Gretta have you as their hostage. They use you to gain full power. I tell you this minute. You keep the secret and aid me by signing the papers I give you I can and will see you free of this hell hole Maxx. I swear if necessary I will smuggle you the fuck out in the night. I only need you to do three things for me to see this plan come to truth."

I couldn't believe my ears that someone was saying they would aid me to escaping at last. I felt the boy's head nodding that I wanted to hear his demands. I felt as if in a trance frozen in time like I had earlier.

Byron smiled with thrill in his expression. "First you must never breath a word to anyone about this business between us. If someone finds out they can block me from gaining the legal right to see you free. Second, you must trust me. I don't want to fight with you over every little thing that must be done to see this happen. Third, you have to remain patient. No more suicide attempts giving up your fighting these bastards that try to hurt you, and no more hating the beautiful boy called the Mad Maxx. I beg of you. Accept the things I offer you: sanctuary, protection, and freedom. I promise you will no longer desire to take that leap off the banister."

I stared at him blankly "What the hell is in this for you, Byron? Are you asking me to trade all the other rapists in this Haus for a single one? I tell you I am straight. I want the Frau and children. I won't settle for less. I would rather be dead."

Byron patted my head with gentleness as he smiled with friendliness. "I am not asking you to do anything you don't want to do. If you want the frau and children then I swear I help you get that too. As for what is in this deal for Byron, that is a simple answer. A chance to do the right thing for someone that deserves the second chance to see his dreams come true. What do you say? Do we have the deal?"

I shook my head. "What if I say nein."

Byron frowned. "Well, after you jump I will likely have to answer for what I know of the reason for it since many saw us together earlier. I will be forced to tell the truth that I heard you say to Gretta about that business below. Your disgrace will leave Almut, Hubertus, and Cary in dire straits, ja?"

I dropped my eyes to the floor. "Oh, you were eavesdropping. That is how you learned of it. You would tell the others? I thought you said you want to be my friend Byron. Friends don't do that to each other."

He nodded. "And they don't abandon each other when given a valid alternative to work things out. You jump then I can safely say we are not friends. Besides, if you die, then who will care for Felicity? I guess I will have no choice but to give that lamb to Jonas. Since he is your guardian he has the right to all your possessions, even her."

I startled and flashed a look of fear at him. "What is this you say? Nein, Felicity is safely with another. I give her a new home far from that fiend. She is safe. I need not worry. I have been a good father to my lamb. She won't even cry for long."

Byron's expression turned stern. "Is that so? I think you are delusional Maxx. I happen to know that Birgit didn't want to assume care for your responsibility. She brought the lamb to me. I have her in this Haus as we speak. Now I ask you do I return her to you, or do I call Jonas to pick up his property immediately? Up to you. You may not care about her proper treatment, but I happen to worry for her a great deal."

Within the wheelroom chaos had broken out once more. I stood there unsure what the fuck to do. I was ready to tell Byron to fuck off and head back to the banister. I didn't believe a word he said, nor did I think for a second I could handle being stuck as this man's whatever he thought I would be. Well, all that thinking changed the second I found out that Felicity's life was in danger. This was bad as things could get.

Maximillian and Mad Maxx backed away from us as we thrashed in anger at the wheel. "Gott dammit. He is holding our poor little lamb. Boys, I say we kill him quick, rescue felicity, and find Cary. We get her to him and Roselina. They will care for her all her days. Then we can finish this bullshit."

Maximillian groaned as he held his head as if it ached. "Nein brother Mad Maxx die Brutale. Cary and Roselina will give our lamb to their children. She needs special care. Besides I don't believe in the boy's ill health we can take Byron with ease. He maybe will end us in the fray. Then the Vampire will rip our girl to pieces in revenge against us."

Mad Maxx nodded. “I have to agree with Maximillian on this brother. Think of what will happen when the Haus finds out about that disgrace. Or worse that we killed the Voter, even the Master of the Haus cannot kill one of his rank without good, damned reason. It will take time to prove we had the right and if we don’t hang around to make sure our name cleared, then the men and woman we promised favor to will suffer the same fate as the boy. We must think of them too.”

Maximillian nodded as he dropped his gaze. “Look, I know it will be horrible being stuck with Byron for a bit, but I don’t see we have a better choice. No one else is offering to help us escape the Haus. I can put up with him for a while I dink. Then once he gets us out to his home outside the walls we run away from him. Easier to escape one than many, ja?”

Mad Maxx sighed. “Maximillian is right. If he is willing to endure this monster than I say we let him. Remember what Mad Lucus told us. You never know what tomorrow can bring.”

Mad Maxx die Brutale glowered. “I don’t think any of us want to know what the fuck tomorrow can bring after the horrors we endured in our yesterdays, fools. I find it hard to believe you are voting to trust this fucking bastard. He is a pervert. They lie to get their way. I bet there isn’t even any money or mother.”

Maximillian shrugged. “Maybe you are right brother, but I do know there is also no Leo, Jakob, or Rolf willing to go this far to lie, or hell even bother to help us at all. We cannot just be the selfish bastard that leaves all those that showed kindness to suffer. I mean even Geraldine maybe will be slaughtered if we are disgraced."

Mad Maxx die Brutale chuckled with evil. "There are people that showed mercy to this boy. I think not fool. I say we jump, let the chip fall where they may. Fuck them all, oh wait, that is your job isn't it Maximillian?"

Maximillian scoffed then crossed his arms with a flounce. "I only say this a million times already, you idiot. I don't fuck anyone, they fuck me. Are we taking a vote on this, or shall we waste more time arguing about my sexual victimization?"

Mad Maxx die Brutale nodded with a wicked smile. "I vote nein. We jump and be shut of it. Oh, and is that what the kids call the slut nowadays? A sexual victim?" He broke out in cruel laughter.

Maximillian glared at Die Brutale. "I wonder why I am the shard selected to handle the sex with a man. After all you are far better at being the asshole than I even can hope to be. I vote we accept Byron's deal."

Mad Maxx trembled as he watched his brother shards. He feared a fight would break out. "I vote with Maximillian. We take the deal and watch for a loophole to improve our lot."

Maximillian smiled in smug victory. "There you have it brother. You are outvoted. We accept the deal. Get to making the arrangements and for Gott's sakes get Felicity before that fucking pervert Lucus comes to claim the boy in a few hours."

Mad Maxx die Brutale frowned, then pointed at Maximillian angrily. "Okay, I agree the vote is against me. However, I fucking refuse to manage this nightmare you are about to agree to. You want to live pussy? Then you can handle the boy by yourself."

Maximillian shuddered. "Uhm, okay? I know you are pissed you are the loser in this decision, but I don't think forcing me to handle that wheel all the time is the proper way to voice discontent about it. I wasn't designed to manage day to day functions of the flesh, only the, well you know."

Mad Maxx die Brutale grinned maliciously., "Oh I beg to differ Maximillian. This latest attempt to save the failure called Christian Axel is the job you were born to handle. I mean after all, taking it up the ass is what you are best at little brother. In fact, after hearing this bullshit you spew today I even believe you love it. Why else would you refuse to take the only honest route that would see it all come to a fucking end once and for all" He pulled away from the wheel forcing Maximillian to rush forward and grab it before the boy fell into a faint.

Byron was looking into my eyes with a tinge of impatience. "Well? Maxx, make up your mind. Will you accept my deal or do I call Gretta and Jonas to clear the air."

I looked at the floor and took a deep breath while I whispered, “I take the offer.”

The Voter leaned in closer to my face raising an eyebrow. “What was that? I didn’t hear you?”

I whimpered in defeat but spoke up. “I said I take the fucking offer, Byron. I will do as you ask me to and keep it a secret, learn to trust you and be patient.”

Byron smiled with joy. “Ah, That wasn’t so hard now was it? I am so happy you are intelligent enough to know a good deal when you hear it. Wait, first let me hear you give me your word. I know you are a man of it. Do that and let the past be gone. Our future begins today.”

I nodded slowly with caution. “I give you my word I will do as you ask Byron. Do I need to sign the contract?”

He shook his head. “You will be signing things soon enough to get that guardianship out of Jonas’s claws, but for now I will trust you the way I ask you to trust me.”

I shrugged. “Can I please have my Felicity back now.”

Byron smiled with pride. “Of course you can Maxx. Hell, in fact, come with me. Let me show you your room. I hope you like it. Remember, decorate it anyway you like. It is all yours anytime you want to just have a little peace and quiet. Here is the key to my apartment. From this day forward, consider anything of Byron’s yours too. We are partners, ja?” He patted my back with vigor as he handed me his apartment key.

I frowned at that and eyed him with suspiciousness. “All this I see is my too, huh? You swear you do did without expectation of my seeing to your special service’s needs?”

Byron chuckled as he stood up pulling me to my feet with him. “Damn you are the paranoid one, Maxx. I told you, I never make you do anything you don’t want to do. I assume you don’t want to be with me like that?”

I nodded. “You assume right. I don’t want you fucking me.”

He shrugged. “Oh well. Too bad for Byron then. Come with me. I cannot wait for you to see the room. You will be so surprised.” He jerked me across his haus to the hallway.

I kept a baleful eye on him as he pointed out his own bedroom door, the bathrooms and finally the room he was giving me at the very end of the hall. He let me through the entry. I stood there stunned to silence in shock. My old bed from the fourth floor, the one Byron originally bought me, sat in the center of the room.

I shot a look of confusion at the Voter as he chuckled. “You recognize all the furnishings in here I bet? Well, when that creep Lucus took your home away, I made sure to repossesses all the beautiful things I gave to you. I brought them up here. He was going to see them put on the trash heap. These were gifts from my heart, dammit. That monster has no respect for anything other than power. He uses others like they are nothing but tissue paper. Hey.

Look over there Maxx. On the mantle, do you recognize her?"

I gasped as I set my sights on the gorgeous China lamb with diamond eyes. "You managed to save Geraldine? Oh, my Gott. I thought for sure Lucus had her crushed or sold away. I rushed over and scooped up my little lamb and hugged her tightly to my chest."

Byron's expression turned cloudy with irritation. "If only I were a lamb. Damn that Geraldine is a lucky one to be loved so much by such a worthy man, ja?"

I didn't respond to his mild catty comment. I was so happy to see that Lucus had not managed to steal the things I had earned the hard way. Well, Lucus did steal my apartment. Nothing could have bothered me at the moment. Okay, almost nothing.

Byron walked over to the far corner of the room where a birdcage under a pretty cover hung from a display hook. "Are you pleased with the arrangement now that you see I am the man of my word Maxx? Have you changed your mind about my honest desire to be your buddy?"

I snuggled Geraldine closer as I caste my eyes about the room and clutched that key. "I guess so. I ask your forgiveness for the initial distrust of your honorable motives, but I have been fooled so many times. Lies is all anyone has ever told me. Until now no one ever did anything for me without wanting far more in return than I was to receive from them."

Byron snickered. “Ja, which sounds about right. Maxx you see that is how the world works. There are those looking to buy and those looking to sell. You know like you do with that pretty ass of yours. The only way to truly get ahead in this world is to be willing to give all you have when trying to pay the huge bill required to obtain your dreams. Do you understand what I say to you?”

I nodded. “I think I do Byron. More than most. If you recall I was willing to tolerate you and that fucking brute buddy of yours, Friedrick, to pay for protection. I had to stay alive long enough to break my metal. Back then I was too small to defend myself. I did what I had to do.”

He laughed as he pointed at my gold collar. “Ja you did and look where that got you? Back where you started. Only now you are not the scared little boy are you? Nein, you are the clever, experienced man. The predators that used to feast on your flesh with ease, they find you a far more dangerous target these days no doubt. The weaklings stupidly resort to bars, chains, weights and a dirty cell to get what they want from you.”

I shrugged as I put Geraldine back on the mantle wondering what the hell he was babbling about. “I suppose you are right Byron. I am the Master of the Haus. Many desire to hold that regent leash. Yet, Mad Lucus won that race. He made the deal with Gretta. He will be named the voice of the Mortar King on my eighteenth birthday. Do you think your mother’s money and those guardianship papers will be secured before then?”

Byron reached out and picked lint from the cover over the birdcage. “Oh, I am sure we will be long gone by then Maxx. Won’t Lucus be the pissed bastard when he finds himself without the throne he tried to steal? Ah and Gretta, if only I could be a fly on the wall when that bitch discovers her precious Priceless has escaped her grip at long last.”

I flinched at his saying that. “Huh? Why would Gretta be upset? She wants me gone. As long as the Master of the Haus is within her walls she is second in power.”

Byron shot me a look of humor. “I am surprised at you, Maxx. As smart as you are you still miss the obvious? The woman is fucking obsessed with you. You are all she has ever wanted. The moment Lucus takes the Regency she plans to make you her Mann or at least her pleasure slave.”

I choked. “Nein, you lie. That cannot be true. She ordered that shit in the Palace. Loaned her own fucking hound too. She has tried to murder me so many times I lost count. That woman hates me, Byron. Stop that disgusting attempt to confuse me.

He crossed his arms. “You are angry because you always knew deep down inside what I say is the truth. The woman has been trying to get possession of you for her lusts since the day they brought you in here kicking and screaming years ago. You forget I am the Voter brother. I know everything about the secrets of the fifth floor. If I tell you that Gretta plans to make you her stud, then you can be assured I tell you the truth of it. Peter may have stolen you and blocked her by forcing you into being the catamite, but Gretta keeps you one. She will not tolerate another woman having what she believes is her own. Cora, well she truly hates you. She would like to see you dead because you stole the heart of the one she wants. Boy, you have been suffering the results of a love triangle you never admitted you were involved in."

I sat down on my bed feeling the room spinning. He was right. I knew what Byron said was true. I just never had been able to face the horrific facts of my sorry lot in life. It was just so farfetched to believe Gretta would be so low as to manipulate everyone into keeping me the one used for schwuler sex. All those deaths, my chronic sexual abuse, the torture, even sending her own hound to do her dirty work just so she could assure I never had conquest other than her. The hopeful Frau, yikes!. This was the obsessed lover at the obscenest of levels.

Byron dropped his head attempting to catch my eyesight with his own. "What's wrong, Maxx? Come on buddy. Don't let that dumb bitch get you down. Now that you are Byron's partner things will change around here at last. Just think, we are going to be the unstoppable team. This Haus will tremble at the very sound of our names."

I looked up at him with a startle. "Wait. What? Nein. I thought you said we are leaving soon Byron. I don't want to be a force in the Haus. I desire to be the forgotten memory of it. Besides, I thought you said I am to keep your association with me the secret."

Byron glared at me with another sudden darkening of his friendly demeanor. "Very good, Maxx. You were paying attention to what I demand of you. Ja, our association is the secret. It would not be in your best interest to forget it either. The fucking Gretta will stop at nothing to see you chained to her bed for the rest of your days. The shit she has done and is likely willing to do to get what she wants, well I can respect that. However, I cannot allow it. You are never going to belong to her."

I nodded. "I thank you for the mercy of helping me keep that from happening, Byron. I don't mean to sound rude, but can I have my Felicity now?"

He smiled showing me all his teeth. "Why of course, Maxx. She is right here waiting for you. You can visit her anytime you want. All you got to do is come see your buddy Byron." He jerked that cover off the birdcage to reveal my lamb locked inside it.

My eyes went wide as they searched the heavy gaged metal bars for the door to the prison. There wasn't any. Byron had welded that cage around my lamb holding her hostage in the room that was deep within his Haus. Far from the prying eyes were the secrets, not me, that reigned as King.

To be continued in book seven of The Collar King Series: "Mortar Transformation"

About Author: Alexandria May Ausman

Alexandria May Ausman in her 16th year was diagnosed with Schizophrenia. She was quickly abandoned by her foster parents. While still only a teen, she was forced to battle this devastating illness alone.

Alexandria has struggled with lack of a support system, numerous psychotic episodes, exploitation, homelessness, and an uncaring mental health system.

Alexandria raised two healthy children. After obtaining her bachelor's degree in psychology she worked as a child abuse investigator and became a diagnostic psychologist while acquiring her Master's in psychology. Alexandria never forgot the experience of 'slipping through the cracks.' Her life's goal is to help people suffering abuse and/or mental illness have access to necessary services. By accident, she became a model of 'gothic attire' and the World Goth Queen.

She began writing a fictionalized account of her life experiences after a catastrophic return of psychotic symptoms. Today, Alexandria is retired, and homebound due to crippling symptoms of Schizophrenia. She currently lives in Tallahassee, Florida, with her loving husband and a loyal support dog.

www.ingramcontent.com/pod-product-compliance
Lightning Source LLC
LaVergne TN
LVHW020657110826
845149LV00012B/2019

9781963335163